MARCUS CRANE : ONE MORE LIFETIME

Sue Gibbons

"…and beyond this Earth are things we do not see;
where eternities gone by and those to come merge as one."

ISBN: 978-1-8381967-0-7

First published in 2020

Disclaimer
This is a work of fiction. Names, characters, places
and incidents are either the product of the author's
imagination or are used fictitiously. Any resemblance
to actual persons, living or dead, events, or locales is
entirely coincidental.

Dedication

*To all the family, friends and associates who have
been the inspiration for the characters in this book.*

*Especially to Bri, my own 'Marcus Crane'.
I love you.*

Contents

Chapter 1 – We Come Into This World Alone....

Marcus Crane had the most surreal sensation of dissociation; a feeling as though he was watching a movie; as he walked for the final time along the darkened corridor of the Semper Fidelis Hospice. He'd experienced this sense of detachment only twice before - the second time occurring when he had walked into the gym of White Friars High School to begin his second-year teaching practice in 1988.

He recalled the dull, rhythmic thud of his own heart beating deep in his ears which drew his concentration away from the muffled drones emanating from the gathered crowd of adolescents, eagerly anticipating the nervous introductions and instructions from yet another fresh-faced student teacher.

The dream-like feeling lasted only seconds and Marcus had found the occurrence oddly comforting and disturbing at the same time. He had thought about that strange state of disconnection many times since then but had not experienced it again until now, almost 16 years later, as he headed for the large, circular entrance hall of the old hospice.

As he entered the hall, the overpowering smell of stale food and bleach which hung in the walls and fabrics of the corridors and rooms of the hospice faded.

Spacious and elegant, with an ornate central ceiling rose and Victorian style coving, the entrance hall smelt strongly of furniture polish and flowers. A pungent aroma drifted from the arrangement of drooping lilies, which scattered copper red stamen onto the large, central oak table, staining the tired, white, lace table cloth.

The sound of his shoes on the stone floor brought him back to awareness and he remembered the first time he had arrived at Semper Fidelis with Ava, his partner of 13 years and his first and only romantic relationship.

Ava had been in the year below Marcus at Loughborough University. An extrovert and outspoken fresher, her energy and passion for life were intoxicating to Crane and he had been immediately attracted to the effusive brunette.

Whilst always being relied upon within the group of Loughborough jocks to lighten any mood with his dry, northern humour, Crane's obvious discomfort when presented with the fairer sex had always been a source of frustration to him. The instantaneous blotching of his fair skin and an almost involuntary, mildly sarcastic response to any small talk offered by women, in an attempt to build rapport, invariably presented Crane as an arrogant oddball and thwarted any attempt to present the cool, unruffled demeanour he saw in his male friends.

The first meeting with Ava had been no different. Crane was already wasted that October evening when she entered the bar. Laughing with two female friends, Ava's voice seemed inappropriately loud to Crane and her shrill tones penetrated the mellow, blurred sounds of his drinking partners' conversation. The interruption irritated Crane and he spontaneously turned to identify the source of the disturbance. Even through the numbing effect of the six strong beers he had consumed, he was aware of that familiar sensation of prickling heat in his neck and the crippling embarrassment as the pretty, petite girl laughed mockingly, reading his expression.

"What? Stopping you guys studying, are we?"

Crane turned back to the group of lads in an attempt to hide the expanding crimson heat raising from his neck into his jaw and cheeks. Oblivious to the intrusion, his drinking partners continued debating the competence of the day's rugby team, but the discussion was only a dampened hum to Crane; the continued animated chatter of the girl group, smothering all other sounds in the room.

Five minutes later, he found himself walking towards the bar, an almost involuntary movement and the very first time he had experienced that sense of total detachment from his surroundings. Crane wondered if the sensation was as a result of the excess of alcohol he had consumed.

He was not unaccustomed to the dizziness and instability which frequently accompanied his drinking binges but somehow, this felt different. As he approached the group of female freshers, Crane felt as though he was standing next to himself, watching his own actions but unable to influence his movement or his speech. He felt almost as if his body was being remotely controlled, a disconcerting feeling but one which provided an element of comfort to the typically awkward, shy student.

"If you girls are going to insist on interrupting our study session, perhaps I can buy you a drink?"

The volume of Crane's voice, as he struggled to be heard over the noise in the bar, jolted him back to reality and he felt exposed and vulnerable once again as the gregarious student turned to face him.

"Well, let's see. You buy the drinks and we'll see how we can improve your study session, shall we?"

Even through his own intoxication, Crane was aware of Ava's slurred speech and glazed eyes and her vulnerability made Crane feel suddenly confident and in control.

"Deal! What can I get for you all?"

Part of Crane had always regretted being drunk that night. Whilst there were never reports of outlandish or inappropriate behaviour as a result of his drinking, he always experienced memory loss and large sections of his student social life were lost forever in a fog of cheap lager. Tonight was no different. He remembered stumbling back to Ava's halls and pouring vodka into plastic tumblers, but the rest of the night was a patchwork of drunken fumbles and blackouts, punctuated with numerous, barefooted trips to a cold, dark, shared lavatory from which emanated a strong smell of stale urine and vomit.

At 5am, as the alcohol content in his blood subsided, he awoke and was aware of the heat in the tiny room, exacerbated by the lack of space in the single bed, pushed tightly against the wall. He could hear Ava's breathing as she slept and could just make out the outline of her face and hair on the pillow next to him. As his insecurities came flooding back, Crane anticipated Ava's rapid rising from the bed on awakening and her eager and unsubtle encouragement for him to leave her halls, in order for her to resign the night to the 'another pissed shag with a drunken sports student' file.

He wondered if he would ever experience a relationship where he could feel completely comfortable to be himself: with someone who loved him unconditionally and could see through the tough but fragile veneer to the sensitive, lonely little boy inside.

To his frustration, Crane felt tears pricking his eyes.

"Get a grip, you dick," he whispered to himself, as he forced his thoughts back to the detail of the previous day's sports events and drifted back off to sleep.

At 7:30am Crane was awoken by the light shining through the thin, ill-fitting curtains. It took him a second or two to remember where he was before he noticed Ava staring at him.

"Good morning, Randolf. Shall I get us some coffee?"

Crane sat up and smiled, a smile which didn't quite reach his eyes. Randolf? How the fuck did she know my middle name?

Randolf was Crane's family name; passed down through numerous generations and one of which his father had been fiercely proud. Crane had always hated it and vowed no child of his would be lumbered with it. He had worked hard to prevent his uni friends from finding out about this unfortunate inheritance, as he knew the discovery would lead to unmerciful piss taking for the entire duration of his degree study.

"You told me," Ava giggled. "You said I was the only person at Loughborough who knew and swore me to secrecy. I promised I'd keep your secret but only if I could call you Randy. So Randy, shall we have breakfast?"

Randy? Jesus! Really? Crane's irritation at his stupid disclosure was immediately tempered by his recognition that this beautiful girl appeared to want to spend more time with him.

"Sure. Let's find some coffee."

Above the impressive oak double doors in the entrance hall of the hospice, Crane noticed a picture, similar to those he had seen many times as a child and reluctant attendee of Sunday school. The faded depiction of the final hours of Jesus Christ hung slightly off centre over the arched entryway to the lobby. Although he had visited Semper Fidelis many times during the latter stages of Ava's illness, he didn't recall ever having noticed the cheap reproduction of Bartolome Esteban Murillo's Crucifixion before. As he gazed at the emaciated, lifeless body of Christ, he became aware of how alone this solitary figure appeared in his final hours and from the most distant corner of his memory came Diogenes of Sinope's famous quote,

"We come into the world alone and we die alone. Why, in life, should we be any less alone?"

As he stepped out into the dark, cold November night, Marcus Crane had never felt so alone.

Chapter 2 – A Special Bond

The only adopted child of Maria and Andrew Moran, Ava demonstrated none of her middle class, conventional South Buckinghamshire upbringing and instead leaned towards her wild bohemian roots. Roisin Collins, her biological mother, had become pregnant with Ava at 19, before fleeing Belfast for London following the 1969 riots. A fierce and outspoken Republican, Roisin had become involved with the Northern Ireland Civil Rights Association during her first year at Queen's University and witnessed first-hand, the violence and destruction which marked the beginning of 'The Troubles', during the Battle of the Bogside. She saw no future for a single, Catholic mother in Belfast, with its escalating unease and intolerable bigotry.

Roisin's parents, shopkeepers and respected members of the Swatragh community in County Derry, had never supported Roisin's radical left views. They had hoped the academic demands of a three-year Bachelor of Music degree would help her to 'grow out' of her wayward ways and when she abandoned Queen's and Northern Ireland's developing troubles, in search of a future in musical theatre in London, they chose not to follow her. They were unaware of the impending arrival of their first grandchild and did not know of Ava's existence until many years later.

Ava had always known she was the 'specially chosen child' of Maria and Andrew Moran. Adopted at two months old, the Moran's had never tried to hide her past and Maria had played an active, if a little reluctant, role in helping her to locate her birth mother when she turned 18.

She had always shown an interest in her biological parentage. Even at three years old she would talk about her 'other Mummy'. She would tell Maria colourful stories of the trips she and her 'brown, me me' would take. The references, wholly inaccurate as they were to her real origins, always generated a pang of painful jealousy in Maria; an emotion she felt guilty and selfish for experiencing.

As the years passed, Ava's stories about her 'brown, me me' diminished. A dedicated and academically gifted pre-teen, she took advantage of Buckinghamshire's continuing 11 Plus system and gained entry to Grammar School where, during her fourth year, she selected History as one of her nine O level options and joined Miss Linh's class.

Ava had always been fascinated by history in general and specifically in modern, international, political history. She had a natural ability to recall dates as well as very specific details about past events and her parents were frequently both amused and amazed at her recollection of the smallest details of family outings, often from many years previously.

Linh Mason didn't fit the usual Wycombe Grammar School profile of the History faculty. A twenty-six-year-old History and English graduate of Durham University, Linh brought an energy and freshness to the school which Ava found magnetic. Whilst having been educated in England from the age of five, she had been born into the repressive regime of President Ngo Dinh Diem in South Vietnam, in 1958. Following the death of her mother in 1959, Linh was adopted by Geoffrey Mason, a Baptist missionary from the US and his wife, Margaret, a UK national who had travelled to Vietnam to teach English as a foreign language. As the strength of the Viet Cong increased, the political climate became unstable and the safety of a Baptist minister in communist South Vietnam became even more fragile, Geoffrey and Margaret returned to the industrial north east of England, to raise their child.

In 1969, Linh left Cook's primary school in Marton, Teesside and having passed her 11 Plus, began attending Eston Grammar School for girls. In 1976 she was offered a place at Durham University where she gained a 2:1 and later joined the history department of a large comprehensive school in Middlesbrough. Following an uncharacteristically rapid rise to Deputy Head of Department, Linh left the familiarity of Cleveland in 1982 and relocated to Buckinghamshire to join her boyfriend. She knew her application to the highly regarded girls' grammar school as Deputy Head of faculty was an ambitious stretch and was delighted, astounded and terrified when she was successful.

Determined to create the passion for history that she felt herself, Linh was quick to adopt new approaches to teaching. Her sessions were interactive and the content of her historical sessions, unfiltered and honest. She was energised by the interest many of these bright kids demonstrated and was a popular teacher.

Ava was always of special interest to Linh. The extrovert child was never afraid to ask questions or challenge the actions of historical leaders and her passion for learning was a delight to her young teacher.

The connection between teacher and student grew stronger during that first academic year. Ava admired and respected Linh but, for her, the connection between them was more than just a teacher : pupil relationship. She felt an unusual closeness with her young mentor and she wondered if the deep affection was because, like her, Linh had never known her birth parents.

It was a great sadness to Linh that she had never known her biological mother. Margaret had told her as much as she could recall from her discussions with the elderly gentleman who arrived with the little girl at the small Baptist gathering in Saigon, one February night in 1959, as the group dispersed.

The dishevelled and frightened man spoke no English and his reluctant and mumbled communication was translated by one of the elderly Vietnamese group members.

The child, he thought, was just over 12 months old. Her mother had been a whore or gái giang hồ, lived locally and had, in the past few days, succumbed to cholera. Her ability to practise her trade had been thwarted by Madame Nhu and the new government influences and these had inflicted hardship and poverty on many of the working girls of the time. The child had arrived with no documentation, no official evidence of her existence and her only possession, other than the rags she was clothed in, was the small, silver plated cross; one of many that had been handed out to visitors at the Baptist mission.

The old man's objective had been simply to leave the orphaned child in the relative safety of the Baptist flock and disappear into the night.

Margaret Mason had often thought about the aged and apprehensive benefactor who delivered her precious child that night and wished she had tried to find out more about Linh's background. Linh had asked Margaret to recount the events of that evening many times during her childhood. What started for her as a child's desire to hear stories of distant lands and people who had once cared for her, had developed during her early adolescence into a longing; an obsession to discover who she was. During her early childhood years, Linh fantasised about travelling to her original homeland. The innocence of youth enabled her to imagine visiting Saigon, locating siblings and extended family and devouring stories of her loving parents and the short time they had before her mother's demise.

As Linh entered her teenage years, her insatiable thirst for any information about Vietnam, the continuing conflict and the threated communist oppression of the south, occupied her mind. She read any publication and listened to every news broadcast about the war; the increasing US military intervention, the advancing of The People's Army of Vietnam into the South and the death of millions of innocent Vietnamese people. The image of 9-year-old Phan Thi Kim Phuc, running terrified and naked, scarred with Napalm, away from her burning village on 7th June 1972, would never leave her.

However, the continued unrest in South Vietnam, following the US withdrawal of troops in 1973, along with the increasing academic pressure of grammar school education, forced the temporary dissolution of her plans to discover her southeast Asian heritage. Her ambitions for university life and qualifying as a teacher began to erode her desires to follow her roots and the secrets of her past occupied her thoughts less and less.

Ava Moran was an attractive and popular teenager. She possessed a rare ability to relate to the others in her year, showing an interest in fashion and the music of the time, while maintaining a consistently high standard of academic achievement. Whilst always attaining top of the class status in her subjects, she skilfully negotiated the mounting pressures of study and home assignments with social activities and as such, managed to avoid the 'swot' and 'teacher's pet' labels, generally awarded to studious high performers.

She had earned herself the reputation of being a committed and talented student with many of the school staff. She admired the dedication, the knowledge and the skills of a number of the teachers but when she joined Linh's class in 1984, it was the first time she had experienced any teacher able to demonstrate such infectious energy and excitement for her subject. Of course, there were still those kids who chose to waste the opportunities which a selective educational system, still available in very few counties in England, presented them with. Those kids who saw little value in understanding the rich history behind some of the world's fundamental monarchical and political decisions and selected, instead, to chatter, daydream or disrupt the lessons. But, on the whole, Linh captivated her audience and enchanted Ava and in 1985 Ava achieved her anticipated A grade GCE O level and embarked on her A level History studies with Linh Mason .

During the months leading to the final A level examinations, in early 1988, Ava regularly stayed behind after classes to discuss the content of the history sessions with Linh. The A level History curriculum included the study of British and Irish Relations, 1791-1921 and with the Anglo-

Irish Agreement having been signed by Margaret Thatcher in 1985, one afternoon the extra-curricular dialogue soon digressed to the current day troubles in Northern Ireland.

As the conversation began to slow, Linh started to pack the various papers and books from her desk into a backpack.

"My birth Mum was from Northern Ireland," Ava whispered, her head down staring at the practice exam paper in front of her.

"She went to Queen's before jacking it all in to live in London."

Linh had often referred to her own Vietnamese origins in class and her well-judged self-disclosure had helped the girls to warm to her and in turn, feel comfortable sharing some of their own experiences and backgrounds. She knew Ava had been adopted shortly after her birth but was not aware of any of the circumstances surrounding her adoption and until now, Ava had never volunteered any personal information.

Linh looked up from the overflowing backpack and sat down at the desk next to her student. "Really Ava? How interesting. Talking about Northern Ireland must have made you think about your past? Do you know anything else about that part of your family?"

Ava lifted her head and smiled.

"I know she was only 19 and pregnant with me when she left Ireland. She had some sort of falling out with her parents, I think. Mum said she intended to keep me, but she got into some bad habits and social services took me into care until the adoption."

"And have you ever thought about trying to find out more, Ava?"

"I used to make up stories about her when I was little. Mum says I would talk about my other Mummy; I called her my 'brown, me me'. Apparently, we spoke with different words and we used to sell food from her funny hat." Ava laughed, "I must have had quite an imagination when I was little."

Linh joined her laughing and the atmosphere lightened but something in what Ava had said had unearthed a memory in Linh's mind.

"I would love to know more about my mother," Linh sighed, "but from the little I have heard, there is no way I could trace her. I don't even know her name, if she had family or more kids or even where she lived. Would you ever consider trying to find your birth mum, Ava?"

Ava bit hard into her bottom lip and gazed back down at the exam paper. Linh noticed a drop of water, a single tear, fall onto the sheet and spread out, blurring the ink underneath.

"Oh, I'm so sorry. Have I upset you?" Linh put her hand on Ava's arm and the young student reached into the pocket of her blazer for a tissue.

"I can't, Miss Linh. My mum and dad would be so hurt if they thought I wanted to find my real mother. They're wonderful parents and I can't bear to upset them, but I've thought so much recently about where I've come from. I might have cousins or even brothers and sisters that I've never met. I know so little about my mother and nothing about my father; I don't even know if they're alive. I started to wonder about my past when we began talking about Northern Ireland in class. I thought it would go but it hasn't, in fact it's occupying my mind most of the time and I don't know what to do."

Linh sat quietly and watched Ava, her head down and shoulders shaking as she sobbed silently. "Would you like me to help?" Linh's voice broke the silence. "Your parents love you and want you to be happy and they will have been anticipating the day when you needed to discover your true identity. Let's make a pact. I know your parents might be concerned about how this journey might affect your studies, so let's get these exams out of the way and then I'll talk with your parents and help you to find your mum. How does that sound?"

Ava wiped her eyes with the fragmented tissue and smiled. "Maybe, Miss Linh. I'll give it some thought. Thank you."

Linh patted her hand and walked back to her backpack.

"What would I call her, Miss Linh? My real mother. What would I call her if I found her?"

Linh smiled kindly and pulled a tattered picture, an old leaflet, out of the back pack and held it out to Ava. It had a picture of a Vietnamese woman carrying a baby on her back and wearing the traditional Nón Lá or Leaf Hat.

In Vietnam they call Mother.." Linh stopped speaking and looked at her pupil, "me me, Ava. Vietnamese kids call their mothers me me."

Chapter 3 – In Search of a Future

The sound of men shouting, the whir of the bin lorry's hydraulics and the banging of the commercial, metal waste bins in the yard below the broken sash window, stirred Roisin from her sleep. Her reaction to the pulsating thud behind her eyes and the sharp pain in her neck, from lying awkwardly on the worn sofa, was to turn over and try to doze back off but the smell rising from the disturbed rubbish bins seeped into the small, dark room and made Roisin feel nauseous.

The tiny bedsit above the Tandoori Spice Tavern on Upper Clapton Road, Hackney, had been Roisin's home for the past six years. Her initial plan, on her arrival to London 18 years before, had been to find work for the remaining five months of her pregnancy, perhaps restaurant or bar work, to fund a small apartment within an easy commute to auditions and theatres. She had worked in a small café during her time in Belfast and could easily double her wages in tips. Roisin had very little money on her arrival to London and the harsh reality of how difficult finding work without a permanent address or accommodation without a regular income would be, quickly became apparent. Even disguising her developing bump did not appear to encourage potential employers to offer her work and her first experience of both living and working in England was cleaning the old B&B in Brixton, where she had managed to find a room she could afford.

The dilapidated terraced house was owned by Vera McManus, a 63 year old East Ender who had decided, following the incarceration of her husband 11 years before, to market her home as 'a cosy and hospitable stay away' in order to replace the ill-gotten gains previously provided by her, now, ex.

Vera demonstrated a tough, no nonsense approach to people on first meeting. Decades of associations with the unscrupulous and often violent misogynists, brought home by her criminal spouse, had taught her that behind every pleasantry was an ulterior motive. She had lost count of the number of times she had been on the receiving end of a drunken punch and the inclusion of his wife, along with his cigarettes and whisky, of things to be 'shared' with the deplorable thugs her husband counted as friends, had created a profound hatred of all things male in Vera McManus.

Vera had never worked. She met and married John McManus, 8 years her senior, in 1922, two months after her 16th birthday and John's crooked dealings and petty crimes had gone someway to funding Vera's dependent and miserable life. An unintelligent and gullible man, John was regularly the scapegoat when he and his felon friends fell foul of the law and he had spent much of their married life in Wormwood Scrubs.

From a very early age, Vera had special friends; friends only she could see and who told her stories and secrets, often late into the night. Her mother and elder siblings had initially humoured Vera, asking their names and details of their conversations. They would tell visitors about 'our Vera's invisible pals' and to Vera's frustration, her mother would set additional places at the meal table for them but, as Vera reached seven or eight, her family became noticeably less tolerant of the little girl's stories and Vera stopped mentioning her visitors.

By the time she was 11, Vera realised that the various men, women and children, waking her from her sleep, attired in clothes she had only seen in old books and talking about their 'passing', were not figments of her imagination; nor were they experiences anyone she knew shared. It was not unusual for her to encounter a fretful old lady or a grubby, giggling child as she reached for the chamber pot under her bed in the middle of the night. But Vera was never frightened by her uninvited guests and was more concerned about the harsh slap or pinch she would receive from her brother or sister, who shared the old, wooden bed, when her conversation with these interlopers inadvertently disturbed their sleep.

As the years passed and Vera entered her teenage years, the visits became less frequent, but they never disappeared entirely. Early in their relationship, John had dismissed Vera's claims to be able to communicate with those who had passed, as the attention seeking ramblings of a hysterical woman. He took pleasure in mocking her in front of his delinquent friends during their many alcohol fuelled gambling evenings and Vera learned quickly, that keeping her counsel about her 'gift' generally resulted in less humiliation and fewer black eyes.

When John became an unpaying guest of Her Majesty once more, in 1958, Vera noticed a significant intensification in the communication from what she had simply begun to refer to as 'spirit'. She noticed that individuals visiting the house, often unwittingly brought spirit along with them; frequently a deceased friend or relative. These unusual house guests would ask Vera to pass on messages or mention past events or experiences to validate their presence. Recalling her husband's often savage response to references about her psychic gift and fearing a similar reaction from her associates, Vera was reluctant to mention these unsolicited guests to their hosts.

An early recipient of the new Hoovermatic Twin Tub washing machine from one of John's illicit dealings and generally only affordable to the well-heeled, Vera had started to take in washing from families in the same street in an attempt to support herself.

On the 26th December 1961, Vera was awakened in the early hours of the morning with the sound of coughing. Alone in the house, she was initially convinced that an intruder had broken in; probably one of John's objectionable accomplices. As she sat up in bed, her concern turned to panic as the smell of smoke filled the room. She grabbed for the light-pull which hung from the ceiling above her bed but before she could illuminate the room, her eyes adjusted to the dark and an outline of a young man appeared in the stream of moonlight coming through the small window. He was leaning on the metal bedstead, blackened and dirty, smoke rising from his clothes. The man said nothing but held out a hand and smiled at Vera, a small cameo brooch perched on the tips of his fingers. As the seconds passed, Vera's pounding heart began to slow and the last fragments of sleepy confusion left her.

As she reached for the brooch, she felt a drop of liquid hit her hand and noticed the man's ear lobe appeared to be bleeding. Still the man said nothing but as she touched the small, cold cameo she heard the words clearly in her head, "For my Marjorie."

Two days later, Vera opened the door to a woman she had not met before. The woman was thin and pale, perhaps in her early to mid-thirties and her eyes were red and swollen.

"My neighbour told me you do laundry. How much for this?"

31

The woman pushed a basket of shirts and underwear towards Vera and as she went to relieve the young woman of her load, Vera heard, once again in her head, "For my Marjorie."

"Come in love. You're letting the heat out." Vera beckoned to her visitor to enter the house and closed the door behind her.

"I was just about to put the kettle on. Fancy a cuppa? It's Marjorie, innit?"

The young woman looked surprised and followed Vera over to the kitchen area.

"I was expecting you sweet'eart. I've a message for you."

Vera pointed to an armchair next to the old fire and poured boiling water into a chipped tea pot.

"I 'ad a visitor a couple of nights ago. Decent bloke. Wanted to give you a brooch. Would you know who that is, duck?"

Vera turned around holding two mugs of steaming tea to see the woman staring at her.

"What bloke?" snapped Marjorie, her lip trembling.

"Didn't say love but he wanted you to 'ave one of them cameo brooches."

Marjorie put the mug down on the floor, spilling tea on the bare floor boards and got up out of the chair.

"What you playin' at?" she gasped. "Who told you about our Michael?"

"Michael is it?" said Vera gently. "Well he must 'ave

thought something of you to wake me from me kip and ask me to pass a message on. Want to hear a bit more?"

Marjorie walked hesitantly back to the chair and sat down.

Vera told her guest about her lifelong gift, explained the details of her Boxing Day visitation and looked to her sobbing visitor for clarity.

"Michael was my old man. He was a dock worker and sometimes went out on the ships as a deckhand for some extra dosh. On Christmas Eve he was returning from a trip when there was a fire in the engine room. They managed to put the fire out, but our Michael had died from the smoke. They found this in his jacket pocket."

Marjorie reached below the torn shirt she was wearing and pulled out a small cameo brooch, tied around her neck with a frayed piece of string.

"They says he sold his gold ear stud to buy it for me for Christmas. He'd had that earring for years. It must 'ave hurt like hell to take it out."

Vera stood and patted Marjorie on the hand before walking over and opening the door.

"I'll 'ave your washing ready by Wednesday sweet'eart."

The daily visits from a few local women requiring laundry services quickly increased to a steady stream of individuals from a significant radius, when news of Vera's unusual talent emerged. Her customers frequently arrived with no laundry and instead offered to pay her for her spiritual advice and messages from their loved ones that had passed. By December 1962, Vera was seeing bereaved individuals from all over London and she started to offer Bed and Breakfast for those travelling some distance for her services as a psychic medium.

When Roisin Collins arrived at the B&B, she had no idea about Vera's unusual occupation. The scrap of paper in the window of the corner store merely said, 'Cleaner Required for local B&B, 67a, Atlantic Road, Brixton' and Roisin had gone immediately to the house to find out more.

As Rosin walked along the bustling street with its imposing overhead railway bridge and fruit and vegetable stalls spilling out onto the crowded pavements, she thought how different this place was to her home, the small village of Swatragh in County Derry.

The only daughter of devout Catholic parents, her childhood had been typical of that experienced by most children growing up during the 1950s and '60s, in rural Northern Ireland. Francis and Annie Collins ran the general store in the village, which they shared, for the first 14 years of their marriage, with Francis's widowed mother.

As well-known and respected individuals in the community, the couple played an active role in the local Roman Catholic Church. Both were members of the Pioneer Total Abstinence Association, having taken 'the pledge' at 16 and both adhered to and promoted a teetotal lifestyle.

The village shop delivered a modest income and the small flat above the shop provided the three adults and little Fergus, the first of Francis and Annie's three children, with adequate accommodation. In 1950, when Roisin was born, the couple bought the small, terraced house next to the shop and this was to be Roisin's home until she left for Belfast and university life, in 1968.

Liam, the last of the children, had arrived in 1953. The little boy had been delivered, as had all of the Collins children, at their home by the Sister Midwives from the Holy Family Convent House. Complications during Liam's birth had resulted in hypoxia and as a result, the child's development was significantly impaired and his normal, physical activities curtailed, as he grew older. Annie was convinced that she had, in some way, been responsible for Liam's unfortunate condition and descended into a deep depression, immediately following the birth, leaving the burden of the shop and care of the older children to Francis and his elderly and ailing mother.

Roisin was particularly close to her paternal grandmother as, during the years since Liam's birth, the old lady had been the primary carer for her and Fergus. Annie's fluctuating mental well-being and preoccupation with her youngest child, had, it would appear to the two older siblings, consumed all of their mother's energy and attention for as long as they could remember. Even in her failing health, their grandmother would prepare the two elder children for school and make sure they were clean and fed. She would tell them stories of her own childhood; how her father had perished in the Great War along with so many millions of other fathers, husbands, sons and brothers and how the post-war depression and its resulting extreme poverty during the 1920s, encouraged solidarity among the remaining women of Ireland.

Roisin was in awe of her grandmother and in the years to come, would justify her radical approach with thoughts of how her brave and progressive role model would have behaved.

The kind old lady was also the person who would hear Roisin's desperate cries, late into the night, as she had another of her recurring nightmares; terrifying dreams of coughing and choking where Roisin was being held down, unable to breath. The nightmares had started when she was around four years old and had been so disturbing to the child that her grandmother had taken her to the village doctor, in an attempt to discover the cause and appropriate treatment. Being aware of the unfortunate circumstances surrounding young Liam's birth and the subsequent psychiatric problems afflicting her mother, the doctor's conclusion was that Roisin was simply responding, somewhat extremely, to the withdrawal of her mother's attention and the night terrors would eventually stop.

Contrary to the doctor's opinion, the disturbing dreams continued and began to increase in regularity and the resulting trauma began to impact on Roisin's behaviour.

She became reluctant to eat any food which required her to chew or which could, potentially, present a choking hazard. She refused to take even the simplest medication which necessitated her swallowing tablets whole and at its worst, her phobia even prevented the child from brushing her teeth.

The disturbed nights continued for Roisin and her grandmother, with the child always describing the same dream and the same alarming sensations and then, just after Roisin turned eight, the nightmares stopped.

The old lady's death, in 1959, left Roisin feeling empty and alone and her resentment for her neglectful mother and her emotionally absent father intensified.

At 11, Roisin won a place at St Mary's Grammar School and travelled by bus, the 12 miles from outside St John the Baptist RC Church, Swatragh, to Magherafelt each morning.

Whilst Roisin was an academically able child, she found the traditional curriculum content and the 'chalk and talk' approach to teaching, adopted by the nuns, tedious.

During her early years at St Mary's, she tried hard to justify her place at the highly regarded Catholic Grammar but, as she entered her third year, in 1963, Roisin was far more interested in the growing global Civil Rights

Movement and the increasing involvement of women in the struggle against discrimination than she was in her O level studies. An accomplished pianist and vocalist, she spent many hours in the school assembly hall playing the old piano. Noticing her natural talent and enthusiasm for her art, her music teacher, Sister Theresa, was the only educator at the school who really inspired Roisin.

As the months progressed, she became increasingly passionate and vocal, at school and at home, about her support of the Homeless Citizens' League; a group of women protesting about the lack of local authority housing for working class Catholic families.

Both Roisin's parents and her teachers, concerned about the implications of her increasingly radical views and her influence on others tried, in vain, to discourage her political affiliations. In 1967, Roisin joined the Northern Ireland Civil Rights movement and later the People's Democracy and whilst she managed to achieve the qualifications required to attend Queen's University, her A level grades were far from indicative of her true educational ability.

Once at Queen's, Roisin's profound interest in civil rights and particularly rights for women, strengthened. As the Women's Liberation Movement became prevalent in the late 1960s, Roisin sought out and absorbed any infor-mation regarding the brave women's causes and advance-ments. She was frequently surprised at the strength of feeling she had towards the discrimination and bigotry women were facing across the world, the imbalance of power and particularly the lack of control women had, even over their own bodies.

Roisin had felt a passionate connection with the fight for women's equality since she was very young and had assumed this had been heavily influenced by the grandmother she had held in such high regard.

At the entrance to the East End B&B, Roisin hesitated before knocking on the shabby front door. The white, dirty paint was chipped and there was a crack in the window which someone had attempted to repair with gaffer tape. An old, dented, metal rubbish bin sat to the side of the door and Roisin could smell fish emanating from it; a smell which clung to her nose and throat. She wondered how bleak and unsanitary the inside of this miserable place would be and spontaneously turned to walk away when she heard a voice at the door.

"What can I do for you, love?"

Vera was standing in the entrance to the house and Roisin was, momentarily, not sure whether to turn around to engage in conversation or run away.

"Cat got yer tongue, has it?" Vera continued, beckoning the timid looking girl to return to the door step.

"I, er, I saw your advert for a cleaner in the shop window," Roisin said, turning around to face Vera. "You still looking for someone?"

Contrary to Roisin's expectations, the house, whilst old fashioned and cluttered, was clean and tidy and felt immediately homely and safe. In the corner of the antiquated living room was an old, brown, upright piano. It had a patterned, varnished keyboard cover and small holes for candle holders on either side of the sheet music stand. The piano reminded her of the one she had played for many hours, in solitude, in the assembly hall at St Mary's and for a second, she felt a pang of homesickness for her green and wholesome Northern Irish home. She walked over to the piano and placed her hand on the smooth lid. Perhaps, in the near future, Vera would allow her to play this lovely old instrument?

Roisin's room was the smallest of the three bedrooms, with a single bed and small, wooden wardrobe but it was adequate and affordable.

Roisin and Vera had agreed a small wage, food and accommodation in return for daily cleaning and laundry activities for the B&B. The evenings were free for Roisin to do as she pleased.

She felt an immediate connection with the brusque and direct B&B owner. Vera seemed to have a sensible, non-judgmental approach and behind her abrasive exterior, Roisin sensed a gentle, compassionate individual.

"What's yer plans for that kiddie then?" Vera asked, as Roisin started up the stairs, towards her room. Surprised that Vera had noticed her pregnancy and relieved that there was no indication of disgust or disapproval in her tone, she turned and smiled at the woman.

"It'll be going to a family that can give it all the things I can't, Mrs McManus."

The B&B on Atlantic Road was to become Roisin's home, on and off, for the next twelve years, although she would remain in contact with Vera for the rest of her life.

Following the birth and adoption of her baby girl, Roisin began singing and playing piano at small local bars and back street clubs and considered her greatest achievement to be attaining the position of pianist in a leading West End show. It was here that she spent some of her happiest days.

Roisin had never shared her parents' dedication and unquestioning loyalty to their faith and as she grew, could not help feeling that Roman Catholic doctrine was in direct conflict with her allegiance to equality for women. Her weekly attendance at Mass had come to an abrupt halt as soon as she had left Swatragh for Belfast and she had never felt the desire to return.

As the months passed, Roisin and Vera became closer. Roisin enjoyed hearing about Vera's unearthly visitors and attending the weekly gatherings, held each Wednesday at the B&B, for the group of Vera's spiritualist friends. She was fascinated by the prospect of deceased loved ones being able to communicate with those they had left behind and the thought that, one day, she might receive a message from her beloved grandmother, enabled her to feel a peace that she had never felt by attending Mass.

To Vera, Roisin was the daughter she never had. When she had married John, nearly 50 years before, Vera had assumed nature would take its course and the couple would have a family but, as the years passed and she failed to become pregnant, she had given up hope of ever having a child of her own. She had reconciled the absence of children with thoughts of John's abuse and criminal choices and told herself that this was not an appropriate environment to expose any child to, but she had always secretly harboured a deep regret that she had never been a mother. She felt protective of her young guest and had held Roisin's hand and tried to reassure her that she had made the best decision for both her and the baby, as the young girl cried her way through the first twelve months following the adoption.

Chapter 4 – A Sign of Things to Come

The gigs that Roisin played in the evenings were a temporary diversion from the feelings of guilt and loss, which her decision to have her baby adopted had created. They honed her musical talent and supplemented her cleaning income, but they also gained her some rather unsavoury associates, who quickly identified a vulnerable and willing target for their illicit merchandise.

The drugs numbed the pain and helped Roisin fall into induced, deep slumbers at night and for short periods of time, until the effects of the dope wore off, she could forget; forget the child she had rejected, forget her indifferent parents, forget her rudderless life.

Vera instantly recognised the tell-tale signs of Roisin's heroin use. The bloodshot eyes, the disinterest in her personal appearance and her ill-fitting clothes, marking her sudden and significant weight loss, were all signals she had witnessed in her husband's lowlife cronies over the years. She was aware of how dangerous a dependency on this terrible drug could be and how difficult an addiction it was to overcome.

The following year brought with it a cycle of painful withdrawal and heart-wrenching re-addiction for Roisin and a recurring pattern of anger, fear and frustration for Vera. Roisin was aware of, and prepared for, the abdominal cramps, anxiety and profuse sweating which always accompanied Vera's cold turkey approach to rehab. What she was not prepared for was the re-emergence, after 13 years, of her crippling night terrors.

Vera understandably presumed that the nightmares and the resulting hysterical outbursts, were yet another cruel and relentless consequence of heroin withdrawal; but, in late 1972, when the other symptoms finally started to abate and Roisin continued to wake screaming in the early hours of the morning, Vera became concerned for the young girl's mental health.

Fearful of inadvertently causing Roisin to be involuntarily sectioned, Vera was reluctant to seek professional psychiatric help. As a young adult, she had heard terrible tales of the practices in mental asylums; electric shock treatment, surgical lobotomy and zombie-like states, as a result of drug therapies. Whilst she knew there would have been significant advancements in the treatment of mental disorders, she was not prepared to put Roisin at further risk and for the first time in many years, Vera felt helpless.

As the regular crowd of spiritualists arrived for their weekly gathering, Vera lacked the usual energy and enthusiasm with which she was renowned for welcoming her Wednesday guests. Roisin had suffered a particularly bad response to a nightmare the previous night and both women had been awake from two thirty, when Roisin awoke choking and unable to breathe, until the light finally broke through the darkness at six forty-five.

"Young Roisin not joining us tonight, Vera?"

Vera shook her head without meeting the eyes of her friend. "She's not up to it today, I'm afraid, duck. 'Ad a pretty bad one last night and she's knackered. We both are, to be honest."

"That's too bad, love," continued the concerned woman. "I had a kiddie come to me a few years ago. Waking up, swearing and in a really bad way. Months and months, it went on for. Mother thought she was possessed, God help her. Responded well to hypnosis though. Maybe your Roisin would benefit, love?"

Whilst Vera never doubted the strange apparitions or messages she received, or the unorthodox, psychic practices she demonstrated, she was unusually sceptical at the suggestion of any alternative treatment therapies.

"Don't want anyone messin' with 'er head, Jeanie."

Vera's visitor put her hand on her hosts arm and smiled.

"It isn't messing Vera. With hypnosis, young Roisin would be in charge. I'm just there to guide her; you know, help her to remember what caused the problem. Then she'll know how to crack it. Give it some thought, love."

Reluctant as Vera had initially been to join her guests that evening, those few hours had provided her with some welcome respite from the worry of her troubled lodger and she felt a renewed optimism.

As she closed the door behind the last of the group, she thought about Jeanie's proposition. Jeanie was about 20 years younger than the rest of the group of spiritualists and was a trained and recognised hypnotherapist. Vera had heard about the positive results Jeanie had achieved, particularly with phobias, and her youth and intellect brought a freshness and a sense of authenticity to the Wednesday gatherings. She decided to talk with Roisin to see if she was receptive to the suggestion of hypnosis.

Roisin was awake and flicking through an old paperback book when Vera knocked on her bedroom door, entered and sat down on the end of her bed. She told Roisin about the events and discussions of the evening, before reiterating Jeanie's story and asking her how she would feel about trying hypnosis, in an attempt to understand the cause of her nightmares. Like Vera, Roisin had formulated the impression that hypnosis was a kind of mind control; something used by quacks or unscrupulous stage entertainers to humiliate their unwitting participants. She was unaware of the increasing use and notable, positive results of the practice, by credible and highly qualified medical professionals but, having done some research in the days following the spiritualist meeting, Roisin decided to contact Jeanie for help.

Roisin was pleasantly surprised and relieved when she entered the small room, which Jeanie used for both her medium readings and her hypnotherapy sessions. She had been anticipating a musty, old fashioned parlour, cluttered with candles, dusty angel ornaments and pictures of kindly looking spirits. Instead, Roisin found herself in a small, sparsely furnished, modern studio. Two large leather armchairs stood in the centre of the room and a small, dark wooden table sat between them with a jug of water and two glasses placed on coasters. A sideboard with three drawers stood under the closed sash window and two cassette players and some loose tapes rested on top. The walls of the room were plain and neutral, adorned with a light cream, woodchip wall paper and were empty, save for a mirror on one wall and a framed charcoal line drawing of a unicorn in the centre of another.

"Come on in then, love." Jeanie smiled, pointing Roisin towards one of the chairs.

"Help yourself to some water and get comfy."

Jeanie took a note book and biro out of one of the drawers in the sideboard and sat down in the chair opposite Roisin.

For the next 30 minutes Jeanie explained what hypno-therapy was, how it worked and what Roisin could expect. Hypnosis was not, Jeanie was keen to point out, the mind control or brainwashing which some books or TV programmes would have us believe. All hypnosis is, actually, self-hypnosis and Jeanie, as the practitioner, simply a facilitator.

Jeanie opened her note book and drew a large circle on the page. In the middle of the large circle, she drew a smaller circle.

"See this?" she said, turning the book around to show Roisin and pointing to the large circle. "This is your conscious mind, love. We can't keep too much in here; there's too much going on." Jeanie chuckled to herself and continued talking. "This here," she said, pointing to the smaller circle, "this is your sub-conscious mind. This is like a filing system; a big archive. We keep all our memories; everything we've done, seen, learnt; it's all in here, forever some say. With me so far?"

Roisin nodded and looked down again at the note book. Jeanie moved the biro so the tip of it was resting on the outline of the smaller circle.

"Now this, this is like a one-way door, Roisin. It's like a filter between our conscious mind and that old archive, storing all those things in our head that we've forgotten."

Roisin nodded again and waited for Jeanie to continue.

"By helping you to relax, just by using some words and a bit of music, I can help your mind to slip through that filter, into that old archive and see if we can find out what happened to cause those bloody bad dreams of yours. You up for that?"

Jeanie's simple but credible explanation had gone someway to easing the trepidation Roisin had felt on her way to her appointment and she sat back into the well-worn chair and closed her eyes.

"Yep, let's do it," she sighed.

Jeanie had spent some time, prior to the session, talking with Vera about the details of the nightmares. She was particularly interested in the choking sensation and inability to breathe which Roisin was experiencing and Vera felt sure that some incident, perhaps in the woman's childhood or even as a baby, had created some innate fear.

"Lots of barmy phobias and fears start like that," she had reassured Vera. "What I'll do is find it and make her remember it differently, love. That'll sort it."

Vera had spent many hours trying to help Roisin recall any event in her early childhood which could have caused the problem. Like the Swatragh village GP, Vera was inclined to believe there was a link between the abandonment Roisin had felt from her parents and the bad dreams. Perhaps Roisin's impression that she had deserted her child and her perceived dereliction of duty towards her baby, had elicited the re-emergence of the feelings. But that did not adequately explain the choking and breathing complications and Vera was not optimistic that Jeanie would uncover anything additional during the session.

Jeanie walked over to the cassette players, inserted a tape into one and pressed the record button. In the other she placed a pre-recorded tape which filled the room with sounds of sea waves, bird song and gentle music. Having asked Roisin to focus on her breathing, Jeanie began to read out a pre-written script which took her young subject into a deep state of relaxation.

Roisin's awareness seemed to peak and trough as Jeanie continued to talk and whilst she knew she could open her eyes, or even get up out of the chair at any time, she did not want to. Instead, Roisin embraced the peace and tranquillity of the moment and felt unburdened and calm for the first time in many, many months.

With Jeanie's guidance, Roisin had mentally visited her safe, special place. She had described the room to Jeanie; a grand school hall, sunshine warming her through the huge windows as she sat at the old piano, completely alone. Relaxed and confident, Roisin had left the familiarity and safety of her special place and now, at Jeanie's behest, imagined she was in an old cinema.

"Feel the soft chair beneath you and your arms on each of the arm rests," Jeanie said.

"Now see the big screen and feel a box in your hand. The box has some buttons on it; stop, start, rewind, fast forward. Can you feel them Roisin?"

Rosin had felt the temperature and atmosphere in the room change, as she had been guided away from the warm school hall and into the imaginary cinema. She felt the velvet of the seats and the sharp corners of the control box in her hands and as she saw the box in her mind's eye, she was aware of the buttons near her thumbs.

"In a second," Jeanie continued, "numbers will appear on the big cinema screen; numbers running backwards from ten to one, just like you've seen them do in a real cinema, Roisin. As those numbers run backwards, feel yourself drifting back in time, back, back in time to the time when you first had one of your nightmares. Can you see the numbers?"

Roisin nodded, her hands gripping the imaginary box.

"When the numbers get to one, an image will open up; an image of that first time you had your nightmare. Can you see the picture now?"

Roisin nodded again, her body beginning to tense.

"Feel for the stop button, love. Stop the picture. Can you do that?"

Jeanie explained that Roisin was in control of the film and she could stop and start it, rewind or move further forward, at any time.

"When you're ready then, love, you can push start and tell me what you can see."

Jeanie was aware of the immediate change in Roisin's posture. She brought her knees up to her chest, holding her legs with her arms and curling into a foetal position.

Small, whimpering sounds, as though from an injured animal, were emanating from Roisin.

"Please don't, no, it hurts!" Roisin started to cough. She looked, to Jeanie, as if she was trying to move her head, but was unable. Her hands were raised to her face, as if protecting herself, before violently waving her arms, as if at an invisible assailant.

"It's OK, love." Jeanie raised her voice slightly, to be heard above Roisin's panic and spoke calmly. "You can push the stop button. Do it now. You're in control, Roisin."

Jeanie saw the young woman's hand go to her lap and appear to grasp something. Her body immediately relaxed and Roisin returned to a calm, restful state, sitting upright, once again, in the chair.

"You're doing so well, girl." Jeanie said quietly. "Did someone try and hurt you?"

Roisin slowly nodded her head and Jeanie was sure that the young woman had just successfully re-visited the traumatic event which had caused her problems.

"They're trying to feed me?" Roisin started to speak.

"Feed you? Who's trying to feed you, love?"

"The women. The guards and a doctor. They're hurting me!" Roisin curled further into the chair again.

"Can you tell me how old you are when they're trying to feed you?" Jeanie waited.

"I'm twenty-eight. I've just had my birthday in this place. They can't make me eat!"

Jeanie was confused. She was sure Vera had mentioned that Roisin was 22 or 23 but, maybe, she thought, Vera had got that wrong and she's older.

"Which place, darlin'? Are you alright now?" Jeanie leant forward in her chair, careful not to touch her patient and anchor any negative feelings.

"Prison. I died in prison." Roisin said, a tear rolling down her cheek, "It went into my lungs. I couldn't breath and they wouldn't stop."

Jeanie wondered if Roisin was recounting the details of a film she had seen or a book she had read, "Which prison would that be then, Roisin? Is this something you've heard about recently, love?"

"I died. I died in Holloway. 1914, I died, the day after my birthday when they tried to feed me. Deeds not words! Deeds not words! I never got to fight with them again."

Roisin was clearly distressed and Jeanie felt this was probably enough for her first session. Five minutes later, Roisin was fully awake and sipping the water Jeanie had poured for her.

"How you feeling, love?"

Roisin smiled, "Desperate tired but OK, I think. That was quick. How did I do?"

Most of Jeanie's hypnotherapy clients could clearly recall the details of their regressions. They were often surprised at the specifics they were able to recall, even from early childhood days, and eager to discuss their findings afterwards. To Jeanie's surprise, Roisin appeared to remember nothing of the 90 minutes she was in trance state and instead appeared calm and composed and keen to hear what, if anything, she had remembered from her past.

"Oh, I'd say we made a little progress, girl, but we've got a ways to go yet." Jeanie patted Roisin's hand, "Don't want to be doing too much too soon now. Fancy meeting up again next week?"

Roisin smiled, "Surely. Anything to get rid of these nightmares."

When Roisin had left, Jeanie listened to the tape recording she had made of the session and tried to make sense of the alarming, apparent memory the young woman had recalled.

As she listened to Roisin's desperate commentary, something felt vaguely familiar and evoked a strange emotion in Jeanie; a memory buried deep and long forgotten.

"What is it?" she said out loud. "What are you trying to tell me?"

Jeanie did not share Vera's clairaudient abilities. She was unable to hear messages from those that had passed and instead had, since early childhood, received what she described as cryptic and veiled clues from her spirit guides, which she would spend endless hours attempting to decipher. This method of spirit communication had long been a source of frustration for Jeanie as, more often than not, only when some significant event had occurred, was she able to see the link to the spirit's clues.

As the years had passed, Jeanie had become more adept at interpreting what the mysterious signs meant and had been able to pass useful messages and predictions to her clients. Today was to be no different.

As the tape of Roisin's session came to an end and Jeanie was still unable to pin point what felt so familiar, she began to browse through the brief notes she had taken during the hypnotherapy session. Jeanie always started her notes the same way: NAME OF CLIENT, PRESENTING ISSUE, DATE OF SESSION. As she started reading the first paragraph, Jeanie became aware of the top line of her notes:-

Roisin Collins. Night Terrors. 9th June 1914

"1914?", Jeanie smiled to herself. "Got it, Ta!" she said.

The following morning, Jeanie walked the one and a half miles from her home in Hackney to Bethnal Green Library. As she walked towards the old, redbrick structure, she recalled the times she had accompanied her mother there. The imposing building had, until 1920, been the notorious Bethnal House, a lunatic asylum, before being converted to a library in 1922. Jeanie was fascinated by the place and by the chilling tales which Mrs Donaldson, the old librarian, would tell her, of the terrible conditions and the cruelty to the inmates.

Whilst the girl's mother would sit in the top-lit reading room, Jeanie would wander around the dark aisles of dusty books and newspapers, where she could feel the energies of the poor souls who had resided and died here over a period of almost 200 years.

Jeanie often returned to the library; sometimes to reflect and read but, more often than not, to research some vague message, containing historic references, which one of her spirit guides had left her. As she walked up the steps and through the imposing wooden doors of the main entrance, she felt the heavy presence which had always greeted her on her arrival.

"Morning love. Could you help me to find newspaper headlines for 9th June 1914?" Jeanie smiled at the young librarian and tipped her head towards the small side rooms, which housed the microfiche machines.

The thin, flat pieces of film, stored in six separate boxes, contained all of the news details from every regional, national and major international newspaper in June 1914. The librarian had placed the boxes next to the microfiche reader and left Jeanie to it.

Jeanie looked down at the boxes full of slides and sighed. "This could take a while," she said to herself, not even sure what she was looking for. She picked up one of the six boxes and read the notes written in thick, black marker, on the outside.

'1ST – 5TH JUNE 1914', the first box read. Jeanie moved the box to the side and lifted the next. '21ST – 25TH JUNE 1914'. Jeanie pushed the box away and looked at the dates on the remaining boxes. 11TH – 15TH JUNE 1914; 26TH – 30TH JUNE 1914; 16TH – 20TH JUNE 1914. The last in the line had a faded, white label, curling at the edges and was marked '6TH – 10TH JUNE 1914'. Jeanie lifted the top of the small, cardboard box and noticed some hand written and some typed notes on the top of each piece of film, providing details of the specific publication and date. Jeanie pulled around 30 slides marked 'Tuesday, 9th June 1914' out of the tightly packed box and placed them on the table. Picking up the first and sliding it under the reading glass at the base of the machine, she searched the headlines looking for anything which could help her to make sense of Roisin's memory or her own strange feeling of familiarity with the young girl's story.

'The Times. London, Tuesday June 9, 1914,' headed the type on the first slide. Jeanie looked through the columns for anything of relevance. The usual births, marriages and deaths, or hatched, matched and dispatched, as Jeanie's old mother would call them, indicated nothing of any significance and were followed with an article entitled 'The Intruder at the Palace' and various details celebrating an apparent drop in London's death rate.

As Jeanie removed the slide and placed it back in the box, she noticed one of the films at the rear of the box was on its side and protruding from the top of the rest. As she went to straighten it, she noticed the writing on the top: 'The Standard. Tuesday June 9, 1914.'

She removed the film and placed it under the warm viewing glass of the microfiche machine. 'Billboard Headline', was typed at the top of the film and under it,

'LET THEM STARVE Views of public men.'

Jeanie turned the knob to the right of the machine, which scrolled down to display more headlines, *'Militant suffragette, Bertha Ryland, slashes painting in Birmingham Art Gallery.'*

Jeanie skimmed the report, "Yes!" she shouted, as she read the final paragraph, thumping her fist on the desk, shaking the machine and scattering microfilms onto the floor. Jeanie read it again, out loud.

'On her apprehension, Mrs Ryland failed to comment, other than shouting, what has become the standard retort for these troublesome women: "DEEDS NOT WORDS!"'

Jeanie stood in front of the section of books entitled 'British Political History' and with her head tilted uncomfortably to the side, read, *'The Suffragette (Illustrated); The History of the Women's Militant Suffrage Movement 1905-1910. Sylvia E. Pankhurst'*

Whilst her logical mind told her that the book's references fell four years short of the date she was looking for, something compelled Jeanie to reach for the book and as she did, the small, hardback book seemed to fly out of her grasp and land, open, on the floor by her feet.

Jeanie bent down to pick up the book and the words on the page jumped out at her,

'Chapter XVIII – "Then why don't you do something? Deeds not words! Deeds not words!" came a clear, bell like cry.'

As a child, Jeanie's mother had talked about the brave women who fought for the vote and who felt so strongly about their cause that they would go on hunger strike in prison. She had always remembered the description of the force-feeding regime which the women endured; the choking, the often mis-placed rubber tubing into the lungs and the resulting pain, bleeding and pneumonia. Fearful of their increasing ill health, the government passed the 1913 Prisoners' Temporary Discharge for Ill-Health Act and would release the prisoners until their condition improved: They would then be re-arrested; a process which became known as the 'Cat and Mouse Act'.

"Well, I'll be damned!" Jeanie said quietly. "Our Roisin was a Suffragette."

Chapter 5 – Opposites Attract

University life created a turbulent relationship for Marcus and Ava. Marcus would have happily abandoned his university friends to spend more time with his vivacious bed fellow, but Ava was less inclined to restrict her social activities to those remotely suitable for couples.

It was not until the final few months of Marcus's three years at university that Ava chose to spend time with him, rather than join her cohort of promiscuous second year students at the local pubs, clubs and mass benders, poorly disguised as student accommodation parties.

His infatuation with Ava had developed rapidly and while his mother reminded him, too regularly for Marcus's liking, that this was only his first relationship, the thought of Ava and him breaking up was far too unpalatable for Marcus to consider. He recognised the differences between them; Ava's wild, untroubled demeanour, her wilful disregard for planning and structure, with either time or finances, and her innocent readiness to embrace and accept anything spiritual.

"Pretty fundamental shit, mate," his uni friends had warned. "Opposites attract but it's the similars that stay together."

Marcus paid little attention to his drinking buddies' insincere cautions. Many times he had witnessed their superficial, alcohol fuelled one-nighters, followed by the juvenile and frequently exaggerated reporting of conquests. Marcus had always found the practice disrespectful and had no desire to replicate their behaviour.

He frequently thought back to his first meeting with Ava and his clumsy approach. The possibility that his inelegant and unsophisticated chat up line could have repelled her, still elicited a strong feeling of discomfort.

After only a month with Ava, Marcus realised he was imagining their future together. Whilst his sensitivity and judgement told him that sharing his feelings so early may well drive his nonchalant girlfriend away, he cherished everything about Ava: her energy, her smile, her intellect and the tiny birthmark below her left ear in the shape of a bird's wing, which occasionally peeped out from behind her wavy, dark hair.

In the summer of 1990, when Marcus graduated with a 2:1 BEd, he and Ava rented a small apartment in Market Street, Loughborough. Marcus had been offered a position of PE teacher at Laylands Way, a comprehensive school on the outskirts of Leicester and Ava supplemented his salary with bar work at the weekends.

From being a small child, it had always been Marcus's ambition to have a career using his sporting skills. He was never a particularly academic high flyer at school and his annual reports reflected the typically average status his teachers felt he demonstrated. Even into his sixth form years, when his studies included only those subjects with which he felt an affinity, he still failed to compete with the top performers; except for physical education. Where Marcus did excel was in sport. Whilst generally being one of the last to be selected for class spelling quizzes or involvement in the science projects, which the school 'swots' initiated, he was always in high demand for games teams and represented the school in swimming, athletics and football.

Never did Marcus experience the stomach-churning humiliation of being the last to be selected for a rounders or cricket team at the beginning of a PE lesson; that honour always awarded to the skinny geek with bottle bottom glasses or the fat kid with mild asthma.

Marcus did not mind being considered average. To him, average meant beige, invisible, inconspicuous. He had always been an introverted and self-conscious child and even as an adolescent on the sports field, where he excelled, he felt uncomfortable with recognition. He never quite knew how to react to compliments from his team mates or to the adulation from the female supporters in the crowd and frequently reflected on how he could have acknowledged their support differently. On more than one occasion, he had awkwardly responded to an ebullient cheer from a pretty, enthusiastic schoolgirl, with a dismissive roll of his eyes or a spontaneous, "Oh, shut up!" only to regret his actions, having later considered how his embarrassed retort would almost certainly have been interpreted.

In fact, modest and self-effacing as Marcus was, he was always completely unaware of the interest he generated among the girls. While not the tallest in his class, at five feet, nine inches, his muscular frame and toned torso presented as a near flawless 'V'.

His intoxicatingly innocent blizzard blue eyes and thick coral red hair, accentuated his pale skin and his straight, white teeth shone through a perfectly symmetrical smile.

Admired as he was from afar, Marcus never attempted to initiate a relationship with anyone at school and as he listened to the indiscreet and lewd accounts of the early sexual exploits of his plainer but more confident team mates, he felt a sense of exclusion.

Marcus was born and raised in Cheltenham, Gloucestershire and grew up in a comfortable, middle class neighbourhood with his younger brother Neil and his parents, Terence and Gwen Crane.

His mother, a nurse at the town's general hospital and his father, a Bank Manager at a small, village branch, as well as a part time lay preacher in the local C of E parish, worked hard to demonstrate and encourage a strong work ethic in their boys. Their objective had always been to provide a secure home, good education and spiritual guidance, the latter of which had always been far better tolerated by Neil than by his elder brother. A pragmatic and stubbornly logical child, Marcus had found the idea of an all-powerful God, the existence of a Heaven and Hell and the prospect of eternal life after death, highly improbable and in direct conflict with the far more feasible scientific explanations of birth, life and death he had learned about at school and on TV.

As Marcus entered his teenage years, his weekly, mandatory attendance at Sunday school became the subject of frequent rows with his father. A mild disdain for what Marcus regarded as tedious and irrelevant nonsense developed into a resentful loathing and at 17, when school sports matches and tournaments required his weekend participation, Marcus finally managed to escape the sessions.

He cared deeply about his parents and appreciated the environment and opportunities their hard work and values had enabled them to provide for him and his brother. Their parenting had taught him a great deal about what was important to replicate, should he ever be fortunate enough to have a family of his own. It had also made him very clear about the omissions he would be making to their approach, not least the intolerable family name, Randolf, passed down through numerous, long-suffering generations and which had always been a source of embarrassment and frustration to Marcus. Even more important to Marcus was that no child of his would ever be pressured into accepting, or even entertaining, the recycled and controlling, guilt driven propaganda he considered all organised religions to peddle.

"Ava, you're dead, you're dust! That's what the science says and that's it!"

Marcus and his antagonistic partner frequently engaged in the, 'What happens after you die?' discussion. Ava was well aware of Marcus's contempt for all things remotely spiritual and revelled in witnessing her partner bite, every time she suggested that there may be a more ethereal explanation around an everyday incident.

Unlike Marcus's parents, Maria and Andrew Moran had never been regular visitors at church and instead considered themselves hardy biannuals, attending their local C of E services at Easter and Christmas, more out of childhood habit than religious compulsion. On the rare occasion that Ava attended seasonal worship with her mother and father, she had besieged her unwitting parents with a barrage of questions and objections afterwards, which they felt entirely unqualified and ill-equipped to answer.

Ava, unlike her irreverent partner, had always had a fascination for all things spiritual. Celia, her maternal grandmother, had entertained Ava and her mother for hours by reading playing cards and tea leaves and whilst Maria was always somewhat disparaging about her mother's claims to be able to predict the future, Ava had noticed that much of what her grandmother forecast, did eventually transpire.

Ava had been around 11 years old when Celia began doing readings for her and although her mother had recommended that she take Celia's predictions with a pinch of salt, Ava was always secretly impressed by the exactness and relevance of her comments.

She was always particularly interested and hopeful of her grandmother's accuracy when, as a teenager, she began asking Celia about her future romantic liaisons.

"Oh yes. I can see him," Celia had said, gazing at the pattern of well-thumbed playing cards on the dining table.

"He's fair. Yes, he has a fair complexion and maybe titian, yes, lovely titian hair. I can see the letter 'R'. Maybe his name begins with an R?"

"So, you're telling me I'm going to marry a red head called Richard, Roger or Robert, Granny?" Ava had said, incredulous.

"Well, that makes a change from tall, dark and handsome," Maria said dismissively, while giving her mother 'the look', which Ava had always known meant, 'That's enough!'

Ava was only 12 when her grandmother had first mentioned the child's future romantic interest, but she had never forgotten the reading. She had told Marcus about it many years later and received the anticipated 'What utter crap' response from her partner and had decided not to expend any further energy trying to validate her grandmother's unusual skill.

"I can see the comedy and tragedy masks," Celia had said one day, tipping Ava's empty tea cup towards her. "You know, the ones that represent the performing arts? Oh, and there's music notes; lots of music notes. Do you know anyone who plays music, Ava?"

Seventeen year old Ava had not been able to think of any musician of particular relevance, during her grandmother's weekend tea leaf reading, but the events of the next year would dispel any remaining doubt about the credibility of Celia's psychic ability.

As fully expected, Ava achieved three 'A' grade, A levels and well exceeded the ABB she needed to read History at Loughborough University.

Miss Linh's offer of support had helped Ava to hold thoughts of finding her birth mother in abeyance, until the end of her A level examinations but, true to her word, Linh had visited Ava's home and spoken to Maria and Andrew Moran as soon as Ava had completed her final paper.

"I know it will never be possible for me to find my parents, Mr and Mrs Moran." Linh had begun. "The lack of official records, my mother's regrettable profession and the increasing turbulence in Vietnam at the time of my birth, means I am already aware of everything available to know about my ancestry."

Ava's parents looked confused. Linh's unexpected arrival had caused some concern, but they had expected the ensuing conversation to be about Ava's A levels and for a second, did not see where Linh's emotional introduction was heading.

"I have become very close to Ava over the last few years. I have seen what a kind and selfless person she is and whilst she is fearful of upsetting you; of making you think you are anything other than the most wonderful parents, I know she would so value your assistance in understanding more about her heritage. Isn't that right, Ava?"

Maria looked over to her daughter sitting next to Linh and smiled.

"Is this true, darling? Do you want to meet your birth mother?"

Ava bit down on her lip, trying hard not to cry.

"I hadn't really thought about it, Mum. You and Dad are the best parents anyone could wish for and when I was younger, I felt angry and betrayed that my birth mother could give me away."

Ava's face crumbled as she surrendered to the tears pricking her eyes. "But when we started studying Northern Ireland, in History, I realised how hard it must have been to be 19, single and pregnant in Ireland and I began wondering about her. I'm so sorry, Mum and Dad. Are you really hurt that I need to know?"

Andrew Moran took hold of his wife's hand and kissed her gently on the cheek.

"Go on love," he said, as Maria stood up and left the room. Andrew winked at Ava before joining her and Linh on the sofa and putting his arm around his weeping daughter's shoulders. Maria returned a couple of moments later, a black box file gripped tightly in her hands.

"Dad and I anticipated that this day might come, Ava. We know you love us but it's natural to want to know where you came from and who your blood relatives…...."

Maria stopped speaking and coughed, trying to disguise the emotion beginning to overwhelm her.

"Your mum decided to do a little research, Ava, in case, well, in case today ever happened." Andrew continued. "She found out your birth mum's name and had an agency, which specialises in these things, find out a little more." Andrew looked at his wife.

"This is for you," Maria said, holding out the box file to her daughter.

Ava looked in amazement at her mother, her father and then at Linh, as she took the box hesitantly from her mum's hands. To her surprise, the file was heavy, and she wondered how information, weighing so much, could possibly have been uncovered about a teenage girl. Placing the box on the sofa between herself and Linh, she opened the lid.

"The agency found your birth mother about a year ago," Maria continued. "At our request, they contacted her and asked for any information we could give you, should you ever ask. This is what she sent."

On the top of a pile of papers was a photograph. The faded photo was of a young, heavily pregnant girl sitting at an old piano. The lid of the piano was up and there was sheet music in front of her. Standing behind her, with her hands on the young girl's shoulders, was an older lady and both of the women were smiling. Ava took the picture out of the box and turned it around to read the neat script hand-writing on the back.

It read, 'Vera and Roisin, June 1970'

Immediately below the photograph was a small, torn theatre programme. Ava lifted it from the rest of the papers and looked at it.

'Jesus Christ Superstar, starring Paul Nicholas, Stephen Tate and Dana Gillespie', adorned the colourful cover. 'Palace Theatre, London'.

Ava assumed the owner of the programme must have been a theatre goer and smiled as she recalled the times her parents had taken her into London to see "Cats" and "Starlight Express", when she was younger. As she flicked through the colourful pages, she noticed the list of performers and musicians and ran her finger down the column of names.

Under the heading of 'Band Members' and the last list of acknowledgements on the programme, Ava read, 'Piano : Roisin Collins'. She spontaneously raised a hand to her mouth in surprise and recounted out loud, her grand-mother's words.

"I can see the comedy and tragedy masks. You know, the ones that represent the performing arts. Oh, and there's music notes; lots of music notes. Do you know anyone who plays music, Ava?"

Chapter 6 – Not Chivalry but Justice

In the days following her initial hypnotherapy, Roisin noticed a feeling of serenity and self-control which she had not felt for some considerable time. Her nightmares, whilst still present, were less intense and were not causing her to wake tormented during the night.

Roisin was intrigued and frustrated, in equal measure, that she was unable to recall even the smallest detail from the latter part of her session with Jeanie. She remembered feeling safe and warm at the piano in her old school hall but, after that, nothing and Jeanie had been reluctant to discuss her hypothesis afterwards.

Even at Vera's Wednesday spiritualist meeting at the B&B, a few days after Roisin's regression, Jeanie was hesitant.

"Well, I'm happy you're doing a bit better, love. Let's have a catch-up this Friday, shall we?"

Jeanie had learnt, over the many years she had been practicing hypnotherapy, not to jump to conclusions too quickly and instead, to research and reflect on her findings. Her regressions had often uncovered hidden traumas and on rare occasions, what appeared to be significant abuse, which needed handling with sensitivity and discretion.

The added dilemma which Jeanie faced, following Roisin's visit, was unlike her other numerous clients, this young girl appeared to be recalling memories from a previous lifetime.

Jeanie had thought about little else, since Roisin's session and her subsequent visit to Bethnal Green Library and had looked, on more than one occasion, for some clarity from her spirit guides but nothing was forthcoming.

"Blimey!" Jeanie had said, exasperated, "When I need nothing, you're all over me like a rash. What the hell is all this about, then?"

She had considered a number of options: Maybe Roisin was experiencing feelings from inherited memories. Perhaps she had seen something as a child, which she was remembering only sub-consciously, or maybe she just had a very vivid imagination. Jeanie tried hard to think of other explanations to justify her young patient's recollections, but the onset of her problems at just four years old, negated most of the potential answers.

Roisin arrived at Jeanie's studio at 15:00 on Friday. Unlike her previous visit, she had felt no apprehension at the thought of hypnosis and was far more curious than fearful.

Jeanie settled Roisin into her chair and poured her some water.

"So, love," Jeanie began, "does the phrase 'Deeds not words', mean anything to you?"

Roisin looked surprised then thought for a second, "No, I don't think so. Should it?"

"Just a thought," Jeanie continued, shrugging her shoulders and opening her note book, "Shall we get going?"

Roisin relaxed into the leather chair, closed her eyes and listened as Jeanie guided her through a gentle hypnotic induction and deepener. Jeanie had noticed, during her first session, that the young woman seemed particularly receptive to hypnosis and as she descended quickly into trance state, her second experience was to be no different.

Once again, Jeanie gently lead Roisin from her safe, special place to her velvet seat in the old cinema, where she held the control box firmly in her hands.

As the numbers on the screen ran quickly backwards from ten to one, she followed Jeanie's direction to press the stop button.

"In a second, when you choose to press start, an image will open up on the big screen," Jeanie said gently. "The image will be of the very first time you became aware of the phrase, 'Deeds not words'. Do you understand, Roisin?"

The young woman remained still for a few seconds before pressing down on the invisible control box. Almost immediately, her face broke into a huge smile and she began to shuffle around in the chair, as if trying to see something located behind Jeanie. Her hands were now clasped together in front of her and slightly raised, as if she was holding something.

"Where are you, love?" Jeanie asked.

"We're in London, in Hyde Park. Goodness, it's so warm," Roisin said, fanning her face with her right hand, whilst keeping the left one firmly in front of her.

Vera immediately noticed that Roisin's strong, Northern Irish accent had been replaced with that of polished English aristocracy.

"What are you doing in Hyde Park?"

Jeanie had so many questions and was conscious not to rush or confuse her young client.

"It's Women's Sunday, of course. It really is terribly warm. There are so many people here."

"What's that you're holding, love?" Jeanie continued.

"It's our banner, 'Not chivalry but justice.' Look at all the banners. How marvellous!"

Roisin continued to move around in the chair, occasionally fanning her face with her hand.

"And what do you want justice for?"

"Votes. Votes for women. The WSPU want votes for women."

"What's your name, love and how old are you?" asked Jeanie, surprised at her increasing unease and aware that Roisin's response to these questions would be eminently verifiable.

"Eveline Lytton," came the reply "This is my first protest. I'm 22."

Jeanie did the mathematics in her head. During her previous session, Roisin had said she had died the day after her 28th birthday, in 1914.

"So, it's Sunday, Eveline? What's the date?" Jeanie heard herself ask, her voice trembling slightly as she waited for the answer that she knew would come.

"It's June. June 21st, 1908."

Once again, Roisin remembered nothing of her regression when Jeanie brought her out of trance state, 70 minutes after the session began.

"How are you feeling?" Jeanie asked, patting her hand.

"I'm fine, I think," Roisin said, rubbing the upper part of her left arm, "Except for my arms. Jesus, they ache something shockin'!"

Jeanie stared at the mirror on the wall behind Roisin, deep in thought, and gently nodded, as if agreeing her thoughts and next steps with her reflection.

"Come on then, Jeanie." Roisin sat up in her seat, blocking the line of vision between Jeanie and the mirror, "What's the craic? I can tell there's something."

Jeanie rose from her chair, walked over to the tape recorder and replaced the recording she had just made with the one from Roisin's first session. She forwarded the tape to where Roisin had first entered the cinema.

"I'd like you to listen to something, love," Jeanie said.

Roisin sat in silence and listened as the tape played through.

"I'm confused," she said, as Jeanie switched off the tape player. "Who's that and what does she have to do with me?"

Jeanie returned to the chair and leaned forward, her hand on Roisin's knee, "That is you, love," she said, taking a folded piece of A4 paper from the back of her note book and handing it to her pensive, young client. Roisin unfolded the paper and stared at the photo copy of the Standard billboard headline, *'LET THEM STARVE Views of public men'* and below it, the headline and quote following the arrest of Birmingham Suffragette, Bertha Ryland:

'On her apprehension, Mrs Ryland failed to comment, other than shouting, what has become the standard retort for these troublesome women, "DEEDS NOT WORDS!"

While Roisin looked dumbfounded at the photo copy, Jeanie removed a small book from the drawer in the sideboard and opened it at the place indicated by a book mark.

The page was headed, 'Cat and Mouse: Force Feeding the Suffragettes'.

Under the headline was a picture of a woman in a prison cell being held down by four other women; women in long, dark grey dresses and hats which looked like uniforms. An official looking gentleman stood next to the women, pouring fluid from a large, metal jug into a funnel and a long tube ran from the base of the funnel into the nose of the distressed and struggling prisoner.

"This is what they did to the Suffragettes, Roisin. This is what they did when the women went on hunger strike, you know, to keep them alive. Except sometimes the tube, well, it went into the lungs instead of the stomach and the poor buggers got really bad infections, like pneumonia. Some of them died, love. I think you were one of them"

Jeanie swapped the tape in the recorder for the one of that day's session.

"I wasn't sure at first, love. But I am now, and I think I know how I can fix those nightmares."

The two women sat silently and listened to Eveline Lytton; her enthusiasm and innocent optimism emanating through her cultured, youthful accent.

"Jesus! She died, choking; not able to breathe, Jeanie," Roisin gasped, "and I'm remembering it and reliving it, since I was feckin' four years old! How is that even possible?"

Roisin covered her mouth with her hands as tears began to well up in her eyes,

"I don't know, love, but I'm going to try and find out."

During the six days before her next session with Jeanie, Roisin read everything she could find about the Women's Social and Political Union, the Suffragettes and their activities. She was fascinated by the women's passion and full of admiration for their bravery, self-sacrifice and unwavering dedication to their cause. She had always attributed her obsession with women's rights to her grandmother but was now beginning to wonder if the forthright old lady merely strengthened a calling in her, that had been implicit long before her current lifetime.

The calming influence, which the introduction to hypnotherapy had on Roisin, remained and intensified following the second session. The nightmares continued and became more graphic and Roisin reasoned that this was, probably, as a result of her research into the force-feeding methodology, practiced by the prison staff on the hunger strikers. The night terrors, however, no longer made her feel out of control and Roisin began to feel the inner fight of her rebellious school and university years, returning. She found herself desperately wanting to believe that she had lived beyond this lifetime. The thought that she had fought and died for a cause she had felt so captivated by thrilled her and the prospect of a person living, learning and dying over many lifetimes, filled the gaping voids which existed in her belief system while growing up and listening to the teachings of the Catholic church.

Vera was relieved and happy to witness Roisin's significant improvement in temperament. She listened, with interest, to Roisin recounting the details of her hypnosis and considered how the possibility of reincarnation fitted with her own, undoubting acceptance of spirit.

As she reached for the part consumed bottle of Harvey's Bristol Cream from the back of the pantry and placed it on the tray of mis-matching sherry glasses, she wondered what the opinions of her Wednesday evening visitors would be. She was considering the appropriateness of introducing the subject at tonight's spiritual gathering, when she felt the light touch of a hand on her shoulder and heard a gentle Irish whisper in her head. "Not Chivalry but justice, Eveline. You were too far from Ireland, my wee girl, but my heart was with you."

Vera laughed out loud. "The special grandmother, I presume?" she whispered, "I'll let her know you were here."

Roisin was excited about her next session with Jeanie and the days running up to what would be her final session, seemed to drag. She had seen Jeanie during the Wednesday gathering at the B&B but knew that she preferred to keep her psychic medium activities and her hypnotherapy work separate, so Roisin chose to avoid the subject.

The following day, she made tea for herself and Vera and sat down at the table in the kitchen. Vera sat down opposite, her hands cupped around the mug of tea.

"That big march you went to when you was Eveline, love; how old would your grandmother 'ave been then?"

Roisin thought for a minute, "Well, she was 74 when she died in 1959, so, 51 years earlier," Roisin did the calculation in her head, "she'd have been 23."

"A year older than Eveline, then?" Vera said, sipping her tea.

"So she was," Roisin replied. "She felt so strongly about women's rights. I wonder if she knew about the march."

Vera smiled at the young woman, "Oh, she knew, girl."

She told Roisin about the visit from her beloved grandmother the night before: the reference to the banner 'Not Chivalry but justice' and the term of endearment 'my wee girl' and any remaining fragment of doubt, which Roisin may have had about the validity of her regression, vanished.

At 16:00, Roisin entered Jeanie's small studio for the last time. Again, she succumbed readily to Jeanie's gentle induction and felt a deep peace as she sat at the old piano in the school hall; the special place that Jeanie's hypnotic deepener had taken her to once more. The sounds of the notes echoing around the hall were still with her as she entered the cinema, sat down in the velvet seat and took hold of the control box.

"As the numbers count backwards, from ten to one, love, imagine you are going back, back in time to an important time in your life as a Suffragette. See the numbers now, ten, nine...." Jeanie waited as the seconds passed then noticed Roisin nod.

"In a second, when you press 'start', you'll see that time on the screen in front of you. Remember, you can press stop at any time, OK?"

Once again, Roisin nodded her head as she pressed her thumb firmly down on the imaginary control box and almost immediately began to shout, "Shame on you,

Asquith! You broke your word and betrayed us. Shame on you!"

"What's your name, love?" Jeanie asked, quietly.

"It's Evie; Eveline Lytton."

The young girl's tone was still loud and angry and she began to struggle, as if someone was trying to get hold of her.

"Where are you, Evie?" Jeanie spoke gently, in an attempt to calm her patient down.

"We're marching on the Houses of Parliament. Asquith broke his promise."

"And what's the date, love?" Jeanie continued.

"Friday. It's Friday, November 18th, 1910."

Jeanie had read about Black Friday during her visits to Bethnal Green library, immediately following her two sessions with Roisin and was aware of the violence and sexual assaults that many of the 300 plus attendees had endured during their six-hour protest. She felt it best not to prolong this memory for Roisin.

"Press 'stop', Roisin. Let the picture fade now, love. Have you done that?"

Roisin relaxed into the chair and appeared to be in a deep sleep.

"Now, in a second, I want you to press fast forward and when you do, you'll come forward, forward in time to June 9th, 1914. You're in prison and they're trying to feed you. You're watching it on the screen, love. You know, like a film. You can't feel anything, OK?"

Roisin nodded her head and raised her thumb, as if in readiness for Jeanie's instruction.

"Alright. You can press it now and tell me when you're there."

Jeanie noticed Roisin's thumb press the button on the invisible box in her lap and a few seconds later, her hands left the box and gripped the sides of the chair.

"You're safe, love. Tell me what you can see."

Roisin's grip on the chair arms tightened, "I'm in a hard chair. I look uncomfortable and someone has tied my hands and feet to the chair. There are lots of people; women mainly. I think they're prison guards. Oh, and there's a man. I know he's a doctor. He's attaching a tube to a funnel. I've heard about this. They're trying to feed me."

Jeanie listened, "Go on, love. You're completely safe. Tell me what happens next."

Roisin began to sound fearful; her voice getting louder, "They're pushing the tube up my nose. I'm turning my head but one of the guards is holding it. I've managed to free one of my arms and I'm waving it, trying to push the doctor away. Now I'm coughing. I'm coughing but they have my head pulled back and I can't breathe properly. One of the guards punched me hard in the stomach and now I've gone quiet, still and quiet. There are bubbles coming out of my mouth and nose and blood, there's blood. I think they've killed me."

"Press stop now," Jeanie said, firmly.

When Roisin had arrived at the studio, Jeanie had explained her intention to rewind and reframe her experience of being forcibly fed.

"Your subconscious mind, the one I described as a big filing system, it can't tell what's true and what's not." She had said to Roisin. "So, If I get it to forget what happened and tell it a different, nicer story, your horrid dreams should go away. Shall we give it a go, love?"

Roisin had been receptive to the idea but, in truth, was more excited about hearing additional information about Eveline and her life as a Suffragette.

"Now, in a second I want you to push rewind and you'll see that whole scene, the one you've just described, play backwards, very, very fast on the screen. You'll see the guards, the doctor and Evie doing everything backwards and so fast it'll look a bit like those funny old black and white films. When it's finished, just push stop, OK? Right, do it now, love."

Roisin nodded and her thumb pressed into her lap. For a brief moment, Jeanie saw her young patient smile before her thumb once again pressed into the imaginary control box.

"Now, when the next scene opens up, it's going to play through just exactly as I describe it, OK? When you're ready, push start and let me know what's on the screen."

Roisin began to speak, "I'm in a hard chair. I look uncomfortable and someone has tied my hands and feet to the chair."

"OK, that chair you're in, love, it's not hard. It's a comfy, soft armchair with a soft cushion at your back and your hands and feet are loose, loose and free. Can you feel that, Evie?" Roisin nodded and Jeanie saw her body relax.

"There's folks around you. There's a doctor checking your pulse and women patting your hands and telling you it'll all be alright. The doctor's pouring water into a cup and handing it to you to drink. Feel the cool water running down your throat. It feels nice, doesn't it?"

Roisin swallowed, as if enjoying the water, her body still relaxed into the chair.

"You feel calm, love. Now they're helping you out of the chair and you're walking towards the door. There's people there to meet you, love. There's your friends and family. Can you see them?" Roisin smiled and nodded, "Now press stop and let the scene fade."

Jeanie brought Roisin out of her trance state and sat back in her chair, awaiting a reaction from her patient. "I think you'll sleep well tonight, love."

Roisin never experienced her nightmare again and as the bad dreams became a distant memory, so did the regret and self-hatred, associated with her baby's adoption.

For a while, she was content. Her brief time as pianist, at the Palace Theatre for Jesus Christ Superstar, was a happy and proud time for her and Vera and was enough to make Roisin feel fulfilled but, as time passed and Roisin became restless, the allure of drugs and alcohol once again, became too much to resist.

Chapter 7 – Blood Runs Thicker

1991 arrived and with it the welcome but unsurprising news that Ava had achieved a first-class degree in History. At 18, her goals had failed to stretch any further than gaining an undergraduate place at Loughborough and she had given little thought to how she might utilise her degree to earn a living, once her studies were complete. Marcus and she had discussed the option of enrolling on a post-graduate course, as she neared the completion of her BA History, but they had both felt that, given their objective to save for a deposit on a home, it would be beneficial for Ava to find paid work.

Having applied for a number of graduate trainee's positions, without success, she responded to an advertisement in the Loughborough Echo. Most of the jobs advertised in the Situations Vacant section of the paper were looking for free-lance telesales people to sell a variety of goods and services, on a commission only basis. A number of Ava's student friends had been call-centre fodder, in an attempt to supplement their grants and most had complained about the long hours, poor conditions and inadequate rewards. Sales had never interested Ava but, as she scanned the columns of lineage ads, a small, semi-display box stood out.

'Junior Production Editor Required. Do you love reading, have a good eye for detail and work well to deadlines? Why not give us a call?

The advertisement was for a small, publishing house based in central Loughborough and having called the number to request more details, Ava managed to secure an interview for the following day.

Gant and Hartness employed 45 people and had been established 13 years. The original partners, Malcolm Gant and John Hartness, two Loughborough alumni, had both worked for various large, national publishing groups for upwards of 25 years. Rapidly approaching their fifth decades and keen to escape the bureaucracy and increasingly frustrating constraints, symbolic of large blue-chip organisations, they had decided to return to their university town and set up their own company.

The constant pressures of work, combined with the many years of over indulgence, as a result of a healthy expense account, contributed to the major heart attack and early demise of John Hartness in 1983. Hartness had been the innovation and creativity in the relationship. An emotionally intelligent and naturally charming individual, he had been the driving, persuasive force behind securing both the initial, significant bank loan and the authors and clients, which made the small business successful.

Malcolm Gant, in contrast, was far more cautious and his analytical, reflective and risk averse nature was both a calming hand and a frequent irritation to his fearless business partner.

Gant warmed immediately to Ava, as had the Production Manager who conducted the initial interview, before asking her boss to meet her applicant and rubber stamp her decision to appoint her. Ava's effervescent energy reminded Gant of John Hartness. He missed his old friend but he also felt exposed and inadequate, aware that his safe, conservative approach to business was no longer being challenged. Whilst Ava was joining the business at a junior level, Gant had the feeling that the bright History graduate would, in time, prove to be good for the company and for him.

She and Marcus celebrated the new job that evening with a meal and several drinks at the China Garden and the optimistic but lucid conversation about their future became giggly and outlandish, as the strong Chinese beer took hold.

"I wish Roisin was here to celebrate with us," Ava said, slurring her words and bringing the jovial mood to a sudden halt. Marcus reached across the table and took hold of her hand,

"Your mum and dad are so proud, honey and delighted for you. That's all you need; your mum and dad and me."

That June day in 1988, when Miss Linh had visited their home, Ava had finally made the decision to contact her birth mother. Having scrupulously examined the contents of the black box file which her mother had given her, Ava had many unanswered questions. As well as the theatre programme and the photograph of Roisin and Vera, taken about a month prior to Ava's birth, there were many other photographs and documents which Roisin had packaged together in the hope of piquing her daughter's curiosity.

A framed, formally posed, black and white photograph had been placed in-between the numerous loose papers. The photo showed an elderly looking woman and a couple, possibly in their thirties, formally dressed, perhaps in preparation for an important meeting or church service, Ava thought. A boy of around ten and a slightly younger girl stood in front of the adults, the hands of the old lady placed on the shoulders of the little girl. A small boy, maybe around three or four, sat in a wheelchair, which had been positioned between the two older children. Ava had noticed immediately that, while everyone else was smiling, the youngest child looked distracted and unaware of the camera. The backdrop to the photograph was a shop, which appeared to Ava to be a small grocery store with newspapers, flowers and an assortment of fruit and vegetables outside on wooden tables. The shop windows were full of handwritten posters, advertising a variety of produce and imminent, local events and the shopfront sign read, 'Swatragh General Stores'. On the reverse of the photograph was written,

Our village shop in Swatragh, County Derry. 1957. Back row - Francis Collins (Dad), Annie Collins (Mum), Granny Collins. Front row – Fergus, Liam, Me.

The black box file contained a number of photographs featuring the members of Roisin's family at various ages. There was a number of young Roisin with her grandmother, although Ava noticed that the old lady stopped appearing in the pictures when Roisin was around eight or nine and she assumed, correctly, that Granny Collins must have passed away. Fergus was tall and dark and any pictures of him, in his teens and early twenties, were either on or around farm vehicles. Ava had thumbed through the contents of the box several times looking for further pictures of the small child in the wheelchair, but there were none.

As well as the pictures, the box housed photo copies of Roisin's passport and driving licence; both displaying recent photos and Ava saw a likeness in the shape of her large eyes, to her own. There were a couple of programmes for St Mary's Grammar school performances, for which Roisin was named as the pianist, and several copies of old school reports, in which the comment, *'Roisin would be more likely to achieve her true academic potential if she was to concentrate more'*, seemed to appear every year.

The single item in the box which puzzled Ava, was a mid-sized, hardback book entitled, 'The Suffragettes in Pictures', by Diane Atkinson. Ava had studied the Suffragettes during her time with Miss Linh and as she flicked through the book, the grainy, black and white photographs of Emmeline Pankhurst and the depictions of the many protests and struggles of the women, brought back memories of the animated discussions she had contributed to during the history lessons. Tucked in the inside cover of the book was a portion of a faded copy of a birth certificate. It read;

CERTIFIED COPY OF AN ENTRY OF BIRTH
REGISTRATION DISTRICT; Highworth
1886 BIRTH in the Sub-District of Swindon in the county of Wiltshire
When and where born; Eighth June 1886. King James Street, Swindon
Name, if any; Eveline Margaret
Sex; Girl
Name and Surname of father; James Arthur Lytton
Name, Surname and Maiden Surname of mother; Caroline Mary Lytton, Formerly Duke

Ava had no idea why her birth mother might have included the book or the certificate in the assortment of papers and wondered if Eveline Margaret Lytton might have been a distant relative. The very last item in the box but to Ava the most important, was a hand written letter from Roisin.

Dear Ava,

If you are reading this letter, your mother will have given you the package of pictures and souvenirs that I have put together for you. I am so happy that you have expressed an interest in your origins and in me, your birth mother.

I have often wondered what you were doing and prayed that you were happy and well and that, one day, we might meet so I can tell you about your Irish family.

There has not been a single day in 18 years that I have not thought about you and would dearly love to be able to explain my excruciatingly painful decision to give you up, all those years ago.

Your parents have my address and I will leave the rest to you.

Much love,

Roisin Collins

On 19th July 1988, Ava's Birthday, Maria Moran and her daughter boarded a train at Wendover station, bound for London Marylebone. Ava had specifically chosen this day to meet with Roisin as she had felt that, selecting the day when she was no longer officially a minor was, in some small way, a gesture of respect and love to the parents who had raised her for 18 years.

Ava had responded to her birth mother's mementos and letter by writing a short note, requesting that they speak on the telephone. It had been over two weeks since she posted the letter and she was starting to wonder if, perhaps, Roisin was having second thoughts about initiating contact with her daughter.

The Moran's telephone rang at 18:30 on 16th July.

"Hello, is that Andrew Moran? This is Roisin Collins, Ava's, er," Roisin stopped to think of the most appropriate way to introduce herself, "I'm, er, calling for Ava, Mr Moran."

Roisin listened to Andrew's muffled voice as he placed his hand over the mouth piece and called for his daughter. "Ava? Telephone. It's Roisin for you."

The call that Ava had imagined for many years had lasted only a few minutes.

"I was so happy to get your letter, Ava. I've dreamt of talking with you for so long and now it's happening, I'm not sure what to say."

Ava listened to the soft, hesitant words and the script which she had rehearsed in her head a thousand times, in preparation for this conversation, suddenly no longer seemed relevant.

"It's OK. It's a bit weird for both of us. I wondered if you might have changed your mind about getting in touch?"

Roisin began to say something when the beeping of the telephone box she was calling from indicated more coins were needed, "Sorry, Sorry Ava. I'm in a phone box and don't have many coins."

Roisin's voice was louder now and Ava detected a sense of panic or confusion in the woman's tone, "Would you like to meet up, Ava? I know you have a big day coming up. Maybe we could celebrate?"

Ava thought quickly, "OK, why don't Mum and I come to your place on Tuesday? I have your address. We could be with you for, say, 11:30?"

Roisin had wished for her first meeting with her daughter to be anywhere other than the dilapidated bedsit above the Indian restaurant in Hackney but, agitated by the possibility of being prematurely disconnected by the avaricious telephone box, she had reluctantly agreed.

She had promised herself that she would 'take a scheme out on the place', a phrase her grandmother would use when the house or shop in Swatragh needed tidying. But, as frequently happened, a gig over the weekend had taken precedence and a hit of dope and half a bottle of vodka, to quell her pre-reunion nerves on Monday night, meant the place was still an unsanitary dive.

As the waste disposal lorry and its jovial team, in the yard below, continued to disrupt her rest, Roisin abandoned the idea of dozing off again. She sat upright on the threadbare sofa where she had fallen into a drug induced sleep several hours before, knocking a partly consumed packet of chips and a mug, still wet with vodka, onto the floor. The small travel alarm clock on the table indicated it was 09:30 and as she waited for her eyes to clear and the crick in her neck to ease, a bolt of panic raced through her body as she realised what day it was.

"Holy Jesus, Mary and Joseph!" she gasped, as she attempted to negotiate her way through the debris which covered the floor, "What the feck was I thinking?"

At 11:28, a black cab arrived outside the Tandoori Spice Tavern, Upper Clapton Road, Hackney. Intending to take a tube from Marylebone but unaware of the scarcity of underground stations in the vicinity of Roisin's home, Maria Moran had suggested a taxi to avoid being delayed. As the cab had travelled slowly along the part derelict row of shops and takeaways, both women felt sure they had got the address wrong but seeing the old telephone box outside the red façade of the Indian takeaway, Ava realised, somewhat disconcerted, that they had not.

The door between the Indian and the deserted newsagent was ill fitting and the blue paint, scuffed and flaking. The bell box to the left of the door had two buttons. The top one was unmarked and was probably, Maria thought, for the flat above the newsagent. The lower button was marked Collins and Ava took a deep breath before pressing it hard.

After a few seconds, the sound of footsteps on wooden stairs culminated in someone pulling hard at the door and a thin, pale woman in a creased, old fashioned dress stood in the doorway.

"Hi Ava," the woman said, smiling, "and you must be Maria?" she said, holding out a hand, which Maria noticed was trembling. "Come up and please excuse the mess. I've been busy this week."

Ava followed Roisin up the dark stairway to a landing with two doors. The door to the left was ajar and Roisin entered and held it open for her guests. As the women entered the bedsit, both became aware of the sickly smell of food which Roisin had attempted, unsuccessfully, to disguise with an incense stick.

"Please, sit down. Make yourselves comfy," Roisin muttered as she removed a newspaper and various assorted items of clothing from the sofa.

Ava, conscious of how awkward the telephone conversation had been, had decided to bring a number of the items from the box file, in an attempt to generate some benign chatter. She pulled a handful of papers and pictures from her hand bag and held out the photo of Roisin's family outside the shop.

"Thanks for the pictures. So, Fergus and Liam are your brothers?" Ava asked.

Roisin moved across the small room and sat next to Ava on the sofa and looked at the photo. "Fergus, he's the eldest. He turned 40 just last month. He's married now and has two children, Cara nine and Aisling six," Roisin pointed to a small photo on the mantle. A bride and groom stood at the entrance of a grey, stone church and Ava noticed how formal and serious they looked.

"They rent a small holding just outside of Swatragh, where I grew up," Roisin continued, her finger moving to the child in the wheelchair.

"Liam was a sick wee boy. He passed a few months after his 16th birthday; something to do with his chest, Mammy said."

Ava noticed that Roisin's hand was shaking badly, as she gestured to each individual in the photograph. The chemical-based smell on her breath, along with inflamed sores on the side of her wrist, which occasionally appeared above her cuff, prompted Ava to look beyond the superficially neatened room for clues which might indicate a drug dependence.

The women spent the next couple of hours discussing Roisin's great friend and ex-landlady, Vera McManus, and Ava was absorbed in the stories of the old woman's notorious gangster husband, ghostly visitors and weekly seances. She wished Roisin was still living at the B&B, partly so she could have met this fascinating woman but primarily because she instinctively felt Roisin really needed help.

"She's early eighties now, God love her," Roisin said, looking at the photograph of her and Vera sitting at the old piano. "I don't visit enough. I should go more, so I should."

Roisin changed the subject and told her visitors about her various musical assignments; her school musicals, her gigs in some of the less reputable London establishments and her short but happy time at the Palace Theatre.

She had, until recently, had a job playing evening piano in the restaurant of a small, boutique hotel near Covent

Garden. She enjoyed the exclusive environment, which was in stark contrast to her living situation, and meeting the diners. The extra few pounds she made each week were always welcome but, in recent weeks, her ability to arrive on time, or even at all, combined with her unkempt appearance and frequent bungled renditions of well-known pieces, had caused the manager to reluctantly terminate her employment.

"I'm sorry, Miss Collins," he had said at the end of her last shift, "but people are complaining about the music and, well, about your personal appearance."

Roisin had not really cared; a further worrying indication of her growing substance addiction and had simply risen from the grand piano, slamming the lid and walked out of the restaurant. The indifference she demonstrated to any negative life event, typically as a result of her own inappropriate behaviour, was constant throughout her lethargic and hazy days and her intoxicated nights. The only exception was the narrow, early morning window of time on Roisin's waking, when shame and regret engulfed her, before a lunchtime score or tumbler of vodka numbed the pain once more.

Today, with her guests having arrived just before lunchtime, Roisin was starting to feel the familiar symptoms of delaying her hit. "Jesus, I've nothing in the place to offer you. Will you take a cup of tea, if I get some milk?"

Without waiting for an answer, Roisin grabbed the coat, hanging on the back of the door and left the room. Ava and Maria had both noticed Roisin's growing anxiety and the small beads of sweat on her brow and upper lip and had exchanged looks of nervous confusion, as their host slammed the door behind her.

"She's a mess," Ava said, rising from the sofa, "I think she's on something. Look at this place, Mum. It's a dump."

Ava scoured the room, looking for anything which would confirm her suspicions. Having found nothing conclusive, she walked towards the only internal door in the bedsit and pushed the door open. The door led into a small, dirty bathroom with a chipped, white corner sink and a lavatory with a broken seat. The bath had no side panel and Ava could see the bottom of the bath and adjoining pipes, all covered in dust. A supermarket carrier bag had been pushed towards the back, right corner of the bath. She bent down and pulled the bag towards her, hearing the assortment of empty vodka bottles rattling together. An ashtray was on the window-sill, partially hidden by a thin, stained curtain. It contained a bent tea spoon, blackened from the flame regularly held to its base, and a small, used hypodermic needle.

Ava heard slow, unsteady footsteps approaching up the bare, wooden floorboards of the stairs and quickly pushed the bathroom door closed. When she heard Roisin's voice, she flushed the toilet and walked back into the main room.

"Sorry, about the bath.." Roisin slurred, her words tailing off, as if she was unable to find the energy to finish her sentence. Maria and Ava watched as Roisin fell back on to the sofa, her coat still on and the carton of milk still in her hand. A drop of blood ran down her wrist and into her fingers, staining the seat cushion beneath and as Maria gently pushed at the arm of Roisin's coat, a pattern of both raw and scaring track marks, confirmed Ava's fears.

When the ambulance arrived at the bedsit, Ava and Maria left and walked in silence along the bleak, dilapidated street. The next few days were a roller coaster of emotions for Ava. On her arrival home, she had expressed the anger of someone wholly unaware of the behavioural implications of substance addiction.

"For God's sake, Dad!" she had cried. "Was it so difficult, just once, for her to demonstrate some level of decency for the kid she dumped? She hadn't even tried to clean the flat."

Andrew Moran had attempted to explain Roisin's lack of self-control to his daughter; more to negate any developing feelings of inadequacy on Ava's part, than to exonerate Roisin.

"Drug addiction is a terrible thing, darling. I've read a lot about it. It absorbs your every waking minute, from the second you open your eyes to the second you feel the effects of the next hit. Everything unrelated to getting high becomes irrelevant, even the things which are most important to you. Those two and a half hours which Roisin was speaking to you without her booze or drugs, were probably excruciating for her, sweetheart."

Listening to her father's balanced, if not entirely altruistic justification of Roisin's behaviour, prompted alternating feelings of disdain and pity in Ava. She thought about the unanticipated delay between her letter to Roisin and Roisin's eventual telephone response. She recalled the disproportionate anxiety which Roisin demonstrated in response to the phone box requiring more coins and she remembered the thin, pale, perspiring woman with shaking hands in the dirty, unkept little bedsit; and Ava felt compassion.

Chapter 8 – The End of a Blueprint

18, Market Square,
Loughborough
August 12th, 1991

Dear Roisin,
I hope this letter finds you well.

I wanted you to know that I graduated from university this year. Studying has always been a joy to me, particularly History, so leaving Loughborough is bitter sweet. I was delighted to achieve a first-class degree, of course, but I will miss the learning.

I have met a wonderful man here. His name is Marcus and he is a teacher and we are now living in a place of our own. No more student accommodation, thank goodness.

I have thought about you a great deal since Mum and I visited. You were clearly going through a very hard time and looking back, I wish I could have helped more.

I guess at 18, I didn't really know how, and Mum and Dad wanted to protect me.

I still look at the papers and pictures you gave to me and have so many questions that I didn't have time to ask you before: I wondered about the book and Eveline Lytton's birth certificate. Was she a relative of yours, or maybe of my fathers?

When you feel ready, please get in touch and maybe we can try again.

Ava

Ava took a deep breath before pushing the white envelope into the post box.

That ill-fated afternoon, in 1988, her mother had contacted Homerton Hospital where, according to the paramedics, Roisin would be taken and monitored overnight. The hospital reception confirmed that she had been admitted but had discharged herself later that afternoon.

Andrew and Maria Moran had been reluctant to encourage Ava to reconnect with Roisin. Ava had been distressed for weeks, following their disastrous trip to London and Maria had felt culpable. They had convinced their daughter that, if and when Roisin was able to overcome her addictions, she would probably try to re-establish communication. Ava, keen to start her new university life and unaware of how to effectively manage a person with a destructive addiction, was happy to be guided by them. She had naively expected Roisin to get in touch, once she had taken time to reflect on her actions, but she never had and for the next three years, Ava built her new life.

She had told Marcus about her heritage when they had been dating for around a year; her adoptive parents and her unfortunate meeting with her birth mother. Marcus's opinion on the matter was predictable and entirely in line with his dispassionate approach to anything which may upset his beloved Ava,

"She's a smack head, Ava. She had her chance and she doesn't deserve you. Frankly, I hope she doesn't contact you."

Ava had accepted her boyfriend's opinion and resisted approaching Roisin but something in her shifted when she graduated and accepted the job offer with Gant and Hartness.

The child's mantle she had been able to hide beneath for 21 years, as she studied and grew, was now gone and with it, the entitlement to be selective about what she wanted to see and experience. Thinking a meal out and several beers would dull the impact, Ava had already made the decision to tell Marcus of her plan to contact Roisin, when they went to celebrate her new job.

Four days after she posted her letter, an A4 brown envelope arrived at their apartment.

It was addressed 'Miss Ava' and was postmarked, London. Ava had been at work since 8am that morning, for the early Friday production meeting and arrived home tired but excited about the weekend ahead. Marcus was cooking when she arrived home.

"You've had a delivery," he said, nodding towards the letter on the kitchen table.

Ava poured a glass of wine and picked up the brown envelope, while updating Marcus on the day's events at Gant and Hartness.

"My boss was really receptive to my suggestion and.." Ava suddenly stopped, mid-sentence and Marcus turned from his cooking to look at her. She was holding a white envelope in one hand while reading from a piece of writing paper, held in the other. He could see from her expression that the contents of the letter were unexpected.

"Everything ok, babe?" Marcus said, waiting for Ava to lift her head from the letter she was reading. "Babe?" he repeated, concerned, as he realised her shoulders were shaking.

She looked up, her face red and wet. "It's Roisin," she said quietly, handing the letter to Marcus.

The letter was neatly written on Basildon Bond paper, probably, Marcus surmised, by an elderly, shaking hand, once able to produce immaculate script.

67a, Atlantic Road,
Brixton
14th August 1991

Dear Ava,
Your lovely letter was forwarded to me. I hope you don't mind me opening it, but I needed to know who to reply to. I have returned it to you now.
I am so sorry to have to tell you that Roisin passed away a

year ago. As you know, she was a troubled soul and finally succumbed to the addiction to heroin, that I understand you and your mother sadly witnessed.

I hadn't seen Roisin for many months when I was made aware of her sad passing but, if she mentioned our friendship to you, you will know that death is no barrier to me communicating with loved ones and I know that she is now untroubled and at peace.

Roisin was always very sad that she had to give you up and even in spirit, wants you to know that she is sorry.

Together, we can answer the questions in your letter, but that conversation is better in person than in writing or over the telephone.

I would be very happy to meet my precious Roisin's little girl.

God bless,

Vera McManus

The journey from Loughborough to London seemed endless to Ava. Marcus had offered to drive but the couple finally decided that the train into St Pancras and a cab to Brixton would probably be easier.

Few changes had been made to the interior of the old B&B, since Roisin's arrival almost 22 years before, but the exterior had benefitted from new, white uPVC windows and doors and the old rancid, metal dust bin was now replaced with two plastic wheelie bins.

When the old lady answered the door, Ava felt compelled to hug her. Vera smiled and waved the couple into the house and Ava thought she looked significantly younger than her 85 years. She showed her guests into the living room, where the old piano still occupied its spot in the corner by the bay window.

"Your mum," Vera pointed towards the piano, "she used to play that for me. Cuppa?"

She left the room and returned a few minutes later with three patterned, china cups and saucers on a tray. A matching milk jug, sugar bowl and tea pot sat next to them and a packet of Rich Tea biscuits balanced precariously on the edge of the tray.

Vera lowered herself into an armchair opposite the sofa where Marcus and Ava were seated. "Let it stew a coupl'a minutes, love. Then you can play mother, Ava."

Ava smiled and waited for Vera to begin.

"So, girl; a first, was it? Smart lass, Ava. Just like Roisin."

"We had so little time, Vera," Ava said, leaning towards her host. "We talked briefly about her parents, her grandmother and her brothers. We talked about her music; just trivial stuff." Ava started to shake her head, "I never got to ask her about really important stuff, Vera. I never got to ask who my father is or if I have sisters or brothers or why she sent me the birth certificate of a woman born in 1886 or…,"

Vera leant forward and put her hand on Ava's, "All in good time, sweet'art," she said, "Pour that tea, duck."

Ava poured three cups of tea, handed one to Vera and returned to her place on the sofa.

"Your dad was at Queen's, love. Jim, his name was. Roisin hadn't long caught with you when she came over 'ere. She never told her bloke that she was in the family way, love, and he never came here, but she did get some letters from Ireland and there might be something in those."

Vera reached down next to her chair and picked up a wad of envelopes, held together with an elastic band. "All manner of stuff in 'ere, Ava," she said, putting the letters back into a carrier bag. "She never 'ad any more kiddies. There were a few blokes around, on and off, but no one special."

Ava reached into her handbag and pulled out the copy of Eveline Lytton's birth certificate. She handed it to Vera, "This was in the pile of pictures Roisin sent to me. It was tucked inside a book about the Suffragettes, Vera. Do you know why she would have sent this to me?"

Vera leaned back into her chair and closed her eyes. "You know I'm a psychic medium, love. There's not much surprises you when you've spent your life talking with thems that 'ave passed but, what 'appened with Roisin, well, I don't mind tellin' you, I was shook."

Vera spent the next hour recounting the details of Roisin's excruciating nightmares, the introduction to Jeanie, the three hypnotherapy sessions and the validation from Roisin's grandmother. "I 'ave the tapes 'ere, duck. They was in the stuff that I picked up from the flat. You can take 'em with you, see'f you can make any more sense out of 'em."

Ava and Marcus chatted with the old lady for another hour before Marcus put his hand on Ava's arm, "We should be making a move, darling, or we'll miss our train back."

Ava stood up and helped Vera out of her chair, "Thank you so much," she said, hugging her, "for everything, Vera; for taking care of Roisin, for being the mum she never really had all these years and for helping me to understand her a little more."

Vera pulled the carrier bag from the side of her chair, "She would've wanted you to 'ave this stuff, duck," she said, handing it to Ava.

She pulled open the door and winked at the young couple. "I'll be sure to let you know if I hear from her, sweet'art."

Marcus had listened patiently to Vera talk of ghosts, spiritual meetings and past-life regression and wished he could, even vaguely, entertain the idea that any of these things could be true. He kissed Vera on the cheek and turned to walk away.

"Oh, Randolf, love," Vera shouted after him, "Dom says to tell you he's still drinking his home brew."

Ava was still laughing when the couple jumped into the black cab and headed for the station.

"You bloody told her, didn't you?" Marcus said, playfully tickling his girlfriend.

"No, no I swear. I didn't say anything. When did I have the chance to tell her about your family name and who the hell is Dom?" Ava objected, slapping Marcus's hand away.

Marcus thought for a minute before realising he had never discussed his Uncle Dominic with Ava or, in fact, anyone outside of his immediate family. Dominic, or 'Dumb Dom', as his parents referred to him, was his father's older brother but, whilst they shared the same parents and the family name, that was all the brothers had in common.

Dom, unlike his moderate and sensible brother, was a chancer; always on the lookout for the next low effort, money making scheme. His private life was as unorthodox as his business ventures and Marcus's father had lost track of Dom's numerous, extra marital affairs and financially disastrous divorces. A significant factor in only the early years of Marcus's life, he remembered Dom as the fun, impish uncle who invariably turned up, more than a little inebriated on home brew, having been ejected by some woman. He had stopped visiting their home when Marcus was around 12 years old and a couple of years later, Dom had died in a road traffic accident. Marcus attended the funeral with his parents and his younger brother, Neil, and Dom had not been mentioned again.

Marcus dozed for most of the return train journey as Ava began to read the letters Vera had given to her. Most of the letters were from a Sister Theresa and dated from March 1970 to April 1982. They referred primarily to developments at St Mary's and general community events in Magherafelt, which Ava assumed was the local town. A letter dated 5th March 1980, referred to Fergus's wedding, 'It was a beautiful ceremony, Roisin. I'm enclosing a photograph.' Ava realised, with sadness, that Roisin had not returned to Ireland to attend her older brother's wedding and wondered if, even then, her choices were being influenced by drugs and alcohol. The paragraphs of pleasantries were punctuated with occasional questions; 'How is life in London? Have you managed to find any work? Are you keeping up with your music practice?' and Ava wondered if Roisin ever responded with answers to Sister Theresa's well-meaning questions.

The letter on the very bottom of the pile had a return address on the back of the envelope;

Swatragh General Stores, Swatragh, County Derry, NI.

Ava opened the small, white envelope and looked at the bottom of the short note, *'God bless you, Mammy'*. She read the letter.

8th May 1970

My Dearest Roisin,
Thank you for your letter telling your daddy and me where you are living. Mrs McManus sounds very kind and I thank her for looking after you.

I am writing to you with very sad news. Your brother, Liam, sadly passed away in March this year. He had failed badly over the last couple of years and his poor wee chest could not cope any longer.

Farther O'Mare took the funeral mass and Liam is now at peace, thank you God.

I wish I could have told you sooner. Please light a candle for him.

Your daddy and me and Fergus are all well.

God bless you,

Mammy

Ava was shocked at the brevity of the letter. She knew that Roisin had left Ireland in February 1970, when she was 4 months pregnant and she imagined the panic, concern and care which her own mother's letter would have reflected, had she not been in touch for three months. She thought of Roisin, alone and heavily pregnant at the time her mother wrote and wondered how difficult their relationship must have been for Roisin to be unable to share her desperate situation with her own mother.

That evening, Ava rummaged through a grey, leather suitcase, under the bed, in an attempt to find her old cassette player. She smiled as she lifted it out of the morass of old exercise books, cheap costume jewellery and obsolete power leads, no longer required but kept, 'just in case'. Having borrowed the required batteries out of a clock and Lady Shave, she placed the tape player onto the coffee table and inserted the tape marked, Roisin Collins, November 1972, Session #1.

"Roisin was a women's rights fanatic, honey. She's bound to have read about the Suffragettes. This is probably just her remembering stuff she's read about," Marcus said, when the recording finished. Ava thought for a minute, "Maybe. I remember seeing programmes about the Suffragettes when I was a kid. The whole force-feeding thing had a lasting impression on me. I guess it's possible she's just recalling something she's seen in a book or on TV."

Ava removed the tape from the player and replaced it with the one marked, Roisin Collins, November 1972, Session #2. The young couple listened to the conversation which had taken place between Jeanie and Roisin just before the hypnosis began,

'So, love, does the phrase 'Deeds not words', mean anything to you?' Jeanie had asked.

Aware that Jeanie was a regular attendee at the Wednesday medium meetings, Ava had expected her to be a similar age and character to Vera and she had been surprised how youthful and pragmatic Jeanie sounded on the tape.

Roisin's reply sounded sincere, *'No, I don't think so. Should it?'*

The induction and deepener had been edited from the tape, a precaution Jeanie always took to prevent particularly susceptible, unsupervised listeners, inadvertently entering a state of trance. Ava was surprised at the level of emotion she felt, hearing Roisin speak; her young voice confident and her Derry accent stronger than she remembered from their meeting. The next time Roisin's voice sounded, the distinctive Northern Irish intonation was gone and, in its place, the cultured, standard English inflection of Eveline Lytton.

Ava and Marcus listened to Eveline's animated description of the WSPU's Women's Sunday march and Marcus smirked, a little too contemptuously for Ava's liking, at Eveline's choice of childlike and inoffensive terminology, "Goodness, it's so terribly warm. How marvellous!" he mocked, "Who speaks like that?"

"Exactly," Ava said curtly, removing the cassette from the player. "No one, not now and certainly not from Northern Ireland but, in 1908, when you're 22, female and English nobility, well, that's just exactly how she would speak."

Marcus laughed, "You aren't seriously telling me you believe all this crap are you, babe?"

Ava ignored Marcus's loaded question and slotted the third and final tape, marked Roisin Collins, December 1972, Session #3, into the player.

Jeanie's voice was the first to be heard on the third tape,

'As the numbers count backwards, from ten to one, love, imagine you are going back, back in time to an important

117

time as a Suffragette. See the numbers now, ten, nine, eight, seven, that's it.... In a second, when you press start, you'll see that time on the screen in front of you. Remember, you can press stop at any time, OK?'

Ava and Marcus listened to Eveline's angry, Black Friday rantings about Asquith and the broken promise, before Jeanie instructed her to move forward in time to her force-feeding encounter.

Ava was familiar with the concept of rewinding and reframing traumatic incidents. She had been aware of a friend at school who had what appeared to be, a completely irrational fear of rodents. Whilst most of the girls in the class could relate to a distaste for the rats that were occasionally to be seen near the school's waste food bins, this particular pupil was unable to even enter the class room if the teacher had, unintentionally, forgotten to hide the class gerbil. While the girl was frequently a victim of derision from others in the school, who were ignorant of the true extent of her crippling phobia, she had confided in Ava about the sleepless nights and increasing agoraphobia, which the terror was triggering.

Her friend's parents had finally, as a desperate last resort, sought help from a hypnotherapist and the young girl had explained to Ava how her fixation had been treated by recalling an incident involving a mouse and a screaming grandmother, when the girl had been a toddler.

"Apparently the memory of my grandmother losing control had stayed with me," her friend had explained. "The hypnotherapist just made me remember it differently and now I'm OK."

Ava had not really understood exactly what reframing was until now, as she listened to Jeanie creating a completely different version of events for Roisin. While according to Vera, the experience was transformational, Ava felt the process was somewhat simplistic and knew she would have a fight on her hands convincing Marcus of its validity.

To her surprise, Marcus did not criticise the reframing approach.

"A mate of mine had hypnotherapy for smoking and it worked really well for a while. I don't have an issue with hypnosis per se, but past lives?"

Marcus looked at Ava in the same way a parent might look at his child, having found flaws in an elaborate fib. "Someone in English aristocracy dying in 1914 and coming back as a Northern Irish junkie, in 1950? Really, babe?"

Ava knew it sounded far-fetched, the way her boyfriend was describing it, but she also felt patronised at Marcus's convenient editing of the information they had.

"Ok, Mr Know-it-all," she said, looking at the note pad she had been scribbling on during the recordings, "So, firstly, what about the miraculous recovery? Roisin had struggled with nightmares and choking since she was four years old. You can't reframe something that didn't happen. Secondly, I know you're totally blinkered to the possibility of any kind of life after death, but Vera has made a living all her life passing on messages from people who have died. She told us what the spirit of Roisin's grandmother had said and she also gave you a message from 'Dumb bloody Dom', who incidentally you have never mentioned to anyone who could have told Vera. Thirdly, why Eveline Lytton; some random, upper-middle class nobody from Swindon? Surely if this was a memory from a film or book, Roisin would have been someone higher profile; Emmeline or Christabel Pankhurst maybe, or the Davison woman who threw herself in front of the King's horse? Roisin believed this stuff, Marcus. I don't think we can just dismiss it as 'crap'."

Marcus had conveniently omitted Vera's parting comment, when rationalising his dismissal of the possibility of anything supernatural, be it spirits or past lives. But unbeknown to Ava, he had secretly wondered how the old lady could possibly have known about his insufferable family name or his unfortunate Uncle Dom.

"OK," he said, feeling guilty at the effect his intransigence appeared to have had on Ava,

"What's the plan then? How do we find out more?"

"I have the birth certificate," Ava said. "I'm going to send for the death certificate. I want to know how and when Eveline Lytton died and I'm going to go into the uni library. They have a computer there and I'm going to see if there is any information on the web about her and then, oh ye of little faith, Randolf, I'm going to meet Jeanie."

Chapter 9 – An Entirely New Perspective on Life

The librarian in the university library handed Ava a list of references for publications which included any mention of the WSPU or the Suffragettes. Given the number of women in attendance, at both Women's Sunday in 1908 and the Black Friday march in 1910, Ava decided to concentrate on events and arrests made in 1914, the year Eveline had been imprisoned and subsequently died.

Many of the books contained indexes and Ava was quickly able to dismiss any which had no direct reference to an Eveline Lytton. The rest, while having sections devoted to the specific marches and high-profile activists during 1914, mentioned few who were incarcerated as a result of the Cat and Mouse Act. The only woman whose death was attributed to forced feeding, was Emmeline Pankhurst's younger sister, Mary Clarke, but Eveline had described a punch to her stomach and Ava wondered if the cause of death might have been registered as something unrelated to the prison's appalling feeding practice.

Having given up on the books, she sat in front of one of the visual display units located at the rear of the library. The librarian had accessed a page on the relatively new World Wide Web, which was headed 'Virtual Library'.

The page listed 16 categories from Agriculture to Society, the eighth of which was Humanities and Humanistic Studies. History was listed as a subsection of Humanities and Ava opened the page as the librarian had shown her. Another list of headings appeared on the page, the last of which was Women's History and as the page opened, she read the words, 'Votes for Women'. She typed the word Lytton into a small search bar and two references to a Lord Lytton appeared, but no further information and Ava had no way of knowing if there was any connection between Lord Lytton and Eveline.

She was frustrated that her library search had produced nothing, but not entirely surprised. The women's movement had counted hundreds in its numbers and very few had been famous or infamous enough to be referenced in print. On the positive side, she thought, with no references to Eveline available, Marcus would be unable to claim that Roisin had read copious amounts of information about Miss Lytton, which she would then be able to recount under hypnosis.

Marcus had called the Wiltshire County Council, Borough of Thamesdown to request instructions for applying for Eveline's death certificate. A letter had arrived confirming his application and estimating its arrival within 10 working days.

Since being involved with Marcus and becoming acutely aware of his inability to recognise the possible existence of anything remotely paranormal, Ava had thought little about the repeated accuracy of her own grandmother's readings. The meeting with Vera and the revelation about Roisin's hypnotherapy had inspired her to think about the feelings and inclinations she had supressed for some time; the ability for some to see into the future, the possibility of life after death and the existence of spirit. Whilst it did not especially concern Ava that Marcus refused to entertain her beliefs; the competitive part of her personality wanted to present him with some evidence he could not dismiss.

"How lovely to meet you, sweetheart. I was so happy when you called." Jeanie hugged Ava as she stepped forward to enter the house. Vera had told her friend about Ava and Marcus's visit and mentioned that she may receive a call from the couple, looking for information about Roisin's unusual regression. Jeanie led Ava into the room which used to be her hypnotherapy studio. The two leather chairs had been replaced with a comfortable three-piece-suite and the small, functional side table with a large, carved, dark wood coffee table. Photographs and artwork adorned the previously plain walls and the room felt far more like a homely lounge than a studio. Jeanie had placed a cafetière and two small coffee mugs on the coffee table and poured the coffee, as Ava removed her coat and sat down on the soft sofa.

"I don't do much in the way of hypnotherapy any more, love; just a bit for friends and family, you know," Jeanie said, "but this is where I saw Roisin all those years ago," she continued, anticipating her visitor's question.

Ava nodded. "We listened to the tapes, Jeanie. Vera had told us about the regression and the emergence of Eveline Lytton. I've always been quite open to the fact that there may be things we can't explain but my partner, well, let's just say he's wired a little differently to me."

Jeanie laughed. "He thinks it's all nonsense, eh? Tries to find explanations for everything?"

Ava felt herself blushing and felt the need to justify Marcus's cynicism.

"He tries to be supportive but he just doesn't believe in anything even remotely unearthly."

Jeanie smiled and Ava guessed she had encountered many non-believers in her time, as both a hypnotherapist and a psychic medium.

"In my experience, love, most people who dismiss stuff they can't explain, do so out of fear. I learnt a long time ago, not to try to argue or persuade but just to present the facts and let them get there themselves."

Ava chatted to Jeanie about her adoption, her upbringing and her psychic grandmother.

"She described Marcus to me when I was about 12. *'He's fair,'* she told me, *'and he has lovely titian hair.'* She said his name began with an 'R'. Marcus's family name is Randolf and boy, does he hate it." Ava said, giggling. "Of course, he won't have any of it; says it's all a complete coincidence."

Jeanie talked to Ava about some of her medium clients, many of whom had arrived determined to prove Jeanie a complete charlatan, only to hear something they were unable to rationalise. As she was talking, Ava noticed Jeanie was staring over her shoulder at a large mirror on the wall.

"Sorry, love," she said, a little distracted, "I don't suppose you could tell me why I'm being shown a red flag? Yes, it's bright red with a yellow star in the middle. Any ideas?"

Ava thought for a moment. "I'm not much good with flags," she said, excited that Jeanie appeared to be receiving some sort of message, "but Marcus is. He'll know. Are they telling you anything else?"

"Hmm, that's the problem," Jeanie said. "They don't 'tell' me anything, love. Show me cryptic, blinking puzzles for me to ponder over; for days on end, sometimes. That's what they do."

Jeanie told Ava about the random date on her note book, after Roisin's first session, which led her to research Eveline and discover her connection with the Suffragettes. She told her about the numerous objects that had arrived and disappeared out of nowhere and the symbols or words which would appear, written in condensation on the windows, which had enabled her to validate messages. Whilst Jeanie attempted to sound frustrated by the vagueness of her spirit guides' communications, Ava could tell that her protestations were not in anger and could even sense a veiled tolerance, almost a fondness, for her unusual associates.

The two women talked for an hour and a half about Roisin's regression and Jeanie told Ava about subsequent past-life regressions she had conducted. "Young Roisin was the first but she certainly wasn't the last. If anyone came to me with a problem, you know, a phobia or some irrational fear and there wasn't an explanation in their earlier life, I'd take them back further. It doesn't work with everyone, of course, but my guides generally let me know if I'm on to something. That flag, by the way, love, that'll be for you. You'll have to let me know what your fella says."

Ava travelled home, more convinced than ever that Roisin had indeed, experienced a past life during her hypnosis session with Jeanie. On her arrival at the flat, she chatted enthusiastically to Marcus, who was keen to hear about her trip and her meeting with Jeanie.

"Vietnam, babe," Marcus said, without hesitation, as he pulled a small book of flags from the bookshelf. "Here it is. Look, yellow star on a bright red background." He pointed to the picture of the Vietnamese flag. "South Vietnam had their own flag until 1976. This one here." Marcus moved his finger to an image of a yellow flag with three horizontal red lines. "When the war ended, the red flag of the north became the flag of the unified country. Why do you ask?"

Ava told Marcus about the image of the flag which Jeanie had seen in the mirror.

"She was certain it was, in some way, relevant to me." To her surprise, he did not belittle the comment or try to contrive some logical explanation for Jeanie's vision.

"OK, so what connections do you have with Vietnam?"

Ava thought for a second. "Linh. Miss Linh, my History teacher. Remember? The lady I told you about that encouraged me to look for Roisin, she's Vietnamese. I wonder if it's something to do with her."

Ava, while not having seen Linh for a couple of years, spoke occasionally with her on the phone and they always exchanged Birthday and Christmas cards. She had visited Linh after the hapless trip to meet Roisin back in 1988. She had also called to tell her about her degree the previous summer, but they had not spoken since and Ava realised that Linh was unaware of Roisin's death or of either of her unconventional meetings with Vera and Jeanie.

Rather than attempt to bombard her friend with the morass of details about her adventures over the phone, Ava decided that she and Marcus should take a trip back to Buckinghamshire to meet with her.

The following weekend, Ava arranged for her and Marcus to meet Linh in a coffee shop near the Moran's home in Princes Risborough. Ava had talked a great deal about Linh to Marcus and she was excited that her boyfriend was finally going to meet her old friend and mentor. Running predictably late, Linh arrived at the coffee shop flustered and apologetic.

"There's never anywhere to park in this town," she said breathlessly, as she hugged Ava.

Ava felt inexplicably tearful as she held Linh. There were very few people in her life that she felt such a close bond with and, embarrassed at her unexpected emotion, averted her eyes to avoid either Linh or Marcus noticing they had filled with tears.

"So, you must be Marcus?" he nodded and shook Linh's waiting hand.

"I'll get some coffee while you two catch up," he said. "What can I get you, Linh?"

"Oh my God! A first, Ava. I still can't believe you got a first-class History degree. What are you planning to do with it?" Linh asked.

Ava told her friend about her job as a Production Editor with Gant and Hartness.

"They're only small but they specialise in non-fiction and seem to be the 'go to' publishers for authors of political and historical books. The people are great and it means Marcus and I can save towards a deposit."

Linh winked at her young protégé, "Wow, sounds serious. Is this the one?"

Ava laughed as Marcus returned to the table with three coffees and croissants.

Linh updated Ava on what had been happening at the Grammar school.

"The Deputy Head is retiring at the end of the Christmas term and I'm going to apply for the position," Linh said, biting her lip, as if suggesting the promotion was a long shot.

"That's fantastic," Ava enthused; "the school needs leaders like you. You'll breeze it."

"So, what's been happening with you guys?" Linh asked, looking from Ava to Marcus.

Ava told Linh about her conciliatory letter to Roisin and Vera's immediate reply, informing her of Roisin's sad death. She described the warm but somewhat irregular visit to Brixton; the details of Roisin's regression and Vera's uncanny use of Marcus's family name and message from Uncle Dom.

"But it was the visit to Jeanie that has really got me asking questions," Ava explained.

She relayed the story of her visit to Jeanie's house; the work of the hypnotherapist and psychic medium and the vision Jeanie had of the Vietnamese flag.

"You are the only connection I have with Vietnam. I haven't even been there on holiday. Can you think of any reason that Jeanie might have received that message for me?"

Linh looked puzzled, "Not really but she sounds like she has a pretty good track record. Have you thought about having a hypnotherapy session with her? I had some hypnotherapy to help me with anxiety when I was doing my BEd. finals. I thought it was a lovely experience. Can't do any harm, can it?"

The three chatted for a while longer before Linh got up, "Marking to do tonight," she smiled, rolling her eyes. "I need to keep up if I'm going to apply for that job. Let me know how your hypno goes."

When Marcus and Ava arrived back in Loughborough on Sunday evening, there was a letter waiting. Through the thinness of the A5 envelope, Ava could feel something rigid inside. The envelope was handwritten but there was no return address on the reverse and the postmark was smudged and illegible. She opened the letter and removed a polaroid photo. The image was covered with a small, pink post-it-note which read,

'Hi Ava. Spirits are at it again! Any idea what this might mean?' Love, Jeanie xx'

Ava removed the post-it and looked at the photo. The picture was of a steamed-up bathroom mirror; Jeanie's, Ava assumed. In the middle of the mirror was written,
'AVA BROWN
ME ME ME ME'

Ava handed the photo to Marcus and resisting the overwhelming urge to suggest Jeanie may just have been responsible for the writing, he simply shrugged, "Ava Brown? That doesn't make any sense and why 'me me me me?"

Unlike her boyfriend, Ava did not question the authenticity of the message, but she was confused and having spent most of the evening trying to figure out what it could mean, decided to call Jeanie the following day.

Ava lay in bed that night, her mind busy and sleep refusing to still it. She thought of Jeanie and wondered if she would consider her close enough to qualify for the hypnotherapy she now reserved for only friends and family. She thought of Linh and how emotional she had felt at seeing her again and her mind wandered back to school days and the extra-curricular chats they would have - and then it hit her,

"Fuck! Not Ava Brown, me me me me," she gasped "Ava, brown me me. The name I called my 'other mummy', Marcus. My brown me me. It's Vietnamese for Mother."

Chapter 10 – Carpe Diem

The wind was blowing hard as Marcus pulled the large oak doors closed behind him. The sky was dark, covered with dense clouds which hid the moon from view and he could feel a cold, light spray of drizzle on his face as he walked towards the car.

The orange MGB GT was parked under one of the decorative street lights, which had been positioned at suitable intervals in the hospice car park. Ava had persuaded Marcus to let her purchase the old car.

"But this one has got character," she had protested, when Marcus had suggested buying a newer and more reliable Ford Fiesta. Marcus complained regularly about the MG: the leak in the driver's side window, the old radio with poor reception and its regular, obstinate refusal to start, for no apparent reason: but secretly he loved the little car and the trips that he and Ava had taken in it. He hoped that, just tonight, the old heap would fire up without protest, despite the hours it had been motionless.

As he searched his coat pocket for the keys, he noticed a motorbike parked in the space next to him. He thought it looked out of place, frivolous and inappropriately informal, for such a sad place, and he wondered who it belonged to. As he reached to open the car door, his coat caught on the handlebars of the bike and Marcus felt an anger he knew was disproportionate to this minor hinderance.

"The car park's fucking empty and you have to park right next to me, asshole!" he mumbled to himself, squeezing into the driving seat.

The car smelt of Ava's perfume and the crystal angel hanging from the rear-view mirror was, she had joked, 'to watch over your crappy driving and keep you safe'. The ill-fitting, rubber floor mats had been a spontaneous purchase of Ava's, the objective having been to keep the thread bare carpets from deteriorating any further.

"Look at the label," Marcus had said, frustrated, before pointing to the list of 'suitable for' cars, none of which were the MG. He regretted it now. With every ounce of his being he wished he could have that moment back, any moment back, so he could hold her once more.

When Marcus leant forward to start the car, he was surprised to notice that the motorbike had gone. He had neither seen nor heard the owner arrive or leave and as he looked at the small clock on the dashboard, realised he had been sitting in the car for over an hour. The rain was heavier now, and the rain drops on the windscreen looked like tiny bulbs as they reflected the glow from the street lamp. The unbearable, crushing agony of grief that Marcus had felt when he left Ava's room had, temporarily, been replaced with emptiness; a suffocating nothingness, where nothing and no one mattered and for the first time in his life, Marcus no longer cared if he lived or died.

It had been a big decision for Ava to take the Senior Book Editor's role in Aylesbury and leave Gant and Hartness, where she had been since leaving university. Her drive for achievement and capacity for learning had helped her to attain a number of promotions and her five years of experience had enabled her to support her boss and friend Malcolm Gant and set the strategy for the business, in time for his imminent retirement.

The call from the Head-hunter was not a great surprise. Ava had established herself as a talented Production Editor and frequently received calls from Recruitment and Search Agencies. She had never been interested in pursuing other opportunities but when she was approached about the prestigious position with one of the UK's leading publishing houses, close to her home town and her parents, she decided to attend the interview.

When Ava secured her new job, Marcus had applied for a Head of Department position with a large secondary school in Hemel Hempstead. The small, terraced house they had purchased three years ago, in a pretty suburb of Loughborough, sold to the first people to view it and Marcus and Ava had purchased a new build in a village on the edge of Aylesbury.

Marcus had always assumed that, at some point, they would get married. His traditional upbringing and his parents' solid and conventional relationship had set a good precedent in his logical mind. His younger brother, Neil, had also been married now for two years and teased Marcus mercilessly.

"It's OK Bro, you've only been with her for eight years. Don't want to rush it, do we?"

Marcus had raised the subject with Ava on more than one occasion.

"Why change things, babe?" Ava had protested. "We're already committed to each other and I'd be a terrible mother, so it's not as if we have to get married for kids."

The comment had surprised Marcus. He knew that Ava had some irrational fear of being responsible for another human being, but he had assumed her reservations were due either to her having been adopted, or her experience with Roisin, and would pass.

"I just know it's not something I'd be any good at," Ava had said, when he had pressed her. He had always imagined having children, but the assumption was, once again, just due to the convention practised by his parents. Focussing on careers and their lives together was, Marcus concluded, a pretty decent alternative.

Life was good. Ava found the challenge of her new job and the increasing time she was spending with bright, new authors rewarding and she was well liked. Marcus had not anticipated the extra administration and general school politics he would face as a member of the school management team. He was not a natural politician and certainly lacked both the ability and desire to compete with some of the more ambitious teachers, but he appreciated the increased influence he had in developing his small team and in making changes to his department.

As the school closed for the mid-term break in February 2002, he drove home thinking about the trip to the Lake District which he and Ava had planned. When he pulled into the drive at 16:30, he was surprised to see the MG already there.

"Hey love, I'm home. You're early. You OK?"

Noticing Ava was not in the sitting room or the kitchen, he went upstairs to find her. The bedroom curtains were closed and the room was silent.

"Darling, what's wrong?" Marcus sat on the edge of the bed, stirring Ava from her sleep.

"Oh, it's nothing. I started feeling a bit crap again at work, so they sent me home."

"Again?" Marcus said, concerned. "When did you start feeling ill?"

"I've felt really weak and pathetic all week. My chest feels heavy and I've struggled a little to catch my breath and then today I had an explosion of a nose bleed. I felt a real dick: it was in the middle of a planning meeting!" Ava propped herself up on her pillows to look at her

139

worried boyfriend and Marcus realised how pale and thin she appeared.

He put his arms around her and pulled her close. "You've probably picked up a bug, babe. Get some rest and we'll see how you are tomorrow. If you're still feeling like crap, I'll call the doctor."

"Your white blood count isn't as high as we'd like, Ms Moran. It's probably nothing that some vitamin supplements won't sort out but, given your weight loss and those nose bleeds you've been having, I think it's important that we get you in for some more tests."

The GP filled in some forms while Ava waited. "I'm arranging for you to have a bone marrow biopsy. It only takes about half an hour and it doesn't hurt but it will answer a few questions for us."

The next few weeks were a blur for Marcus. He had been unnerved by the speed at which the seemingly endless invasive tests had been arranged for Ava and while he tried to convince himself he was over-reacting, he had noticed her rapid weight loss, increasing breathlessness and fatigue.

"You have something called Acute Myeloid Leukaemia. It's serious but there are treatments."

Marcus gripped Ava's hand as she sat, devoid of any emotion, in the Consultant's office. "What we need to do is get you in for something called a lumbar puncture. That'll tell us if your headaches and that numbness in your legs are being caused by the leukaemia."

The news that Ava's cancer had spread rapidly to her central nervous system, brought with it the knowledge that any further care would be palliative. Her relocation, at her own insistence, from the hospital to Semper Fidelis Hospice, just one week before she died, had marked the abandonment of any further hope of recovery.

Marcus spent the week following the funeral with his parents in Cheltenham. The thought of returning to the house in Buckinghamshire terrified him. He knew he would see Ava in every picture, ornament and soft furnishing. He would hear her laughing in the kitchen and singing in the bathroom and he would smell her in the perfumed air of the bedroom and in the fabrics of their sitting room.

As he lay in bed, in the room in which he had spent so many hours as a child, Marcus thought about his home, his work, his life goals and none of it felt important or even relevant any more. He wondered how Ava would have felt if it had been she who had been left. Her unshake-able faith, that this life was just one of many and that we enjoyed various lives and different relationships with the same nucleus of people, would have given her some peace. Her certainty that our deceased loved ones are never really gone and simply on a different plane, awaiting our return 'home', would have eased some of the excruciating pain of loss; the pain he was feeling now. For the first time, Marcus envied people with faith and wished he too, could relieve some of his unbearable and unrelenting heartache with some of Ava's beliefs. He could not envisage how any aspect of his life could possibly return to any semblance of normality and he could not imagine laughing, smiling or even feeling at peace again.

"You need to grieve, son." Terry Crane handed Marcus a beer. "I know it's a cliché, but time really is a great healer and we can't rush the process. I've counselled too many bereaved parishioners over the years to know there are no short cuts, Marcus. Everything is going to remind you of Ava: people, places, music, everything."

Marcus looked at his Father and wondered where this candid address was headed. The honesty of his words stung as they echoed the fears drumming in Marcus's head: that nothing in his life would allow him to escape, even briefly, from his loss.

"Why don't you take a sabbatical, son? Go somewhere you've never been; maybe somewhere out of your comfort zone. Do something different with people you've never met before and turn this terrible time into a period of learning. Of course, you won't be over Ava when you return, but the acuteness, the rawness of the pain will have numbed a little; enough to help you to cope and think more clearly about your future. What do you think?"

As Marcus processed his Father's words, his immediate, logical reaction was to dismiss the suggestion. "Ava was the spontaneous risk-taker, Dad. I'm the boring, practical one. What about the mortgage, the job, the house?"

He watched his father's eyebrow raise and recognised the half smile, which had always said to him and his brother, 'Do you really think I came down with the last shower of rain?'

"We both know your school would allow you some time out, Marcus. Your house is new and low maintenance and would be no problem to leave for a few months and, yes, you're the practical one, which is why you have made sure you have savings. What good is money, if you can't call on it when you really need it?"

The following day Marcus noticed a missed call on his phone. He recognised the number as the main school switchboard and dialled into his voicemail to listen to the message.

"Hello Marcus, Brian Evans here." Marcus could hear discomfort in his Headmaster's voice, which was out of character for the ordinarily confident, austere man.

"I can only imagine what you must be going through and the entire staff and I want you to know that we are thinking of you. You may wish to get back to work: I know that's how many people deal with grief, but I wanted to let you know that, if you feel you need some time, we can cover your classes until you're ready to come back. If there is anything I can do, you only need to ask."

Marcus replayed the message and knew, instinctively, what Ava would have said,

"It's a sign, babe. He's normally such a curmudgeonly old bugger and he's offering you time off. You should take your dad's advice."

143

Marcus climbed into the MG and followed the country road up to Birdlip. As a teenager, he would often drive up to the layby near the Air Balloon pub and watch as the sun faded and the lights began to appear over Cheltenham. Inspiration point, he had named the place. He had told Ava about it; how he used to go there to make decisions or work through a problem, but they had never been there together and Marcus was glad that his special place was, in part, free of her presence.

As he stared at the familiar panorama, he heard a motorbike pull up beside him. His initial feeling of irritation, as his solitude was disturbed by the popping exhaust of the bike, was replaced with interest, as he noticed the bike was the same make and livery as the one which had been parked next to him at the hospice on the night Ava had died. Marcus watched as the rider dismounted, stretched and removed his helmet. He was, Marcus guessed, about 40 years old. The bike was a blue and white BMW Dakar F650GS and was fully loaded with side panniers and a large amount of additional luggage and fuel cans, strapped to the back.

Marcus was staring at the bike when he was startled by a tap on his window.

"Excuse me, mate. I'm going to the Premier Inn on the Lansdown Road. Am I headed in the right direction?"

Marcus gave the man directions to the hotel and watched as he climbed back onto his bike and rode away.

144

As an adolescent, Marcus had always wanted to ride a motorbike, but the idea had rapidly been quashed by his mother.

"Have you any idea how many kids' lives have been ruined by those death traps?" she had said. "You wouldn't be considering even going near one, if you had seen what I've seen coming into the hospital. Lives destroyed; I tell you. They should all be banned!"

Marcus had considered arguing, but decided it was a battle he was not going to win. Even using slightly manipulated accident statistics and a promise to ride carefully, which all young bikers rely on in an attempt to persuade reluctant parents, was not going to work on this battle-worn, orthopaedic nurse.

As Marcus drove along the road towards Leckhampton, the thoughts of his childhood, the time before Loughborough or Ava, the time when he felt optimistic about his future, filled his mind. He remembered the long summer days playing cricket with his friends and without making a conscious decision to re-route, found himself driving towards his old cricket club.

As he headed towards the tall, iron gates which marked the entrance to the club, Marcus noted that this was another place he had never visited with Ava and whilst he knew so much about her childhood, he realised that there were large segments of his old life he had never shared with her.

To Marcus's surprise, the gates at the entrance to the car park were closed. He parked the MG on the kerb further down the road and walked back towards the club. The sound of bike engines and voices shouting met him, as he approached the gates. As he peered through the bars, he noticed white markings on the tarmac and numerous orange cones, replicating a road layout. Three small bikes with riders in high visibility tabards weaved in and out of the cones and practiced U turns and emergency stops, as a man in full biking gear shouted instructions from the side. A large sign on the side of the cricket pavilion read,

'Karl's Motorcycle Training, CBT, Direct Access, Back to Biking, Advanced Riders Courses'

For the first time since that final night at the hospice, Marcus smiled to himself. "Are you trying to tell me something, Ava?"

The instructor led Marcus into the office at the front of the building.

"Direct Access will take you about a week, mate. If you're any good, I'll sort your test for the end of the week. Got any plans, once you've passed?"

Marcus signed the form on the table in front of him.

"Yep, I have," he said, "I'm going away for a while, just me and a bike and I know when I come back, I'll be a better person."

Chapter 11 – We'll Meet Again

"Well that fits, love," Jeanie said cheerfully, when Ava had explained the message on the steamed bathroom mirror.

"Why do you think you talked about your 'other mummy'?" Jeanie asked. "Has your mum told you anything else that you said as a kid?"

Ava told Jeanie about the stories everyone had believed she had concocted as a child.

"Mum said I told very imaginative stories. Apparently, I explained to people that my brown me me and I used to sell food from a funny hat," Ava went on, mimicking a child's voice. But as the words were leaving her mouth, she instinctively knew what Jeanie was thinking.

"Vietnamese people; they wear big hats, don't they, Jeanie?" Ava still had the leaflet that Linh had given her in school, all those years ago.

"It's called a leaf hat, love. They all wore them; men and women and sometimes they would carry fruit and veg in them, you know, to sell at market. Don't suppose you fancy a bit of hypnotherapy, do you; just to see if we can find out a bit more about this 'brown me me', love?"

Ava felt relieved that Jeanie had pre-empted her request for a regression.

"Do you think there's more to my stories than just a toddler's imagination, Jeanie?"

"Well, let's find out, shall we? How about Saturday; about two, eh?"

Ava had felt excited about her hypnotherapy with Jeanie. To her, Roisin's experience had been conclusive and having listened to the tapes and seen the birth certificate and had confirmation of the existence of the death certificate of Eveline Lytton, she was convinced that her birth mother had lived a previous life.

Like Roisin before her, Ava was particularly receptive to hypnosis and having been guided from her special place to the empty cinema, she responded well to Jeanie's request to, "Remember a significant time with your brown me me."

"There's washing. I help me me to hang it and she lets me pull the string to make it hang over the street to dry. There are baskets in the street. They have chickens and other animals in, and wooden tables with lots of things that people are selling."

"And where are these baskets and tables, love? Are you in a town or a city or maybe a village?"

Ava laughed, "We're in Saigon, of course. It's busy here. It's my home."

"You're doing so well, sweetheart. What's your name?" Jeanie waited, and watched Ava as she played with her fingers, as a shy child would.

"Chau Hang. It means Pearl Moon. It was my bà nội, my granny's name."

"And how old are you, Chau Hang?" Jeanie said, softly.

"I'm ten. I'm a big girl now. Me me takes me to sell cai lan, it's like broccoli, and bitter melon. We carry it in a basket. Sometimes the basket is too full and me me puts it in her hat. People buy it."

Jeanie was amazed at the fluency and detail of Ava's recall. "OK, Chau Hang. Now I'd like you to come forward, forward in time to a time close to your final moments in this lifetime. Press the fast forward button and stop at a time that is significant for you."

Ava went silent, her posture returning to that of a relaxed adult.

"When the image on the screen opens up," Jeanie continued, "you'll be at that significant time, ready? OK. Tell me what you can see."

Ava looked tense and Jeanie noticed beads of sweat on her brow. "Please. Please look after my baby. Please. Take this, my cross, and go to the mission. They'll know what to do." She opened her hand and pushed her arm forward, as if offering something to Jeanie.

Jeanie probed for more, "How old is your baby, Chau Hang?"

A tear rolled down Ava's cheek, "She's only 14 months old. We're all alone, me and my baby. Please don't let her die."

"What year is it, love, do you know that?" Jeanie strained to hear as Ava's voice faded,

"It's 1959 and I'm 19 but I'm really sick and I think I'm going to die." Ava's body went limp and the tension in her face, eased.

"Where are you now, love? Tell me what you can see," Jeanie whispered.

"I can see myself. I'm lying on my mat. I've gone now. I think I've passed but I can still see myself. Some of the people that live near are around me. Minh Huy, the old man that brings me herbs; he's with my baby. I can see my baby. Oh no, she's crying for me. Please look after her." Ava started to cry and sound distressed, "How could I leave her? I've failed her, my baby, I'm a bad, bad mother. Please, Minh Huy, take her to the mission."

Jeanie asked Ava to stop the scene and gradually brought her out of trance state.

Unlike Roisin, Ava could clearly recall most of her regression.

"I was Vietnamese, wasn't I? I died and left a child and that's why I can't face having children, Jeanie. What happened to my child? How did a one year old survive without her mother in Vietnam? Oh God, Jeanie. What did I do?"

Jeanie held Ava's hands tightly. "I believe that we all have a blueprint, sweetheart, and we all have to live that blueprint," she said, squeezing her hands. "We write it ourselves, long before we come here. It's specially designed so that we learn the life lessons we have to learn to, well, to progress, to develop and evolve as spiritual beings. Your child, I know it's hard to imagine, but your little girl, well, her me me dying was on her blueprint too. She needed that to happen so she could progress."

Ava wiped the tears from her face. "What about our loved ones, Jeanie? What about my mum and dad and Marcus? When we come back, do we get to be with our loved ones from our previous lives?"

Jeanie smiled. "I believe so, sweetheart. I believe that we stay with the same nucleus of people. We might change relationships, roles and even genders but we stay with the people who help us to grow. I believe, somewhere in your life as Ava Moran, you have, or will, know your baby in some way and you'll know, love; you'll know when you meet her. You'll feel it."

Ava listened to Jeanie and felt a lightness, a clarity and sense of peace that she had never felt before.

"When we've learned what we need to, I believe we go home, Ava. We call it dying but, really, it's just starting on a new path. We rest for a while; we might even be able to communicate with the people we have left behind for a little while. People like me are a conduit for those spirits, but then we choose a new path; a journey in this world and this time, or maybe another place and time entirely, to continue our evolution, our growth as a spiritual being. Don't ever worry about passing, my lovely, even if you're not old. It's just part of your progression and that of your loved ones."

The session with Jeanie had a profound effect on Ava. The knowledge that we remain with the people we love, albeit in different guises, provided an inner peace for her but the reasoning behind her aversion to being a parent, the awareness that she had left a small child an orphan, had created a sadness and a guilt that Ava found hard to shake.

Jeanie had given Ava the recording of the session and, initially, Ava had intended to play it for Marcus. Having considered his likely dismissal of the session as rubbish, in an attempt, no doubt, to make his girlfriend feel better, she decided not to share and instead chose to be economical with her version of events.

"I seemed to have memories of Saigon as a ten-year-old," she said casually, as Marcus listened. "I helped my mum, or my me me, sell produce. It seemed real enough but hey, who knows?"

Marcus had expected Ava to return effusive about her session and entirely convinced about the legitimacy of reincarnation. He was surprised at how brief her recounting of events had been but, also, secretly relieved that, just maybe, this would be the end of their frequent debates about past lives and spirits.

What Ava did share with her partner was Jeanie's blueprint analogy. "We design our own path, good and bad, babe. The choices we make about our lives are designed to develop us and the people we share our lives with. They help us to achieve our goals, our learnings. Once we have learnt what we need in one lifetime, we move on to the next."

Marcus tried not to show the exasperation he was feeling. "So, what Jeanie is saying is that sick people, drug addicts, murderers; they choose that path? People who live in poverty, people who suffer torture or injustice; they choose that? It's all part of their, their evolution? Really, Ava? Have you any idea how crazy that sounds?"

"I know, darling. I know it sounds, well, ridiculous but I get it Marcus. It makes sense that if we have to learn abandonment, injustice or tolerance, that we experience things which help us to accept these things."

Ava thought frequently about the hypnotherapy session and the implications of her recall being accurate. If her child had been only one in 1959, she would be only in her mid-thirties now, assuming she had survived at all. Ava reflected on Jeanie's deeply ingrained belief, that we create a blueprint for each of our lives; a blueprint which exposes us to people and events which help us to evolve. She wondered about Roisin's last blueprint and what this sad lady had learnt by being estranged from her parents and siblings, alone throughout her pregnancy, guilt ridden at giving up her child and dying, alone, an addict.

This was, she thought, at least the second lifetime when Roisin had died prematurely. Maybe she had completed her blueprint and learnt her life lessons quickly? Maybe there was some truth to the old saying that, 'only the good die young'?

When the brown, official looking envelope eventually arrived at the flat, Ava quickly picked it up and wandered into the bedroom to open it. She knew the contents would confirm what she was certain about already and wanted to avoid recommencing the whole past-life conversation with Marcus.

The certified copy of Eveline Lytton's death certificate confirmed her death as 9th June 1914.

Her age was, as Roisin had recounted, 28 and the place of death listed as HMP Holloway.

The cause of death surprised Ava. It was recorded as pneumonia, but Roisin had talked of being punched in the stomach and Ava had expected to see some trauma related cause of death. Nevertheless, it was there, in black and white; Eveline Lytton had lived and died a Suffragette.

Chapter 12 – Ignore the Head. Listen to the Heart

"Well done. You're a natural, mate. I knew you'd pass first time." Karl shook Marcus's hand, "This trip you're taking; got any details?"

Marcus looked at the montage of biker photographs which covered the office walls.

"Actually, I was going to ask you." Marcus paused and considered how best to ask Karl where the best place would be to take a motorbike trip, which would give him time to reconsider his entire future.

"I've gone through some shit recently, Karl; you know, some life changing stuff. I've got an opportunity to take some time out and I want to travel. I'm naturally a creature of habit; no risks, nothing new and it's time that changed. I want time to reflect but also to see and experience new things; you know, push the envelope a bit. If you were me, no ties, no responsibilities, no timetable; where would you take your bike, Karl?"

Karl laughed, "Have you any idea how many of the blokes I ride with would sell their mothers for a chance to sod off on their bikes, with no agendas; just to escape for a bit?"

Marcus shrugged. "Trust me, mate, it wasn't how I'd planned my future but, given my situation, it beats drinking myself into oblivion and slitting my wrists."

"Ever heard of the Pan American Highway?" Karl asked. "I'd bloody love to take the guts of a year out and do Alaska to Argentina. Wouldn't do it on the Honda though." Karl gestured towards the school bike which Marcus had just passed his test on.

Marcus was surprised at how energised he felt at Karl's suggestion.

"No? What would you do it on, you know, if you were flying a bike out to Alaska and planning to end up in, let's say, Buenos Aires?"

"BMW, mate. Dakar, F650GS. Hardy little bugger but pretty easy to maintain and repair. Get yourself down to the Beemer garage. They'll find you one."

To Karl's surprise, Marcus laughed out loud at his instructor's recommendation as he recalled both the bike at the hospice and the appearance of the blue Dakar at Inspiration Point in Birdlip.

"Why did I know you were going to recommend a Dakar?"

A number of the BMW dealerships could offer Marcus a new or nearly new Dakar. The Marcus of the past would have happily purchased one of the more readily available yellow or red liveried bikes, if they had been cheaper or newer or closer to Cheltenham but only Wollaston in Northampton had the blue and white bike, which Marcus was sure he was supposed to complete his journey on. The bike was just under a year old with 4,000 miles on the clock and came with the decent screen and Metal Mule side panniers, which Karl had advised were essential.

The Dakar was very different from the smaller road bike Marcus had completed his training on, but he felt at one with it almost immediately and he knew it was the right bike for his journey. "I'll sort some insurance out and collect it next weekend."

"No problem, Mr Crane. You'll need the model details and the registration number. Here you go." The young salesman looked alarmed as Marcus repeated the plate number and swore under his breath. "WF 51 AVA? For fucks sake!"

"I have to go back, Mum. I have to sort the house out before I fly."

Gwen Crane was concerned about Marcus returning to Buckinghamshire alone.

"It'll be distressing for you, going into that house alone. Why don't you let me or your father go with you?"

Marcus was so grateful to his parents for the love and support they had shown him over the last four weeks. He knew how hard it was for his mother, particularly, to see him so broken and he had heard her crying on more than one occasion.

"I feel so helpless, Terry. He's hurting so badly and all I can offer him are useless platitudes."

Marcus had shared his travel plans with his father, who had been aware of his son's motorbike lessons and subsequent test. They had agreed that, unless either of them was in a position where they would have to lie to Gwen, it was probably better to significantly edit the information they gave her, to prevent her worrying unnecessarily.

"I'm off travelling for a while, Mum. I've done some research and I'm going to start in Alaska and work my way down to Argentina, stopping off in various places along the way."

Terry had attempted to manage his wife's expectations, prior to Marcus's announcement but she was still noticeably alarmed at the extent of her son's travel plans.

"But that must be over 20,000 miles," she said, locating both Anchorage and Buenos Aires on the map, which she had unfolded onto the dining table. "How long will it take you and how will you do it?"

Terry Crane caught his son's eye and winked. "It will take just as long as he needs to start to heal, Gwen. He's a big boy now, love, and he'll find a way."

The trip back to Aylesbury was largely uneventful but Marcus noticed his heart beating stronger and faster as he approached the road into the housing estate. The green wheelie bins were dutifully positioned at the end of every drive; the postman, with his trolley of parcels and letters whistled happily as he marched up and down the uniform, tarmac driveways and a woman that Marcus had, on occasion, exchanged pleasantries with, walked her black Labrador along the otherwise empty pavement. The normality of the place struck Marcus hard. He knew he was being irrational, but he could not help feeling aggrieved at the world continuing as if nothing had happened and he had an overwhelming desire to stop the car and shout at the bin men and the postman and the overly cheerful woman to, 'JUST STOP!'

The sign outside the house surprised Marcus. He had only agreed to the marketing of the property two days before and had not expected the 'For Sale' sign to have been erected so quickly. He had considered letting the property whilst he was away but, having discussed with his brother the many potential pitfalls associated with tenants and realised that he no longer wanted to live in a property which he and Ava had shared, he opted to sell.

The house was cold, and the pile of accumulated letters and flyers blocked the door but, other than that, everything was as he had left it. Marcus was not sure why he was surprised at that and wondered what he had expected to be different.

Among the multitude of junk mail were a number of letters; bank statements, mobile phone bill and numerous clothing and toiletry mailings for Ava. Marcus noticed a small, white envelope and recognised the address from something Ava and he had discussed. He opened the envelope and read the neatly written letter:

1st June 2002

Bell House

Narbourne Avenue

Hackney

Dear Marcus,

I have deliberated for a while before writing to you. I had the pleasure of meeting with your delightful partner a couple of times and she shared with me that, whilst you were always supportive, you found the idea of past lives very difficult to accept.

I know that the last regression I conducted with Ava was lifechanging for her. Whilst the circumstances around her passing and leaving a small child were initially uncomfortable for her, the knowledge that both our ability to evolve and our relationships continue beyond each lifetime, were a great comfort to her, as she began her journey 'home' in May this year.

She has asked me to contact you and ask that you listen to the recording from our last session, which she never

played for you. I hope the enclosed will help you to locate it and will validate Ava's message of love to you.
Best wishes,
Jeanie

Marcus sat down at the kitchen table and read the letter several times. He clearly remembered Ava returning from her regression with Jeanie, way back. It must have been 1992 or 1993 and she had seemed surprisingly under-whelmed by the session. He remembered feeling relieved at her lack of enthusiasm and her reluctance to discuss the session in any depth. He would certainly not have surmised, given her demeanour, that the session had been lifechanging and she had never mentioned it, or Jeanie, again.

Marcus looked back inside the envelope and removed a small, folded page which had been ripped out of a book. In the centre of the page was a flag and Marcus recognised it immediately as that of Peru. In the middle of the flag was a hand drawn heart with an arrow running through it, much like a child would draw. Above the flag was a drawing of a suitcase and below it, a child's sticker of a cartoon motorbike. Marcus's immediate reaction was to laugh. The page was clearly a childlike depiction of his forthcoming trip: the suitcase, the map of Peru which he would visit in the latter half of his journey and the motorbike. But how the hell did Jeanie know this stuff? The only people he had told about the trip were his parents, his brother and Karl, the instructor, and even his mother was blissfully unaware of the motorbike.

The following day, the removal packers arrived. Marcus had already begun sorting crockery, glassware and ornaments into three boxes marked 'storage', 'charity' and 'Mum'. He was surprised how quickly the house began to look empty and soulless and made the decision to stay at the Green Dragon in the centre of the village, once the packing was complete, until he left for the airport in five days' time.

"What do you want doing with this, Mr Crane?" The shout from one of the removal guys jolted Marcus from his thoughts, as he sorted stacks of old statements, letters and utility bills into piles he had mentally marked as 'keep' and 'chuck'. Marcus climbed the stairs and went into the small guest room, where the young man was standing.

"This was under the bed. Do you want it to go into storage as it is?"

Marcus hadn't remembered seeing the grey, leather suitcase before and assumed it must have been Ava's. "It's OK, mate, I'll take it," Marcus said, as he carried it back down to the paper-covered study.

The suitcase was quite heavy and the rattle inside indicated that it was probably full of discarded junk, which Ava had hoarded and moved from one residence to another, rarely opening it. As he opened the stiff zip on the case, he saw the cassette recorder on which Ava had played

Roisin's regression tapes. Strings of brightly coloured, plastic beads, ungainly paste brooches and costume rings, were the items responsible for the clatter, as Marcus had lifted the case down the stairs. Old school exercise books and power leads, from appliances long since disposed of, were knotted into a spaghetti of wires and at the side of the case was a cassette tape in a plastic holder. Marcus picked it up and looked at the writing on the spine of the little plastic case, *Ava Moran, October 1992, #1*

The image of the little, hand drawn suitcase, on the torn book page included in Jeanie's letter, immediately sprang into Marcus's mind, along with the passage she had written.

'Listen to the recording from our last session, which she never played for you. I hope the enclosed will help you to locate it and will validate Ava's message of love to you.'

The Green Dragon was not the most salubrious of establishments, but the food was decent and the choice of local craft beers, more than acceptable to Marcus. The room, in which he had piled everything he would be taking on his trip, was dark and cramped but it had a small ensuite and TV and the bed was comfortable. Ava had developed a dislike for the pub when, on the couple's first visit, a dirty wine glass was followed with an uncooked piece of chicken.

"The place isn't sanitary, Marcus. We'll end up with food poisoning."

A complaint to the duty manager had been met with a patronising roll of the eyes and no reduction in the bill and Ava had refused to go in again, even though it was, technically, their local hostelry. Marcus ordered a burger and pint of IPA from the bar and returned to his room. He had brought the cassette player and Ava's regression tape with him and sat on the bed to listen to the recording of the 1992 session.

Marcus thought he was prepared for the sound of Ava's voice but as she started to speak, the shock was akin to a physical pain and left him breathless. He listened to the tone and pitch of Ava's voice change as she adopted the persona of the ten-year-old Vietnamese child and realised he would not have recognised Ava from the voice, had he not known who it was. Marcus rationalised the first part of the regression with the fact that Ava had always talked about her 'brown me me with a funny hat'. Surely, she would be able to create a story in her head, if asked to imagine a previous life.

The second part of the regression alarmed him. This voice, this person, was not his Ava. The accent, the tone and the intonation were those of someone he did not know and the anguish this poor woman was clearly feeling was disturbing to Marcus. He listened again to the young girl begging the old man to take her baby to the mission and wondered about the accuracy of the content. Did missions even exist in Vietnam in the 1950s? Would a 19-year-old be allowed to die without any medical assistance? After all, this was 1959 not the middle ages.

"I was Vietnamese, wasn't I? I died and left a child and that's why I can't face having children, Jeanie?"

Marcus listened to Ava sobbing and had to pause the tape for a minute to catch his breath. "Why didn't she tell me? Was I so narrow-minded, so parochial that she couldn't share this devastating, life-influencing knowledge with me?" Marcus wiped away the tear rolling down his cheek as he restarted the tape and listened to Jeanie explain her blueprint and after-life philosophy.

"You gave her peace, Jeanie," he whispered to himself, "and maybe you've given me a little, too."

He thought about Linh, Ava's friend and mentor and decided to ask her for clarification on the details he had questioned about the mission in Saigon and the availability of medical help for a poor, single girl. Marcus had no idea about Linh's origins or the marked parallels between Ava's past life and her teacher's start in life. Sending Linh the tape would, unbeknown to him, create an elation and a regret in Linh that she could never have imagined.

Chapter 13 – Highway to Healing

The cargo company at Heathrow Airport had advised Marcus to leave the bike for the processing of documents, packing and shipping, at least a week before his own flight to Anchorage. The entire process of locating the company which Karl had recommended, arranging the documentation and dropping the Dakar off was, Marcus felt, remarkably straightforward. His natural default was to comprehensively plan every last detail; routes, hotels, even potential bike servicing and maintenance centres, but he had resisted the urge to arrange or book anything for this trip. His insistence on having a structured itinerary every time they had travelled had been a constant irritation to Ava. Frequently, during a weekend trip or a holiday, they had been given recommendations for events or locations which they were unable to attend due to planned and pre-paid commitments elsewhere.

"For God's sake, darling," Ava would groan, "let's just be spontaneous for once."

With the house now cleared and on the market, Marcus had decided to take a trip to Hackney to meet with Jeanie, prior to following his bike out to Alaska to start his Pan American journey. The tape had raised a number of questions and in an attempt to be more open-minded, he had wanted the opportunity to meet the lady who had made such an impression on Ava.

"I'm so sorry for your loss, love. Such a lovely girl, she was." Jeanie linked her arm through Marcus's and led him into the room where she had met with Ava ten years earlier.

Marcus had relied on Ava's parents to inform most friends and family about his partner's death and he had wondered if, perhaps, her mother had contacted Jeanie.

"No, love. It was Vera that told me. She's 95 now, you know. Lives in Holly View, the old people's place in Brixton Hill. She needs a little help now."

Marcus was still puzzled, "Did Ava's Mum contact Vera? I didn't know she knew her, Jeanie."

Jeanie smiled and shook her head teasingly. "Ava said you were a hard nut to crack, sweetheart." She winked at her confused guest. "Vera doesn't have to wait for people to give her important messages, love. Ava told her, herself."

Not waiting for Marcus to comment or question, Jeanie sat on the edge of her chair,

"Anyway, love, what can I do for you?"

Marcus reached into the inside pocket of his jacket and removed the torn-out book page which had accompanied Jeanie's letter.

"I found the regression tape. It was in an old suitcase of Ava's. I have a motorbike trip booked and the route takes in Peru, but no one knew that stuff, Jeanie. Only my father, brother and bike instructor even know that I ride a motorbike. The three illustrations on this sheet, they're all completely relevant and pretty impossible to guess at so.." Marcus stopped talking and looked at Jeanie.

"So, how did I know, son?" Jeanie asked. "I didn't, but your Ava did. The page you have there, it was on the sofa where Ava had her hypnotherapy session; sitting on the cushion, clear as day, on 14th May. All I did is fold it and send it to you. To be honest, I had no idea what it meant, love, but I thought you would."

Marcus sat in silence for a few seconds. The date that Jeanie had found the torn page had not gone unnoticed. Ava had lost her short fight with cancer that day and his life had changed forever. Part of him, the logical, scientific part, desperately wanted to be able to rationalise what Jeanie had just said, but he could not.

"The regression, Jeanie, it had a massive impact on Ava. The thought that she had abandoned a baby, albeit unwillingly, well, it appalled her, changed her. With all of your experience, not just as a hypnotherapist but as a very spiritual person, a psychic medium, do you really believe we have lived before or could it be our imaginations?"

Jeanie put her hand on Marcus's cheek and smiled, kindly. "It doesn't matter what I believe, love. Part of being at peace, for me anyway, is not having to substantiate everything, analyse everything and instead just see, listen and feel what's given to me. There's none so blind as those that don't want to see; so true that is. I don't blame you for wanting answers, sweetheart, it's the way you're made, but maybe this trip of yours will help you to accept that there are things we can't define. That's what makes life so magnificent, love."

Marcus was not sure what to believe, as he travelled the 35-minute rail journey back to Aylesbury. Jeanie was right, he needed answers and struggled with weak or unsubstantiated explanations; he always had but, until now, he had seen that as a strength. No one could fob him off with statements like 'It just is' or 'No one really knows why'. To Marcus, there was always a reason, an explanation, an answer; except today. Today Marcus had no answers.

At the end of their meeting, Jeanie had handed Marcus a tape. It was a pre-recorded tape of a guided meditation.

"It's a decent introduction to hypnosis," Jeanie had said. "I had considered asking if you'd like a short session while you're here, love, but I think this is probably a better option for now."

Marcus took the tape and looked at the illustration on the front of the case,

'Meet Your Spirit Guide, a guided introduction to self-hypnosis'.

Back at the Green Dragon, he closed the curtains, put the tape into the cassette player and lay on the bed. The mellow, female voice was softened further with the sounds of gentle instrumental music, the kind he had heard once when Ava had talked him into going for an aromatherapy massage at the local spa. The music was punctuated with sounds of the wind and of waves crashing on a beach and the narrator provided instructions on deep breathing. *"Imagine your body filling with light, bright healing light, that's it, now exhale."*

Initially, Marcus concentrated on the woman's directions but, after what felt to him to be far too long on breathing instructions, he noticed his mind had wandered to airport cargo depots, visas and motorbikes. Frustrated, he tried again, *"and in, count to five, hold, count to five and exhale, good. Now, you're on a beach, a beautiful, golden sandy beach. Feel the warm sand between your toes and hear the sea lapping at the shore. Notice the warmth of the sun on your shoulders and back. Doesn't that feel good?"*

The tuneful hum of the narrator's voice continued. Marcus shuffled on the bed. The pillows were too high and his neck was uncomfortable.

"Feel that warm, clear water lapping at your toes."

Now he felt cold and frustrated, as he wondered why the hell he had taken his sweater off. "Oh bollocks!" he snapped, sitting up, irritated at the woman for her monotonous drone, annoyed at himself for not concentrating and pissed at the world in general.

The weather in Anchorage was overcast and cold when Marcus landed. The plane had arrived at 22:10 and he had decided to stay at a local hotel overnight and travel back to the cargo building early the following morning to collect his bike. The little hotel was on the waterfront and offered a clean, functional room and a small restaurant and bar. Having taken a quick shower, he walked down to the bar and ordered a beer. He sat down at a small table by the window and unfolded a map of the Dalton Highway. Deadhorse in Prudhoe Bay, the unofficial terminus of the Pan American Highway, was to be Marcus's northern most stop on the trip and would, he anticipated, require at least three days' riding.

He stared out of the window into the dark night, the lake lit with the reflection from the ornamental lights in the hotel grounds and he wondered if his decision to travel solo to such a remote, unforgiving environment had been hasty.

He had adapted well to riding but, other than a few additional off-road hours with Karl, his experience was almost entirely on well made, well maintained, well populated British roads.

The internet photographs of the dirt tracks and pot-holed roads from Fairbanks, his next stop and the beginning of the Dalton Highway, up to the Arctic Ocean at Prudhoe

Bay, had not concerned Marcus unduly. He had viewed the many pictures of the bleak landscapes and harsh weather conditions from the comfort of an arm chair at the Green Dragon and with the soothing influence of a second and third beer, Marcus was in no doubt that he would be up to the challenge. Now, however, alone and jet lagged following his 18-hour journey from Heathrow via Seattle, his confidence was waning.

"Mind if I join you?" Marcus turned his gaze from the window towards the voice. A man in dirt stained and wet biker textiles stood next to his table, a bottle of Budweiser in his hand.

"Sure." Marcus gestured towards the chair opposite. "Where have you come in from?"

"Just back from Prudhoe Bay. What a trip! Good to meet you, man. I'm Tommy. You?" Tommy held out a cold and dirty hand, stained from the sodden leather of his black biking gloves.

Marcus shook his hand. "Marcus. Marcus Crane. Good to meet you, Tommy. I'm setting off towards Deadhorse tomorrow. How was it?"

Tommy laughed. "Can I use profanities?" he said, shaking his head. "It was, er, character building. The roads, well, it's a stretch to call some of them roads; more like muddy, gravel dirt tracks. What you riding?"

Marcus sighed. "Dakar, 650. What about you?" Tommy swigged from his bottle of beer.

173

"Yamaha Sport Tourer. Nice enough bike but my mistake was taking the trip on road tyres. Hope you've got dirt-track tyres on the BMW?"

Marcus did not comment but made a mental note to get the tyres on the Dakar changed the following morning. "Any other tips, Tommy," he asked, wondering if the first day of his trip would be spent ensuring his entire bike and equipment were suitable for purpose.

"The Haul Road, as it used to be called, was built for the big rigs to deliver machinery to the oil fields and for the construction of the Trans Alaska pipeline. It's not meant for tourists and didn't even open to the public until 1994. The trucks have the right of way, so use your mirrors; I didn't even notice one sneaking right up on me, I was concentrating so hard.

Don't want to end up in a ditch now, so mind your manners. Take a couple of extra fuel cans: there are some pretty long stretches without gas stations. Oh, and take a bear spray and something to keep the mosquitos at bay; there are trillions of the critters and they hit you like bullets."

Marcus listened to Tommy and was glad of his recommendations. He ordered another couple of beers and gave one to his new drinking buddy.

"So, what made a Brit want to do the Pan Am on his own then?" Tommy asked.

Marcus had never found it particularly easy or comfortable to disclose personal details to anyone other than his closest friends and family. Even expressing his feelings to his parents, following Ava's illness and death, had taken him well out of his comfort zone. Tonight, discussions about a shared challenge with a stranger, along with the soothing impact of the beers, seemed to inspire Marcus to talk. He told Tommy about Ava and his father's recommendation to take some time out.

"It's probably not the best time to make life decisions, you know, when I've just been through some major emotional trauma, but every time I came up with an excuse for not taking the trip, something just seemed to happen to encourage me," Marcus explained.

He told Tommy about the Dakar at the hospice, the touring biker, on the same blue and white F650 at Inspiration Point, his impromptu trip to the old cricket club, which just happened to have shared use with a motorbike training business, and his lessons with Karl.

"It sounds crazy, I know, but the coincidences just seemed to keep happening and I ran out of reasons to ignore them."

Tommy listened intently to Marcus. "The Universe has a funny way of making us do the stuff we're meant to be doing. Never did believe in coincidences. The Pan American; she must be on your blueprint man and, you know what, you'll have a blast."

Whether it was Tommy's encouraging words or the effects of the alcohol, Marcus noticed his anxiety had turned to excitement as he lay down for the night.

" 'The Pan American; she must be on your blueprint.' That's what Ava would have said," he whispered to himself, as he drifted off to sleep.

The following morning, Marcus located his crated bike in a carpark near the cargo centre.

Having completed the documentation required to finalise the import of the Dakar, he limped his almost empty bike to the nearest fuel garage. A poster on the wall near to the cashier's desk was advertising motorbike servicing and repairs. Marcus noticed the logos at the bottom of the poster; Harley Davidson, KTM, Yamaha and BMW.

"Is this place local?" he asked the woman behind the desk.

"Sure, just around the back here," she said cheerfully, pointing towards the rear of the service station.

The motorbike garage was buzzing with bikers and repair technicians and a number of fringed-leather clad, bearded Harley riders sat on plastic chairs, drinking coke from a vending machine. Marcus watched as one by one the various bikes underwent their required oil or tyre changes and his thoughts drifted to the many hours of riding ahead of him.

"Your chain's not in good shape, bud. Want it changed?" Marcus's day dream was interrupted by the young garage worker. "You planning on going far? You don't need it breaking and damaging the bike."

Marcus was relieved that the young guy had spotted the potentially calamitous problem and authorised the chain change. He thought about the chances of meeting Tommy the previous night and his opportune mention of his inadequate road tyres, encouraging Marcus to change his own. He thought about the poster in the fuel station and the motorbike repair shop that just happened to be on site and he imagined being hundreds of miles from anywhere, in hideous weather and with a broken chain; and he smiled at the serendipity.

Marcus returned to the repair shop reception to pay for the repairs to the Dakar and purchased the bear spray, mosquito repellent and two additional empty fuel cans, as Tommy had advised.

The initial leg of the trip was to Fairbanks, 360 miles and around six and a half biking hours from Anchorage. This would be Marcus's first opportunity to fill up with fuel and then begin the real adventure.

The journey from Fairbanks to Prudhoe Bay evoked a range of emotions in Marcus. The riding conditions, which had been standard, paved roadways between Anchorage and Fairbanks, were now largely dirt track. The inclement weather had caused large stretches of the highway to be muddy and peppered with pot holes and the gravelled surface necessitated him standing up on the foot pegs for many hours at a time.

For the first 200 miles, the hills were covered in dense fir trees and he could smell the aroma, even though, for much of the time, the mist prevented him seeing the greenery.

A stop at the entrance to the Arctic Circle and the obligatory photograph presented a brief, welcome rest. Fearful of the powerful and dangerous trucks which kicked up showers of stones, rocks and mud in their wake, Marcus was disinclined to take breaks at the side of the highway, and he could feel the burn in his thighs and calves as the miles passed.

The 800-mile, grey Alaskan fuel pipeline, which runs from Prudhoe Bay in the north to Valdez oil terminal, the nearest ice-free port, lined the majority of his route and was the only constant as the weather, terrain and visibility went from poor to torturously bad.

The Yukon River crossing presented the first fuel stop since Fairbanks and Tommy's words rang in Marcus's ears: "I recommend you go steady and don't waste fuel. If the weather is too bad for you to keep going, you'll need enough fuel to get back."

The view from the bridge over the crossing was breathtaking, although the wooden surface of the bridge was wet and slippery and Marcus had felt his heart beat increase several times as he noticed the Dakar wheels slipping underneath him.

The final part of the journey up to Prudhoe Bay from Coldfoot, the last available fuel stop, took him six and a half hours. As he rode into Deadhorse the mist cleared enough for him to realise the nothingness of the place.

An assortment of white and grey dilapidated buildings greeted him. The town appeared to be a combination of sheds and structures built on stilts, many of which reminded Marcus of the prefabricated classrooms from his childhood primary school, and the place felt soulless.

Industrial plant, trucks and containers were scattered indiscriminately across a dank and desolate landscape and he wondered who would ever choose to visit this Godforsaken place. As he got off the dirt-caked bike, the bitter Arctic wind cut through him and Marcus could not remember ever feeling so cold.

At Tommy's recommendation, he had called the Prudhoe Bay Hotel from Fairbanks and booked a room for the night.

"The hotel nearly always has vacancies," Tommy had said, "but you don't want to get up there and find you don't have any accommodation."

Marcus laughed to himself as he entered the tiny, wood panelled cabin with two single beds and considered what the $105 per night charge would have bought him in Buckinghamshire. He had learnt from his pre-trip research that Deadhorse was a dry town, with no alcohol allowed to be either purchased or consumed in the area. So, with a beer in the hotel restaurant not an option and having bought some food from his last stopover in Wiseman, he planned to eat quickly and settle down to a good night's rest, before embarking on the return trip the following day.

As he lay on his tiny bed, his mind played his Dalton Highway adventure over and over and he hoped the return trip would be easier. He had just dozed off when there was a knock at the door. At first he thought the loud tapping had been part of his dream but a few seconds later, it came again. Reluctantly he climbed out of his warm bed to undo the bolt on the door and find out who was disturbing his much-needed rest.

The woman from the hotel reception stood at the door looking embarrassed,

"I'm sorry to disturb you, Mr Crane, but we have a guy in the lobby, just arrived on his motorcycle and, well, we have no more vacancies. Would you consider sharing your room?"

Marcus rubbed his eyes and sighed. He thought about how relieved he had been to finally arrive at the hotel. He knew he had probably only been able to get a room because he had been fortunate enough to have received Tommy's recommendation to reserve one. As he looked past the woman, down the hallway towards reception, he was aware of the tired and grubby biker hovering in the doorway, "Sure, no problem. Send him in," he said, wearily. He left the door to the room ajar and returned to his bed.

"You're a life saver. Thank you so much." The bedraggled biker was soaking wet and covered in dirt and mud from the long road. Marcus smiled and propped himself up on his pillow. "You're welcome. I've just survived that

God-awful journey myself. Dump your stuff and grab a shower. Beer is a no go so fancy a coffee?" Marcus pointed towards the small kettle and the pot of instant coffee sachets.

His new roommate was Grant Bruton and ten minutes after his unexpected arrival, the pair were exchanging details of their arduous journey from Anchorage. Marcus suddenly felt wide awake and was unusually interested in what might have motivated this polished young man, who was significantly now more fragrant than on his arrival, to take this hideous trip.

"I spent the last 200 miles wishing I'd turned around at Coldfoot," Grant grumbled into his steaming coffee. It was a mother of a journey but, shit, it still beats the hell out the office! What about you?"

Marcus shrugged, disinclined to mar the atmosphere with the story of his bereavement,

"Just fancied a challenge, I suppose," he said, avoiding Grant's gaze.

Grant looked unconvinced. "Yeh, right. You fly 20 hours from the UK and ride a death trap on the highway to hell to the asshole of the world because 'you fancied a challenge'?"

Marcus laughed. "OK. So, I needed to escape before I bored my miserable self into an early grave. What about you?"

Grant poured out his story as if he had been waiting for a receptive ear for years. The 29-year-old lawyer worked for his father's law firm in New York City. An only child, he was a natural academic and, being ruthlessly driven by his father, had achieved good results at high school and been Valedictorian as well as top performer in the school league football team. Grant considered himself a people person and had always imagined using his intellect and emotional intelligence to, in some way, help people who were disadvantaged; those who had been presented with significantly fewer opportunities than he had been in his short, privileged existence. Life had turned out differently for Grant and his talents were, he regretted, being used to make fat business cats even fatter.

"Dad had other ideas. Only a law degree and fast-track in the family law firm were ever on the radar and only Harvard or Yale was acceptable." Grant tutted to himself, "And like a weak, freaking jerk, I let him push me around. Now, oh yes, I'm smart and rich and fucking bored out of my mind and I hate myself for being a dick."

Marcus was fascinated. In his limited experience, affluent and avaricious adults typically produced entitled and equally avaricious off-spring; he had seen it as a teacher. He had, for a short time, many years previously, been a substitute teacher at a prestigious boys' public school. He had witnessed the pressure from wealthy, influential and ambitious parents, to give 'little Montague' a place on the 1st team, when little Montague could hardly tie his boots, let alone hold his own on a rugby field. Whilst the sycophantic persuasion fell on deaf ears when aimed at Marcus, the promises of donations to school charities and improvement projects always had the desired effect and managed to persuade the Head that 'little Montague' was just the man for the team. As the little Montagues of the world grew up, they invariably expected the same level of favouritism and Marcus felt lightened by Grant's unusual modesty and refreshing honesty.

"It was Mum who actually persuaded the old man to let me take the time out to do this trip; the SOB said 'No' when I asked. He only re-considered when I threatened to quit."

For a brief moment, and for the first time since Ava died, Marcus felt fortunate. Other than his father's well-meaning insistence on Marcus's attendance at church and Sunday school, he had never felt manipulated or controlled.

"So, what's the plan when the trip's over, Grant?" Marcus asked.

Grant paused, as if considering whether to confide in his new friend. "I met someone, last year in Delhi. I was on vacation and I met a woman who I initially went to see for anxiety." Grant paused and took a deep breath. "Christ, I can't believe I'm saying this; my father would freak if I even mentioned anxiety to him."

Marcus waited for Grant to compose himself and continue, "She was a hypnotherapist and she specialised in something called past-life regression." Grant looked at his roommate and expected Marcus to laugh, or worse, mock the subject. To Grant's amazement, Marcus did not flinch. "Go on, mate. I'm more than familiar with past-life regression," he said, noting Grant's nervousness immediately subsiding and waiting for his somewhat emotional roommate to continue.

"I'm not sure where to start; you see," Grant took a deep breath, "I believe I've lived before, dude. Actually, that's not true: I know I've lived before." Grant looked at Marcus and waited for the patronising dismissal or the ruthless sarcasm he believed he deserved, but it never came.

"I feel an unrelenting, uncontrollable empathy when I meet people who have been unfairly treated, sometimes even ruined, by wealthy people who can buy victory when they don't deserve it. I know that my destiny is not to be a corporate lawyer; it's just not what I'm here to learn. I think I'm meant to have the balls to do the right thing; leave the law firm and help the poor schmucks that the rich bastards I work for exploit." Marcus noticed Grant's head lower and guessed he was crying.

"It's OK, mate," Marcus said, quietly, "my partner; she believed she'd lived before. That knowledge had a fundamental impact on her life but it gave her a peace; a clarity that enabled her to pass without any fear and I'm so grateful for that."

Marcus explained the journey Ava had taken, having established that her birth mother had also lived a previous life. "It's taken me a while, mate," Marcus felt the emotion rising inside him, "but I'm starting to wonder if there may just be something in this stuff. Follow your heart, Grant."

Marcus woke at 4am. The proximity to the Arctic Circle meant it was light outside and the glare through the poorly covered window woke him. As he turned over in his small bed, he became aware of the crackle of paper and noticed the handwritten note on his pillow,

"Thank you, Marcus. You'll never know how much you helped me. Hope to meet you again, in this life or the next. Grant"

Chapter 14 – Pay it Forwards

The ride back from Prudhoe Bay felt much easier to Marcus. Completing the long stretch of mud track from Coldfoot to Deadhorse without serious injury had given him a renewed confidence.

"Better weather today," the Receptionist had said, as Marcus checked out. "Enjoy the ride but don't get complacent; the pot holes can catch you out and there's a lot of big, fast rigs out there."

The weather was significantly kinder as Marcus set off and whilst still being cold, the previous day's wind, which had cut through the many layers of his clothing and chilled him to the bone, had dropped. Large patches of blue sky allowed the sun to break through and he became far more aware of the patchwork of colours and the smells of the vast landscape as he rode through the miles back towards Fairbanks.

Having rested overnight in Wiseman, Marcus set off early the next day. The conditions were, once again, favourable and as the hours passed, he became less conscious of the bike and allowed his thoughts to wander.

"20,000 miles, son," his father had warned. "That's a lot of time alone in your helmet. Make sure you use it positively."

Marcus knew his dad was right. It would be so easy to allow feelings of self-pity and thoughts of what could have been to absorb this time and he had tried hard to remain focussed on the experiences he was having each day; the places, the people and the learnings. His mind drifted back to the night in Prudhoe Bay and his unexpected conversation with his surprise room share. Marcus pondered the chain of improbable events which led to his deep discussion with Grant. He wondered what the chances were, in Deadhorse of all places, of being asked to share his room with not just an advocate of re-incarnation, but an individual who had seemingly come to the same realisation as Ava and Roisin; that he had lived before this life. He had liked Grant and had felt an enormous amount of respect for a man who could walk away from a comfortable life in order to follow his calling. Marcus thought about his own career as a teacher and realised that he had never really given much thought to a vocation. He had applied to Loughborough to do a Bachelor of Education simply because he was good at sport and primarily because his own Head of Physical Education had suggested it. Hearing Grant talk with such passion about his preferred professional route had made Marcus recognise the indifference he felt about his job. He liked the kids, or at least most of them, most of the time, but he despised the increasing need to toe the party line in order to progress. He had seen his colleagues climb high onto their metaphorical soap boxes in order to support a personal principle, only to perform a complete U turn when it was professionally lucrative to do so. He thought about returning to his job in Hemel Hempstead and felt a sinking feeling. Maybe it was time to do what Grant was doing, and move on?

The truck came out of nowhere, scattering debris from the road and a deluge of pot-hole water over Marcus and the bike. Marcus's mind had been so occupied with other things that he had been completely unprepared, and his automatic reaction was to grab the front brake. As the front wheel dipped and the rear wheel skidded around to the left, he put his right leg to the ground, in the vain attempt to stop the fully loaded bike from falling. As the 230kg bike bit the dust, he realised his mistake in attempting to save it,

"It's nearly three times your weight, mate. Let the fucker drop!" Marcus could hear Karl's voice ringing in his ears and knew, as soon as he had felt the twinge in his back, that he had committed a school boy error.

He estimated he was about an hour and a half out of Fairbanks as he looked at the Dakar, bent and filthy, its load of rolled luggage and panniers shed across the deserted highway. With the exception of the truck, Marcus had not seen a single vehicle for over two hours. His somewhat antiquated mobile phone indicated that there was no mobile reception and as he dragged the fallen luggage to the side of the road, he felt angry with his lapse in concentration. The bike had fallen clear of the centre and Marcus had managed to push the rear wheel, so it was now out of the way of any further inconsiderate rig drivers. He perched on a rock on the road verge, wondering what to do next and noticed a small, red coloured bird on the branch of a fir, on the far side of the highway. As the bird pecked at the needles on the branch and its delicate wing dropped down to support its balance, Marcus noticed how the shape of its wing was exactly the same shape as the tiny birthmark below Ava's ear. He watched the bird for a while and thought how out of place the bright little creature looked in the otherwise grey and green environment. He knew nothing about birds and began to rummage in one of the panniers to find his camera. When he turned back, the bird had gone and he was just about to re-pack his camera when he realised it was perched on the deformed handlebars of his damaged bike.

"Brave little chap, aren't you?" he said, as he scattered a few crumbs from a half-eaten cereal bar he had found in the pocket of his jacket. He took a couple of pictures of the bird pecking at the crumbs before noticing the small ripples in the water filled potholes, indicating the oncoming downpour. As his feathered companion flew away, Marcus became aware of the distant sound of an approaching engine.

"You OK, man?" A heavily built man adjusted his Anchorage Bucs baseball cap as he jumped out of the pick-up. "Looks like you had a spill. You hurt?"

Marcus shook his head, "Only my pride. Don't suppose you could help me lift the bike? I think I've stuffed my back up."

The good Samaritan was Jake, a police officer from Fairbanks and was taking Mikey, his young son, up into the mountains to fish. He helped Marcus stand the bike and shook his head. "That ain't going anywhere with bars like that. Let's get it onto the truck and I'll take you to get that back of yours fixed."

Marcus felt bad about ruining the pair's day but neither Jake nor Mikey seemed bothered at the interruption or about their premature return to Fairbanks, as they chatted to their passenger about his ride from Deadhorse.

"It's a real bad road, that highway," Jake warned. "Claims a few riders every year; and truckers. It's sure not unusual to see a rig on its side in the fall or winter, when the ice hits."

Marcus shuffled as the pain in his lower back intensified. "The local wildlife is friendly though," he said, showing Jake's son the picture of the little bird in the display window of the small, digital camera.

"That's a white-winged crossbill," Mikey said excited, "We just call it the 'Wing'. The females; they're yellow or green but the males are either red or orange."

Jake sounded surprised. "You hear the Wing a lot in these parts, but you don't often see them. They stay high and feed from the seeds in the fir cones. I don't think I've ever seen one on the highway and they sure wouldn't generally go anywhere near a vacationer."

Mikey laughed, "Maybe he was taking care of you 'til we arrived."

The osteopath was closed by the time the pick-up arrived back in Fairbanks, so Jake took Marcus back to the red and white, cabin style house he owned on the outskirts of the main commercial area. "We have a spare room. You'll be more comfortable here than in a motel," he said, lifting Marcus's muddy panniers from the back of the truck. "I'll drop your bike into the shop while you get settled. Joe's a buddy of mine. He'll have it sorted by the time you've had your back looked at."

Jake handed some of Marcus's luggage to Mikey. "Get our guest a beer, son. I'll be back in 15."

Marcus felt embarrassed at the inconvenience he had caused Jake and Mikey and had objected when Jake first suggested he stay with them. "I couldn't possibly. You've done more than I could ever have asked for, Jake. I'll be fine at a motel."

Jake had ignored his protestations. "Mikey and I will be glad of the company. I'll cook us all a steak."

The following morning Jake drove Marcus to the osteopath and went to check on the Dakar. The small waiting area was dark with posters of various sections of the human anatomy and a full-sized model of the human skeleton hanging from a hook. The telephone rang every few moments and tripped to an answer phone. "Hi. This is Kelly-Anne. Thank you for your call. Please leave your name and number and I'll get right back to you."

Marcus was relieved at the apparent demand for Kelly-Anne's services. His previous aches and pains had only ever been addressed by fully qualified, old, wrinkly medical professionals and whilst Ava had always sworn by the local chiropractor and osteopath, Marcus had always preferred the GP and inevitable regular doses of Ibuprofen.

"Marcus?" A cheerful young woman in white scrubs and crocks held out her hand. Marcus was relieved to see the formal medical attire; the type a doctor in the emergency room would have worn, had he gone to the hospital.

"I hear you've been giving your back a hard time. Come this way."

Kelly-Anne waited for Marcus to push himself slowly out of his chair and walk towards her.

Having examined his posture and noted the limitations of his movement, Kelly-Anne asked him to sit on the edge of the massage bed.

"OK," she said, "this isn't a spinal problem, Marcus. It looks like your muscles went into spasm when you tried to hold the bike up. You have options but what you do depends on you." Marcus looked at Kelly-Anne and waited for her to continue.

"I can massage your back and recommend Advil; that's a pretty effective anti-inflammatory. It'll help but more than an hour on a motorcycle will hurt like hell."

Marcus sighed. "What's the other option?"

"Reiki," Kelly-Anne said, shrugging and waiting for Marcus to dismiss her suggestion out of hand.

"Reiki?" Marcus repeated. "Isn't that, like, hands-on healing? Like energy healing?"

Kelly-Anne nodded. "It's originally a Japanese practice; used for stress reduction and healing; healing the mind, body and spirit. Most medics don't recognise it, but I've had pretty impressive results. That's what all those phone calls coming through were for."

Marcus thought for a second about the constant ringing of the phone while he had been waiting for Kelly-Anne. "So, how does that help my back?"

"It works on energy, universal life force energy. That's what the 'ki' stands for.

Your body knows how to heal itself; I simply facilitate it."

Kelly-Anne turned away from Marcus. She had made a judgement that her patient was probably not one to wander too far from convention and she did not want to place undue pressure on him to consent to something he was not entirely comfortable with.

"This trip is throwing me all kinds of curve balls," Marcus said, lying on the massage table. "Let's try something new then. What do I need to do?"

The Reiki lasted for 45 minutes and Marcus had never felt so relaxed. He had been concerned when Kelly-Anne had put on the familiar spa type music and asked him to focus on his breathing, as he wondered if this might be a repeat of his futile self-hypnosis session. Initially Kelly-Anne made sweeping movements over his entire body, at no time making contact.

"I start by clearing," she said, quietly. Marcus had decided not to question the procedure, no matter how bizarre it seemed. His eyes were closed throughout the duration of the treatment, but he was aware of the heat on various parts of his body and at times could feel a power, an energy, running from his head, right down to his feet and warming every muscle, nerve and fibre.

"You have a bit of a block around the heart and sacral chakras, Marcus. That usually indicates relationship issues and emotional isolation. Does that make sense?"

Marcus grunted, sarcastically, "Yeh, you could say that." He didn't want to appear rude but neither did he feel inclined to spoil the relaxation by discussing his life story. "Recent bereavement. The trip is to help me deal with it."

Kelly-Anne held her hands above his lower abdomen. "Einstein famously said, 'Energy can neither be created or destroyed'. Lots of spiritual people believe, when we die, our energy, some call it our soul, remains and is re-born into another body."

Marcus tried not to laugh, concerned that Kelly-Anne may think he was belittling her efforts, but the irony of flying nearly 5000 miles and meeting two sensible, professional adults within three days who chose to talk with him about reincarnation, was not lost on him.

'You couldn't write this stuff,' he thought.

Marcus had excused himself at 9pm that night. "Sorry Jake, I'm wiped out. Must have been the treatment. You mind if I hit the sack?"

Jake and Mikey had been incredible hosts for the two days since his altercation with the truck. The father and son lived together; Mikey's mother having left when her son was only two. "She couldn't handle the job," Jake had said. "I get that. Not everyone can be with a cop but, crap, what kind of woman abandons their kid? She's never been in touch with him, not even his birthday or Christmas. It breaks my heart."

Marcus shared his host's indignation and as he lay in bed, he thought about Ava's guilt at the thought of leaving a child, even in a previous life and wondered if Mikey's mother ever thought about her child.

The following morning, Marcus felt refreshed and significantly more comfortable. His nine and a half hours of sleep had been undisturbed, unlike the previous night when the discomfort in his lower back had kept waking him. When he went into the kitchen, Jake was in his Fairbanks PD uniform and he and Mikey were already eating breakfast.

"Morning. How's the back?" Jake asked.

While he was desperate for his back to be improved enough to continue his journey, a tiny part of the old-school Marcus; the part that needed science and logical justification and the part that trusted medical degrees and prescription drugs, almost wanted the pain to still be evident. Apart from the remotest echo of an ache, however, it was gone.

"Great, thanks. Must have been the massage and Advil," Marcus replied.

"Course it was, bud," Jake said, winking at Mikey. "The Dakar's out in the front yard, waiting for you."

As Marcus pulled away, he thought about how different the last two days could have been. Jake had rescued and cared for him, selflessly giving up their dad and son time together and generously cooking and providing accommodation for a complete stranger. He had arranged for Kelly-Anne and his mechanic friend to repair both Marcus and the Dakar and had refused any payment. The generosity of spirit, which both Jake and his young son had shown Marcus, made him feel quite emotional. They had truly 'paid it forwards' and Marcus vowed to be a better person and do the same.

Chapter 15 – A Tiny Speck in the Universe

It was the second week of July and a further 2400 miles by the time Marcus reached the outskirts of Seattle. His journey through Canada, over the snow-capped Rocky Mountains into Jasper National Park and on to Roger's Pass, in the stunning Glacier National Park, was exactly as the brochures and internet sites had promised. The road conditions were, on the whole, reasonable, although some of the higher mountain tracks reminded him of the Dalton highway; effortless for the bike, less so for the amateur biker.

He had spent two nights at Lake Louise and armed with the bear spray, had hiked up the peaks overlooking the glacier-fed, turquoise blue lake, in the hope of catching sight of a grizzly bear, snatching salmon.

"They fish in late August or early September," a fellow walker had told him. "The fish fatten the grizzlies up before the onset of winter. You might see a female with her cubs this time of year but be careful, if they feel threatened, or you get between her and her littluns, you're toast." Marcus had heeded the advice and beat a hasty retreat, hand firmly on the aerosol spray in his pocket, back through the electric bear fence around the lodge.

The crisp air and tranquillity of the mountains were a welcome interlude from the internal dialogue, which Marcus struggled to keep at bay during the miles of solitude on the bike. Memories of Kelly-Anne and her miraculous healing had led to thoughts of Grant and his past-life and had then morphed into thoughts of Ava. Recollections of Jake and his kindness had turned into sympathies for Mikey and his absent mother and had morphed, once again, into thoughts of Ava. All thoughts seem to turn to Ava and while Marcus had no desire to forget his partner, he had made the decision that this trip would be a catalyst for transforming his negative, self-pitying, uncontrolled thoughts, to happy memories that he would invite into his mind and savour.

The time off the Dakar also offered some respite to his aching shoulders, arms and neck, which had been permanently tensed in anticipation of a second fall which, fortunately, had not occurred.

An article that he had read in the May edition of Motorcycle News had been submitted by Steve Lloyd, an ex-pat bike enthusiast living in Seattle. Marcus had noted some of his suggestions for travelling safely and relatively cheaply through Central and South America and he had torn the article out of the paper and packed it for his trip. Steve had mentioned in the feature that he frequently welcomed touring bikers and had included his e mail address at the bottom of the piece and Marcus had decided to mail him, prior to leaving London.

Hi Steve, I really enjoyed your article in MCN. I'm planning a motorbike trip from Alaska to Argentina and found the suggestions you made about travelling from Mexico City to Buenos Aires, very useful.

I'm aiming to arrive in Seattle at some point during mid to late July and wondered if you would like to meet up for a beer? I'm not sure how much access I will have to e mail during the early part of the trip, but my mobile number is below. Maybe you could send a text and let me know if you'll be around?

Marcus R Crane

Marcus had received a reply before he had even boarded his flight for Anchorage.

Hi Marcus, Glad you enjoyed the piece in MCN. It would be a pleasure to meet you and you would be more than welcome to stay with me and my wife while you're in Seattle. If your trip started in Alaska, you'll have done a few miles by the time you get to us, so maybe we can give the bike a health check while you're here and get you ready for the next few thousand miles? Cell number is below. Call me when you have an idea of your arrival date.

Regards, Steve.

Marcus had been pleased to receive the amicable reply and relieved that Steve had sounded significantly more technically competent than he was. He knew he would have put the Dakar through its paces by the time he had reached Seattle and it had concerned him that his motorbike maintenance skills were substandard, at best. He had enjoyed the privacy and reflection which the single rooms in the various lodges and hotels had awarded him, but to his surprise, the conversation-filled overnight stays with Grant and Jake had been particularly enjoyable and he was looking forward to his time with Steve and his wife.

As he approached Seattle, the imposing Space Needle structure loomed in front of him. He had seen the famous observation tower in numerous films and documentaries and he felt excited to see it in the flesh. Steve had agreed to meet him at the main entrance to Pike Place Market and as Marcus approached the huge, red letters which read, 'Public Market Centre', he immediately saw the lone biker waiting on the BMW GSA.

Steve's house was a ten-minute ride from the market and Marcus followed as Steve indicated right and turned into a garage in a smart, residential part of the neighbourhood. The garage was at street level and appeared to be built into the side of the hill. The house was set back and positioned several metres above and initially, Marcus was unable to see how the residence could be accessed from where they had parked the bikes. At the very back of the garage was a dark grey, metal door and as the men unloaded the panniers on the Dakar, the door opened and a woman in an electric wheelchair emerged from what Marcus could now see was an elevator.

"Marcus this is my better half, Karyn. Karyn, this is Marcus, our guest, and I'm guessing he's ready for a beer."

Marcus could see immediately that Karyn had very limited movement; the chair being operated entirely by small, subtle movements in her right hand whilst the remainder of her body appeared motionless. Her head was slightly tilted against the high head rest and her voice was slow and slurred, "No problem, I'm on it."

Marcus lifted his hand and waved from behind his bike. "Lovely to meet you, Karyn. Thank you so much for letting me stay."

The wheelchair turned quickly and in one movement, Karyn was back in the small elevator.

"She does so well," Steve said. "Lou Gehrig's; it's a bastard of a disease. She puts us all to shame with her positivity."

Marcus had heard someone on TV refer to Lou Gehrig's. The term was frequently used in the US, following the death of the famous American baseball player and was better known in the UK as Motor Neurone Disease.

"Started with symptoms five years ago. That's why we came back to the US," Steve sighed and pressed a button on the wall next to the grey door. The elevator buzzed to signal its arrival back at ground level and the men loaded Marcus's panniers into the small lift and waited for the clunky construction to take them up to the house.

At first Marcus worried that, with the speech impediment caused by the disease combined with her strong American accent, he may find Karyn a little difficult to understand and he was apprehensive about inadvertently offending her. Within a few minutes, he realised he had not needed to be concerned. Karyn was bright, charming and a natural comedienne. Her ability to laugh at herself, as well as mercilessly teasing anyone around her, currently Steve and Marcus, quickly enabled anyone to warm to her; seeing past any disability.

"Bikers are usually happy when they meet me," she said giggling. "They know I'm not going to steal their bikes."

When Karyn had disappeared to bed, the two men stayed up talking.

"Medical advances seem to be happening all the time, Steve. Are there any new drugs that can stop the progress of Karyn's sickness?" Marcus asked.

"Oh sure. There's lots of drugs," Steve replied, sounding frustrated, "but in our experience, they ease one symptom and cause another. The list of potential side effects for some of these drugs is terrifying; they give her more anxiety than comfort."

Marcus thought of Kelly-Anne and her insistence that most illness was a combination of mind and body turbulence.

"Has Karyn ever tried any alternative therapies; you know, like Reiki?"

Steve's reply surprised Marcus. "She isn't interested in cures or even treatments. Karyn describes herself as an old-soul and she feels she is learning what she needs to learn by experiencing this dreadful disease. I know it's hard to get your head around, it was for me for a while, but she's not scared of what will happen. I fought with her for a while: I'm a stubborn old bugger and I thought I was right and she should try anything which might prolong the time she has left, but I was wrong and she has me convinced that, well, this one short life on a miniscule speck in the universe, can't be all there is."

Marcus smiled. "My Ava; she would have been exactly the same, Steve."

He told his host about Ava and his inspiration for his Pan American adventure.

"I feel that every day I am learning something I would never have known, if Ava hadn't died. She used to say, 'If you don't listen, the Universe has a way of making you.' Maybe she was right and her death was the Universe making me listen?"

The following morning, Steve took Marcus down to the garage and showed him how to carry out some basic maintenance on the Dakar.

"The valve clearance adjustments are really important. Incorrect clearances will cause running problems. Your engine can't breathe properly if there's too little clearance; too much will cause damage."

Marcus nodded, as if he had any idea what his host was saying and Steve laughed,

"You have no idea what I just said, have you? Just get them checked once more, before the end of your trip, or you're screwed."

Marcus spent the remainder of the day with Steve and Karyn, visiting the must-see tourist spots.

"People love sightseeing with me," Karyn whispered to Marcus, as they waited to enter the Space Needle. "I get to go to the front of the line, every time." Steve patted his wife on the shoulder. "That's why we brought you," he said, winking at Marcus.

"Oh, you're so funny," Karyn said, pushing in front of the two laughing men, through the entrance to the busy building. "Don't let these two jokers in," she said, smiling at the doorman.

Marcus took his hosts out for a meal that night to thank them for their incredible hospitality. He was shocked and angered at the snooty and insensitive greeting of the first restaurant; a high-end, half empty bistro in the centre of the city. The woman at the bistro door, patronisingly directed her comment at Steve, as though Karyn was unable to understand,

"We have quite a wait at the moment, I'm afraid, and we don't really have the facilities for those clients with special needs."

"Well you'd better get your fucking facilities into the 21st century, you philistine," Steve said, incredulous. The restaurant receptionist looked suitably embarrassed as Karyn laughed and turned her wheelchair around.

"I've heard your food sucks, anyway!" she shouted.

Marcus followed his friends in silence and wondered if this was the reception they could expect at the next restaurant.

"Let's go to Majo's," Karyn suggested. "I fancy ribs."

Steve kissed his wife gently on her cheek. "We can go where ever you like, darling."

Majo's Diner was a small place on the edge of town and Steve and Karyn often ate there. It was owned and run by Matty and Joe, two native Oklahomans, who had realised some ten years earlier, that the heart of the Bible belt was not the best place to be in a gay relationship. Joe's sister had suffered with mental health problems and he and Matty had taken responsibility for her four-year-old son, Lucas, who had cerebral palsy. Majo's was comfortable and easy; and a haven for those made to feel like pariahs by the insensitive, ignorant and intolerant, and Karyn loved it.

"They're just fantastic with little Lucas," Steve said, holding the door open for Karyn and Marcus. Marcus smiled to himself as he noticed the sign above the door to the eatery,

'Never Lose Your Majo'.

"Karyn! Sweetheart. You still with that old Limey? Leave him and marry me!" Joe ran towards Karyn, kissed her on the cheek and struck a pose as he noticed the stranger standing between her and Steve. "Oooh," he said, his finger to his lips and his eyelashes fluttering at Marcus, "well, well. Who's this handsome hunk, Karyn?"

For the next two hours, Marcus and Steve watched as Joe and Karyn threw friendly abuse at each other.

"I just can't believe that husband of yours hasn't bought you a Harley and got your lazy ass out of that totally uncool crap-heap, Karry-baby," Joe laughed, pointing at the electric wheelchair.

"You're so full of shit, Joey boy," Karyn replied. "You wouldn't know what to do with a Harley if it bit you on your gay ass."

"They do this every time we come here," Steve said to Marcus, getting out of his seat to head to the Gents. "It keeps me amused for hours."

The following morning, Marcus was loading his bike when Steve arrived in the garage.

"Got everything you need?" Steve asked.

"Thanks to you, Steve. Is Karyn coming down to see me off?" Steve's gaze dropped to the floor. "She's having one of her bad days. She asked me to say goodbye for her."

Marcus tried not to look disappointed, "No probs. Send my love and tell her to feel better soon. I'll get in touch when I get back to the UK."

Steve gave Marcus a thumbs up and Marcus instinctively knew that the gesture was a replacement for the words which would probably have caused Steve's cool exterior to crack with emotion.

Marcus climbed aboard the clean, newly serviced Dakar and turned out of the garage. He felt refreshed and happy to be continuing his adventure, but he was also aware of the disturbing knot in the pit of his stomach. He realised his sadness was at the thought of those two gracious and generous people, having to accept the implications of such a dreadful illness. Karyn was an inspiration; her humour, her acceptance without complaint, and Steve was her rock. Marcus wondered if he would have been as strong and supportive of Ava's beliefs if she had refused all medical intervention. He admired the remarkable couple and felt humbled by their strength.

As he rode south, the July heat became more intense with each mile he travelled and he decided to head towards the west coast, as soon as he could, to benefit from the ocean breeze. An overnight stay in Medford, Oregon led to a further day's ride to San Francisco; a stay which would be another significant development in Marcus's journey.

Chapter 16 – Belonging; The Brightest Light.

Linh had been devastated by the news of Ava's death. Even a few weeks later she had found herself crying inconsolably and on more than one occasion, had to excuse herself from class in order to compose herself. She had known Ava was seriously ill but had not allowed herself to consider the possibility that she may not recover. Andrew Moran's phone call had shaken her to the core. "I'm afraid our beloved Ava has lost her fight, Linh," Andrew had sounded completely broken. "She passed a couple of nights ago. Marcus was with her."

Linh had been speechless and now, thinking back to the call, was ashamed and regretful at her inability to say all the things she should have, to comfort her friend's father.

Andrew sounded concerned, "Are you alright, love? I know it's a terrible shock, even though we all knew she was very ill."

Linh took a deep breath and tried harder than she had ever tried, not to cry.

"Oh God, Mr Moran, I am so sorry. You and your wife must be devastated, and Marcus, how is he doing?" Linh held her hand over the mouthpiece of the phone to prevent Andrew hearing her sobbing.

"He's just about holding up, love. Maria and I are letting people know about the funeral arrangements. The service will be at 2pm on Tuesday at Aylesbury Crematorium. It's just close friends and family and no flowers; Ava asked for donations to Semper Fidelis Hospice."

Linh managed to force a whispered, "I'll be there, thank you," before breaking down.

The days following the funeral were hard for Linh and she had picked up the telephone to call Marcus a number of times, only to hang up again, unable even to think about Ava without crying. "That's the last thing he needs, me blubbing all over him," she had said to herself.

When she received Marcus's letter in the post, she had felt remorseful that she had not persevered and contacted him.

Dear Linh,

First of all, I wanted to thank you for attending Ava's service. I know It was a tough day for you but Ava would have been so happy that her dearest friend was there.

I know that she mentioned, a number of years ago, that she had been to see a past-life regressionist and If I remember rightly, it was you who suggested it to her when we all met in Risborough, years ago. She didn't discuss it very much when she returned home and I had assumed she was unimpressed with the session. However, the hypnothera-pist contacted me recently and suggested I listen to the tape. It raised some questions about culture and lifestyle in Vietnam in the late 1950s and I thought I would send it to you. I'd love to hear your views.

I am leaving the UK in the next few days to travel for a while. I'm not sure how frequently I will be able to access my e mail, but the address is below.

Very best wishes,

Marcus

Linh knew that hearing Ava's voice would upset her, so she had left the tape for a couple of days before playing it. She had been confused at first, as the sound of a child she had never heard before, rang out from the cassette player.

"There's washing. I help me me to hang it and she lets me pull the string to make it hang over the street to dry. There are baskets in the street. They have chickens and other animals in, and wooden tables with lots of things that people are selling."

From Linh's years of study about her home country, she knew about the tendency for residents in the poorer parts of the city, to hang their washing out of the upstairs windows. In the same areas, vegetables and live produce would often be traded in the street and bitter melon was frequently referred to in the many text books she had read.

Her adoptive parents had, years before, confirmed that it was not unusual to see people carrying produce in the large leaf hats, worn by men and women throughout the country.

Linh smiled as she listened to the ten-year-old Chau Hang talk happily about her life in Saigon and as Jeanie brought Ava forward in time, Linh froze as she heard the distressed voice of the sick, young woman,

"Please. Please look after my baby. Please. Take this, my cross, and go to the mission. They'll know what to do."

Linh had cherished the small, silver cross which her parents had returned to her as soon as they considered her old enough to take care of it. She had changed the delicate chain, the original having perished over time, but the cross still hung around her neck to this day. Linh had never been a religious person, so the memento had remained hidden beneath her clothing, but she had worn it every day since her tenth birthday.

She did the calculations in her head and the dates matched. Chau Hang's little girl was 14 months old, the age everyone thought Linh probably was and the age which the medics back in the UK, had confirmed that her development was in line with. Then there was the old man, Minh Huy, who brought the child to the mission. What, Linh wondered, were the chances of all these specific facts - the date, the cross, the old man and the delivery of the baby to the mission - occurring twice? Her parents had not been aware of any other Christian missions in the area and Linh was the only orphaned child ever trusted to their care. Linh sat motionless, finding the information she had just been presented with, difficult to process. She tried hard to think back to the after-school conversations she had enjoyed with Ava. She knew that, while her pupil was aware that Linh's birth mother had died and Linh had been adopted in Vietnam, she had never shared the circumstances surrounding her mother's death, the old man or the existence of the small, silver cross. She wondered if her parents had kept any details of visitors to the Baptist mission and decided to call them.

"Your father had a small visitor's log, pet," Margaret Mason confirmed. "I'll see if I can find it and have a look for the name. Chau Hang, did you say?"

Linh spelt out the name and asked her mother to call her with any news.

In her teenage years, Linh had researched the documenting of birth and deaths in Vietnam back in the 1950s. To her frustration, there was no systematic recording of either of these events until the 1960s in the north and the 1970s in the south of the country. Whilst Tu Du Maternity Hospital had existed since 1923, Linh had been informed that a local prostitute would have been unlikely to have been admitted and would probably have given birth at home, assisted by other local women.

At around 8pm that evening, Margaret Mason called her daughter,

"We found it, Linh. Your father has looked through every page and eventually found the name you mentioned. Chau Hang visited the mission on 16th November 1958. I don't remember her, pet; we had lots of visitors and many only came once, but your dad says he vaguely recalls a heavily pregnant young girl coming to one of the meetings."

Linh felt elated. In her heart she knew her long search was over but while the facts were startling, they weren't conclusive enough for her. The following morning, she looked at the small, plastic case which the tape had arrived in and read the white sticker. Jeanie's name was printed on it and underneath, 'Certified Clinical Hypnotherapist', with her address and phone number. Linh took a deep breath and dialled the number.

The telephone rang a few times before a mature, female voice answered.

"Hello Jeanie," Linh said, nervously, "my name is Linh Mason and, well, I know this is going to sound crazy, but I think Ava Moran may have been my mother in her previous life as Chau Hang." Linh listened to herself as the words poured out and felt embarrassed at how ridiculous she sounded. "The dates and all of the details of my mother's death, they're just too similar to be a coincidence and, well, I've spent my entire life not knowing who I was until now, Jeanie, and I need to know for sure."

Jeanie listened to the emotional woman and to Linh's amazement she did not sound even remotely surprised,

"Well, my lovely, Ava would have been so very happy that you figured this out and I want to hear all about it. I've often wondered if we would solve this particular puzzle."

On Saturday morning, Linh set off to meet with Jeanie at her home in Hackney and explained how Marcus had sent her Ava's regression tape. "As soon as Chau Hang mentioned the silver cross, I just knew, Jeanie," Linh reached below the neck of her sweater and pulled out the small silver cross.

Over the next hour Linh told Jeanie about the name in the register and the matching dates.

"How would you feel about a little regression yourself, Linh?" Jeanie asked. "I know you were only tiny, but we don't forget anything we've seen, heard or experienced; it's all there, logged in our subconscious."

Linh had no fear of hypnosis, having experienced it before, for her pre-degree exams anxiety, but she was concerned that she would not be especially receptive to regression.

"I'm not very visual, Jeanie. I struggle to imagine images so I may not be very good at this."

Jeanie smiled. "Have you ever been so absorbed in a book or a film, that you haven't heard someone come into the room?"

Linh nodded, "Sure, lots of times."

Jeanie continued, "And how many times have you got into your car and driven somewhere and not remembered large chunks of the journey?"

Linh nodded again and laughed, "Yep, too many times, why?"

"We spend most of our time in trance state, love. That's all this is, me supporting you into a nice, relaxing state of trance. If there's something to see, something to remember, you'll see it, love, don't you worry about that."

The gentle music encouraged Linh to relax as Jeanie's soft voice helped her to focus on her breathing and, as Ava had before her, Linh eventually imagined herself in the empty cinema with a remote control in her hand. Having explained that Linh was completely in control, Jeanie asked her to go back in time to her first, significant happy memory.

Linh snuggled into the armchair and smiled. "It's my birthday," she said, her voice high pitched and childlike, "I have my new dress on and all my friends are here. Daddy is playing the piano and Mummy is in charge of bumps."

Jeanie waited until Linh stopped. "Bumps? What are bumps, Linh?" Linh tilted her head to the side and looked surprised. "Bumps, you know, musical bumps. Mummy's in charge of who bumped last. They have to leave the game."

Jeanie laughed before asking Linh to press stop on the remote control, "You're doing so well. Now I want you to travel back, back in time to the last day you were with your birth mother. Take your time and let me know when the image appears on the big screen."

Linh went silent and a few moments passed before Jeanie spoke again, "You're about a year old, Linh. Do you see anything?"

"People are in our home. The herb man is here, he comes to see us a lot. He makes my mummy special drinks to make her better. Mummy is sick a lot and has tummy ache. He's nice to me."

Jeanie probed further, "The herb man, Linh? Do you know his name?"

Linh pulled a face, as though trying to remember. "Bright Light. That's a nice name, isn't it?" Linh sounded sleepy.

"It's a lovely name," Jeanie whispered. "Can you remember the last time you saw Bright Light, Linh?"

Linh's face crumbled and tears seeped out from her closed eyes. "It's dark. Mummy isn't with me. Bright Light is giving me to a lady I don't know. She smells nice but her words sound funny. She's holding me and I'm crying. There are other people here. The lady can't understand what Bright Light is saying. Now he's going. He's leaving me with the strange lady with funny words. I want my mummy."

Jeanie asked Linh to let the scene fade and gently brought her out of trance state.

Like Ava, Linh could recall all of the details of her hypnosis and sat quietly reflecting on what she had just experienced. Jeanie remembered Ava talking, during her regression, about an elderly man who brought her herbs. She had known his name but Jeanie was unable to remember it. "Can you remember the Herb Man's name from the tape, Linh?" she asked. Linh nodded, "Absolutely. It was Minh Huy, but I have no idea what that means."

Jeanie reached into the pocket of her cardigan and pulled out an old mobile phone. She slowly pushed the keys and put the phone to her ear. "Hello sweetheart, it's Mum. Could you have a look on that computer of yours? I want to know what Minh Huy, that's M I N H space H U Y, means in English. It's Vietnamese, love. I'll wait."

The pair sat in silence until Linh could hear the sound of a distant voice leaking from Jeanie's mobile. She watched Jeanie's face closely, unable to make out what the voice was saying.

"Thank you, darlin'. See you next weekend." Jeanie smiled at Linh, "Minh, love, it means Brightness and Huy, well that means Light. Bright Light, Linh. Ava was your Mother."

Chapter 17 – The Consequences of Clarity

A further 360 miles and almost six hours in the saddle, brought Marcus to Downtown San Francisco and the hotel which Steve and Karyn had recommended for the next three nights. The boutique hotel was fairly easy to find and had secure parking for the bike and while Marcus had been surprised at how expensive accommodation in the area was, it was in a convenient location and boasted office and e mail facilities.

Marcus was conscious that he had not picked up any e mail since his arrival in the US and wondered if there would be any news from his family, school colleagues or the estate agents. He knew he should probably have made an effort to find an internet café before now, to check if there had been any viewings, or even better, any offers on the house. The thought of normal life back in the UK had, however, created a heaviness, a lethargy in him and he justified his tardiness with the knowledge that he could always be contacted on his mobile, had there been an emergency.

The reception area was empty when Marcus arrived and having pressed the buzzer to alert the receptionist to his presence, he wandered around the spacious lobby in the hope of locating the business centre. A wooden display rack housed a large number of promotional leaflets for tourist activities around San Francisco and Marcus selected one for Fisherman's Wharf and one for boat trips to Alcatraz Island.

The Standard Executive room, as the receptionist had described it, was functional and very small but had a wall-mounted desk and what looked to Marcus like dial-up cables. He plugged his old lap top into charge, attached the cables and waited for the familiar tuneful sound of the system connecting to the internet. Having negotiated his way around the 'plug, pay and play' instructions and cursed the extortionate additional charge for internet use, he clicked on his e mail and waited for it to download. Slowly, the stream of messages began appearing on the screen and frustrated at the pedestrian pace of the system, Marcus began unpacking one of his panniers.

When he returned to the laptop, he was surprised to see the note at the bottom left of the screen, '38 unread messages'. He knew a significant number would be spam, but he was still surprised how a technophobe like him had managed to accumulate so much e mail.

He browsed the e mail addresses and deleted the unsolicited approaches from travel firms, storage companies and insurance organisations, without opening them. The bulk of the e mails were from estate agents, marketing details of properties for sale in the Hemel Hempstead area, which Marcus had registered for before he left the UK. These he ignored, intending to read them closer to his return. There were two messages, both with 'Property Viewing' as the subject and looked to Marcus like a standard template in which the address, date and time could be altered, as required. Both viewings on his house were over a week ago and with no further e mails from the agent, he assumed that neither had resulted in an offer.

As he scanned the remainder of the messages he noticed one unusual address, 'Mason, Linh', and it took him a second or two to realise that the mail was from Ava's friend and teacher. The mail was dated 30th June, just a few days after he had left for Anchorage. It was a long e mail and Marcus felt guilty that he had not read it earlier.

Hi Marcus, I know you are travelling so it may be sometime before you read this note. Thank you for the letter and for sending me Ava's hypnotherapy tape.

Marcus had completely forgotten that, rather than attempt to explain Ava's regression and ask the questions he had about Vietnam, he had sent Linh the tape so she could interpret it herself.

I wanted you to know that the tape was a revelation and in fact, quite life changing for me.

Linh's e mail contained a number of details about her very early years, some of which Ava had already told Marcus.

I knew very little about my origins, other than that an elderly gentleman had taken me to my adoptive parents' Baptist mission. Everyone thought I was a little over one year old and my mother had been a working girl and died of what appears to have been cholera. There was no birth certificate; apparently Northern Vietnam had a rudimentary census in 1960 but nothing significant before that and nothing at all in the south until the 70s.

Marcus wondered where Linh's detailed note was heading.

My only possession, other than the clothes I was wearing, was a small, silver cross, which the old gentleman gave to my adoptive mother.

The mention of the silver cross immediately caught Marcus's attention. Didn't Ava give a silver cross to someone holding her baby, during the regression?

My adoptive parents recognised the cross as one that they gave to new visitors to the mission but, as they knew my birth mother had died, they thought nothing more of it.

You can imagine my surprise when I heard Ava, or should I say Chau Hang, give the old man the cross and beg him to take her child to the mission.

Marcus sat bemused, trying to make sense of what Linh was saying.

Until I received your letter and Ava's tape, I had no name, nothing to even start with.

My father still has the service register, a small book which new visitors to the mission were asked to sign. I have enclosed a copy of one of the pages and want to thank you with all my heart.

Stay safe on your travels, my friend.

Linh x

Marcus clicked the tiny paperclip, indicating an attachment and a photograph opened up on the screen. It was a page of dates and names, not unlike the school register he remembered as a child at school. About half way down, on the left-hand side of the page, Linh had circled a name and date with red marker. Marcus looked closely at the child-like hand writing,

Chau Hang, 16/11/1958.

Marcus replayed Jeanie's words from the regression tape in his head.

"I believe that we stay with the same nucleus of people. We might change relationships, roles and even genders but we stay with the people who help us to grow. I believe, somewhere in your life as Ava Moran, you have, or will, know your baby in some way and you'll know, love, you'll know when you meet her; you'll feel it."

Marcus felt breathless and could feel his heart beating fast. He wondered what the likelihood would be of Chau Hang attending the mission, in what would have been the eighth month of her pregnancy, and not being the mother of the abandoned, cross-wearing child, 15 months later. His uncomfortable conclusion was, that was just too great a coincidence to accept.

Marcus spent the next two days exploring San Francisco and felt a particular affinity for the place, with its steep hills and cable cars. He had ridden across the Golden Gate on his way into the city and been stunned by the views before the fogs descended later that same day. The afternoon of the next day was spent wandering around Fisherman's Warf and Marcus made the decision to take a boat tour to Alcatraz Island the following morning.

Ava had been fascinated with the infamous island prison, ever since she had watched Escape from Alcatraz with her father, when she was a small child. She and Marcus had frequently discussed taking a trip to San Francisco and visiting the old prison and he now regretted not having found the time to arrange it.

As he joined the line at pier 33 for tickets, he was aware of the people around him. Marcus had never taken an interest in watching the interaction of others. He had always regarded the people in pubs or at theatres and social events, as more of an inconvenience than something to be observed. It had always been Ava who had initiated any conversation with strangers and Marcus had always felt mildly irritated at her inclination to involve him in inane chatter.

Today, as he waited in the summer sunshine with the locals and many tourists, he wondered about the lives and stories of the individuals around him.

An elderly woman was sitting alone on a bench a few meters from the Alcatraz boat trip queue. She was wearing a heavy coat, opaque tights and a headscarf, which seemed incongruous with the 25 degrees of the late July sunshine. She was nursing a Starbucks cup and Marcus wondered if the large, fraying storage bag, similar to the one Ava had used to hide the ever-increasing piles of pending ironing, was simply filled with shopping or, as he suspected, her entire worldly possessions. He wondered if she had a husband or children or if she was alone in the world and he wondered, if Jeanie's hypothesis was true, what she was meant to be learning from this life.

The queue for the ticket booth seemed to be moving annoyingly slowly and the couple in front of him were finding occupying their small child increasingly challenging.

"I don't want the boat now, Mommy. I want to go swimming in the pool."

Children had always gravitated towards Ava. While Marcus would sigh at the realisation that a baby or toddler was in the aeroplane seat directly behind him and antici-pate the inevitable screaming and irksome kicking of his seat, Ava would happily entertain them for hours. Games of peek-a-boo between the seats or long chats about the most recent Disney characters or children's book, would enchant kids and delight their weary parents who, no doubt, had been expecting little respite during the flight.

It had always confused Marcus that someone so natural and comfortable with other people's children, had no desire to have her own. Jeanie's regression tape had finally given him some clarity.

The queue for the boat finally began to move and Marcus took his seat. The couple with the small child sat opposite; the child's shoes, socks and hat now removed, much to the despair of his mother, who was now negoti-ating with the small boy to leave his T-shirt and shorts on. Marcus chuckled to himself as the poor woman resorted to the bribery he had frequently driven his own parents to.

"Put your shoes and hat on and maybe we'll find some candy when we get off the boat."

He wondered what kind of parent he would have been and as he acknowledged that he would more than likely have played bad cop to Ava's good, he felt a stab of sadness at the realisation that parenthood was evidently not on his blueprint this lifetime.

Route 1, the Pacific Coast Highway through Santa-Cruz and onto Carmel, presented Marcus with beautiful winding roads; the steaming hot air cooled slightly by the ocean breeze. Tired after his long ride, he decided a shower and early night was probably the best idea.

As he arrived at the hotel, a group of Harley riders were busy checking in and, keen to hear about the amateur

Brit biker's experience on the infamous Dalton Highway, persuaded Marcus to join them for a beer and dinner at the famous Hog's Breath Inn. The group was travelling from Portland, Oregon to San Diego for a Harley rally and was made up of a father, two sons and two further friends of the family.

The Hog's Breath was buzzing with patrons when the noisy mob arrived and Marcus found a table with Ted, or 'Vic', as the group had nicknamed him, whilst the four younger guys ordered beer and food.

"This place was owned by Clint Eastwood until 1999," Vic told Marcus. "The guys were determined to get a Dirty Harry Burger while we were in the neighbourhood."

Marcus thought Vic looked very young to have two adult sons and noticed how happy he seemed to be travelling and spending quality time with his family.

"Why Vic, Ted? What's the story behind the nickname?" Marcus asked, expecting the moniker to be Harley, or at least motorbike, related.

Vic laughed. "It's short for Victory," he explained. "I've just had the all clear for the second time. Cancer, but I beat the SOB, twice." Vic sounded jubilant, "And I'll keep beating it."

Marcus felt a lump in his throat. Ava had said that. "I'll beat it, darling and if it comes back, I'll keep beating it." He smiled at Vic and lifted the pint which one of the boys had put in front of him, "Cheers to that, Vic!"

The two-day trip to Las Vegas took Marcus briefly onto the historic Route 66 and through the Mojave Desert, with its crystal blue skies, unbroken sunshine and temperatures which constantly exceeded 37 degrees. As the heat burned through to his skin, he wished he had bought some lighter textiles and it was hard for him to remember how the grey, damp riding hours in Alaska had felt, when his fingers and toes had been numb with the cold from the Arctic wind and he wondered if he would ever feel warm again.

Marcus loved the camaraderie which came with being part of the global biker community. He had been pleasantly surprised when bikers in the UK nodded as they passed each other and had assumed it was a British thing. But the custom of recognising a shared passion seemed to cross oceans, borders and state lines. Every biker he passed or met waved, regardless of the size or make of bike and the gesture made the endless miles of road, shared only by the mountains and Joshua trees, feel safer.

As the miles passed, Marcus pondered what Ava would think about his new pastime. She had always had to cajole him into trying anything new and persuade him to take even the slightest gamble. The old MG had been a classic example of Marcus's risk aversion but, having allowed himself to be coaxed, he quickly realised the thrill of stepping out of the safe zone and living a little.

This trip had necessitated abandoning everything that was comfortable to Marcus. 20,000 plus miles on a bike he had been able to ride for only a few months, across numerous countries, none of which he had visited before, with no technical skills and very little pre-planning, was a big deal for him. He had reflected on his uncharacteristic spontaneity, during the first few days of the trip. He had often woken during the early hours of the morning and wondered if he should, perhaps, return home and resume his innocuous life. But as each impromptu day presented new experiences and inspirational people, Marcus became more comfortable with the unknown and he knew Ava would approve.

Chapter 18 – Peeling Back the Layers

'Mystic Marvel, Spiritualist and Psychic Medium to the Stars,' the posters had said.

A photograph of a gregarious young man, wearing a bejewelled suit and performing in front of an adulating audience, adorned the advertisements at the entrance to most cafés and restaurants along The Strip. Scheduled to perform *'for one night only'* at one of the smaller hotels outside of the main Las Vegas streets, Marcus decided it may be interesting to watch someone with a similar gift to Vera.

Ava would be very pleased, he convinced himself, as he purchased the ticket for a show which not so long ago, he would have labelled as 'complete and utter crap and a total waste of money'.

"Don't tell me, don't tell me! Yes, I'm getting roses. Oooh, yes. I can see them, lovely pink roses, yes and I'm seeing a 'P'. You, the gentleman in the blue shirt, this is for you. Who do you know who has passed recently, with a name beginning with 'P'?"

A middle-aged man in the third row of the audience turned to look at the expectant group immediately behind him, before realising, with an embarrassed blush and an uncomfortable shuffle down into his chair, that the question was being aimed at him.

"Yes, yes, definitely a 'P'. Could be Patricia, Paula, Pearl?" the medium continued.

The mortified man, now feeling the eyes of the entire room on him, felt under significant pressure not to disappoint either the audience or the affected and demonstrative stage medium.

"Er, Sarah, my wife. She liked roses," came the stuttered response from the reluctant participant.

"Sarah, Sarah, Sarah," the performer repeated to himself, closing his eyes and pinching the top of his nose as if deep in thought. "Oh yes, she's telling me off for getting her name wrong and I can see her holding a pink rose. Sarah says she has a message for you: She says take care of that bad back of yours. Do you have a bad back?"

The man in the blue shirt gritted his teeth and looked apologetic, "Er, no, sorry, I don't." Conscious of the disappointed silence in the room, he continued, "But I broke my leg a couple of years ago?"

Mystic Marvel had clearly encountered this type of impediment to his performance in the past, "Oh dear, dear, dear, she's telling me off again. 'Bad break!' she's shouting at me. Not bad back but bad break." Marvel rolled his eyes and chuckled as he playfully slapped his own wrist as the audience laughed. "Silly old me!"

The hum of a disturbance sounded from the back of the room and an elderly man with a walking stick was encouraged to stand up and take the microphone, offered by one of the show assistants. He spoke quietly into the mic, "Hello. My sister was called Prudence. She liked roses and I have a touch of arthritis in my lower back."

To Marcus's amazement the audience gasped and clapped enthusiastically as the Mystic Marvel took several bows and appeared to revel in the praise. Marcus looked around the room, astounded, as the two people sitting with the old man rose to their feet and applauded and someone in the front whistled in admiration. Had he missed something? Marcus wondered to himself. Was the show really a humorous spoof and he had missed the entire point of the performance? Marcus looked at the advertising flyer which he had picked up on entering the room, '*Mystic Marvel, Spiritualist and Psychic Medium to the Stars.*' No mention of comedy or improv.

The performer disappeared briefly behind a flipchart stand which had been positioned to the left of the stage and scribbled briefly before tearing off the sheet and showing it to the audience. On the flip chart page was a crude line drawing of a vehicle, the type a small child might produce when asked to draw a car. "I want to say 'Chevvy'," Marvel squealed, pointing at a woman on the far left of the room.

"Why oh why do I want to say 'Chevvy'? "

The woman looked confused. "Er, my old boss's wife's sister had a Chevvy, I think. But she sold it about six years ago."

"Was it blue? I'm hearing Blue Suede Shoes." Marvel began to dance on the stage.

The woman looked uncomfortable. "No, it was white, with a red stripe. It might have had blue seat covers?" The audience fell silent, waiting for Marvel's next psychic prophecy.

"My first car was a blue Chevrolet Camino. It was a pain in the ass! Always in the shop."

The voice came from a man about Marcus's age, sitting towards the back of the room.

"Yeh, mine was a Chevvy Corvette!" a woman in the middle of the room, with bright purple hair and a number of facial piercings, shouted.

"My Grandad has a blue Sting Ray," a young girl, around twelve years old added, "but he's not dead yet." The audience laughed.

Marvel pointed to the woman with the piercings and the unorthodox hair colouring.

"Tattoo. I'm hearing tattoo. Someone likes your tattoo."

Even from where Marcus was sitting, he could clearly see the blue ink peeping above the collar of the woman's turtleneck sweater and he struggled not to laugh as the woman's hands rose to her mouth and she stood, starting to cry hysterically, "Oh my God! It's my Mama." The woman rolled up the arm of the sweater, revealing a sleeve of coloured ink.

"I knew she'd like it."

Once again, the applause sounded and most of the room stood and cheered.

"Thank you. Thank you, my friends. This gift is truly a blessing and a curse."

Marcus watched the people around him, astounded. Surely these people could not possibly have believed that this eccentric fraud was really receiving messages from the dead.

He left his seat and walked to the exit.

"He's really something else, isn't he?" the young woman responsible for selling ticket on the door said, enthusiastically.

"Yep," Marcus said, pushing past her, "he really is!"

The sham performance occupied Marcus's mind for the next hour, as he wandered through the crowds and bright lights of the busy Strip, looking for a coffee shop. Not too long ago he would have laughed, wondering how people could be so gullible to believe that anyone could deliver messages from deceased friends and relatives. His support would, without doubt, have been with the opportunist fake: If he can make good money from these deluded idiots, good on him. Today, to his surprise, he felt different as he considered the comfort and peace of mind which Vera had given to Roisin and Ava and numerous others, no doubt, over the years. He felt compassion for those people in tonight's audience, who had attended the performance in the desperate hope of hearing from their wife or husband or child, only to encounter this ruthless phoney.

As Marcus sauntered back to his hotel, he was approached by two young girls, scantily clad in pink, sequin and feather covered basques.

"Come and have a photograph with us, hansom." One of the girls gestured seductively and walking up to Marcus, threw a pink feather boa around his neck. Marcus felt awkward but not wishing to appear aloof, struck the required pose between the two girls while another young woman took a picture.

"We suggest tips of $30 per model, Sir," one of the girls said to Marcus, as he struggled free of the girls' hold. Marcus felt foolish; of course there was a charge. This is Vegas and here everything is an opportunity to extract as much money from tourists as possible. He walked away shaking his head. He had expected the contrast to be stark; the peace, isolation and unspoilt landscape of the empty roads with the noise, neon lights and commercialism of Las Vegas, but he had not expected to feel this level of disdain and contempt for this superficial place.

As he reached his accommodation, he walked through the throng of anonymous faces, all feeding cups of coins and wads of dollar bills into glutenous slot machines. He stood for a few minutes at one of the numerous roulette tables and watched excited smiles turn to contrite frowns as the emotionless croupier scooped up the forfeited chips. As he walked past the Cashier's cage, Marcus wondered how much money would be won and lost tonight; how many homes and businesses and livelihoods would be gambled and how many lives would be ruined, and he decided that tomorrow he would leave.

Before Marcus left the hotel the following morning, he visited the small business centre to check his emails. Having disposed of the usual junk, he scanned the remainder of the messages and opened one, dated the day before, from the estate agent which was marketing Marcus's house.

Dear Mr Crane,

Following their second viewing on your property, 53, Carmarthen Gardens, Weston Turville, Aylesbury, Buckinghamshire HP22 5TX, we are delighted to confirm that Mr and Mrs Phillipson have offered the full asking price of £525,000, to include all carpets and curtains. As the purchasers are currently in rented accommodation, they would request exchange and completion to occur as soon as possible.

Please contact us on your receipt of this mail to confirm your acceptance of the offer.

Regards,

Sally Parker

Marcus had expected to feel relieved at the sale of the house. He had never been able to envisage living there without Ava and even spending time there to clear the place had felt strange. To his surprise, he felt sad; a sense of finality making him doubt his decision. He thought about what Ava would have said.

"It's on your blueprint, babe. Time to move on." Marcus took a deep breath and clicked 'send' and his acceptance letter had gone.

His abridged stay in Vegas had enabled him to plan a longer visit to the Grand Canyon National Park and, having grown bored of characterless hotel rooms, decided to purchase a small tent and camp. The South Rim would offer easy access to the interstate and routes to Sedona, his next stop. Marcus smiled at the continuation of the ever-present ethereal theme running through his trip, as he confirmed his reservation with the 'Shining Angel Canyon Camping Co.'

He secured the bike and pitched his tent, ramming the two panniers and the rest of his luggage into the tiny canvas shelter which would be his accommodation for the next two nights. Grabbing his camera, he began to walk the ¼ mile to the ridge of the Canyon, expecting to take the requisite snaps of the famous landmark before returning to camp for a much needed cold beer. As he approached the South Rim, Marcus realised that any description he had heard or read about the Canyon was in no way representative of its true magnificence. The scale and colour of the mile-deep Canyon took Marcus's breath away and for the first time, he could understand why people had described this glorious place, one of the seven natural wonders of the world, as awesome. He stood for some minutes, gazing at the remarkable vista and felt a spiritual presence he had never experienced before and knew that this was a truly magical place.

The camping area was busy and the Shining Angel staff circulated around the various tents and RVs to inform campers about the catering, which would be available during the day and into the evening. A number of cyclists, bikers and hikers were seated around a BBQ area when Marcus left his tent to find some dinner. A young woman shuffled along one of the benches to make room for him as he approached, precariously balancing a chili dog, corn and a full plastic beer cup.

"Quite a sight, isn't it?" she said, gesturing towards the view of the sun disappearing into the Canyon. Marcus nodded, his mouth full of bread roll, as chili and sausage spilled out onto his lap, most having missed the inadequate paper plate it had been served on. They both laughed.

"That doesn't sound like a local accent," Marcus said, wiping his mouth with a napkin. "What brings a Scottish lass to the Grand Canyon?" The young woman pointed to the expensive looking camera around her neck. "I'm an artist," she said, "I take pictures of beautiful things and then I paint them. I'm Isla, by the way." Isla held out her hand before realising Marcus's hands were otherwise occupied with somewhat messy, disposable tableware.

Marcus looked around for something to wipe his hands on. "Wow, and you can make a living doing that? You must be good. I'm Marcus; pleased to meet you, Isla."

Isla smiled, "I wish. It's more of a hobby really. My proper job is a Special Ed. Teacher. The kids love to paint and I love to show them how to create something they can be proud of, you know, give to their parents or hang on their bedroom walls."

Marcus remembered it was August now and UK schools were on Summer break,

"You out here for all of the school holidays, Isla?"

The young woman shook her head, "I've actually been travelling for five months; took some time out to sort my head out."

"And have you managed it; sorting your head out?" Marcus said, interested to hear more.

"I'm getting there. It's a long story." Isla sighed and lowered her head.

"Well, I'm not in a hurry, if you need to talk to a random stranger, you'll probably never see again." Marcus nudged Isla and laughed and the young woman stood up.

"OK," she said. "Shall we walk?"

The pair walked along one of the many tree lined paths away from the throng of music and voices.

"So, what's messing with your head so much that you disappear for five months?" Marcus asked, sipping from the pint cup he was still holding.

"Something strange happened and the easiest thing to do was to run away. I met my partner three years ago; we both play squash in the local league. It was lovely; love at first sight and all that jazz." Marcus listened to Isla talking and waited for the 'but'.

"We bought a place just outside Edinburgh together; he's from Bristol and got a job as a Manager for a brewery. He looks after 30 pubs throughout Scotland." Marcus said nothing. "And then, about a year ago he asked me to marry him." Isla looked down at her hand and straightened the diamond solitaire on her ring finger. "I was thrilled, and we immediately arranged to go to Bristol so I could meet his father. His mother had passed away when my fiancé was very small."

By now, the darkness was closing in and Marcus was conscious that they were wandering well away from the camp site. He turned and beckoned Isla to join him but instead, she sat on a tree trunk by the side of the path and began to cry. Marcus was uneasy; listening to the personal problems of complete strangers was becoming habitual on this trip but his experiences at school and university had made him wary of saying anything insensitive or crass. He sat down next to Isla and waited.

"When I met his father I felt really scared, Marcus. Not nervous or uncomfortable but terrified and sick to my stomach. I couldn't bear to be in the same room and I couldn't breathe if he was near me. The poor man hadn't done anything wrong. He's actually a kind of innocuous little guy and I have no idea why I reacted like I did, but I made my fiancé leave at 8pm the day we arrived and find a hotel."

Marcus listened and tried to think of practical, logical reasons why Isla might have reacted this way. "Maybe he reminds you of someone; someone that hurt you or scared you as a child," he suggested. "What about a teacher or maybe the parent of a friend, when you were little? Did anyone shout at you or hurt you as a child, Isla?"

The young woman shook her head. "It's more than feeling scared, it's as though my survival was dependent on getting away from him; a pathological dread. Luke, my fiancé, is understandably hurt and confused. At first, he was sympathetic but now he thinks I'm being over-dramatic and won't listen. I love him so much, but I can't marry him while I feel this way about his only parent."

Marcus sat with Isla until she had calmed down and the pair then walked back to camp. As he lay in his tent, the hum of fading voices around him, he thought about the dilemma the woman was facing and wondered how he would have felt if Ava had displayed such a vehemently negative reaction to his father.

The following morning, he saw Isla eating breakfast at one of the picnic tables and went to join her. "Morning. How are you feeling this morning?" he asked, cheerfully.

Isla looked embarrassed. "I'm so sorry, Marcus. I shouldn't have dumped all that stuff on you last night. It must have been the wine lubricating my vocal cords," she laughed, nervously.

Marcus sat down next to her. "Have you ever thought of getting some kind of treatment to help you understand this seemingly irrational fear?" Isla looked at him quizzically and Marcus continued, "Maybe hypnotherapy could help. I've heard lots of good things about it."

Isla shook her head. "It's not really me. I've always found alternative treatments to be a bit fluffy, but thank you, so very much. I really appreciate how kind you've been and maybe, when I've sorted all this mess out, I can contact you back in the UK and tell you that I'm finally getting married to Luke."

As Marcus prepared to leave the Grand Canyon the following morning, he noticed that Isla's tent was already gone and he hoped she would find a way to solve her problem with Luke's father. He thought about what he had learnt about himself over the months he had been on his journey; how his opinions about things he had previously dismissed as ridiculous had changed, how he had been able to listen and sympathise with people he had barely known and how he wondered if the direction his life had been taking before his partner died, was now still appropriate or even relevant.

He climbed aboard the Dakar once again, and headed for the lonely Route 64, on the way to the red rocks of Sedona. Marcus would shortly have answers to his question.

Chapter 19 – Red Rocks and Blueprints

'The Cathedral without walls' was how Sedona had been described in the tourist literature which Marcus had stuffed into his biking jacket. As he descended 1000m on the winding mountain roads which swept down from the university city of Flagstaff, he became aware of the array of bright red and gold sandstone formations and pine forests.

A number of the people he had met so far on his trip had recommended a visit to the 'spiritual mecca', so named because of the location of vortices; moving centres of energy, believed by many to promote healing.

Marcus had been interested to hear more about Sedona's history and experience the beauty of the red terrain. The brochures all mentioned the New Age shops and numerous psychics offering readings and until his unfortunate experience with Mystic Marvel in Las Vegas, Marcus considered arranging a private reading on his arrival. Now he was not so keen.

The city, which looked to Marcus more like a large village, was busy when he arrived. He was hot and thirsty and having attempted, unsuccessfully, to find accommodation close to the centre, he followed the directions of the woman in the tourist information office, out of the main area and up towards the tiny regional airport. The Redstone View Hotel was located about three miles away from the main restaurants and shops. The cabin style rooms were tired and small but clean and the views from the grounds, spectacular.

"We offer a shuttle service down to the centre," the friendly receptionist had said. "Just give us a call when you're ready to go."

The hotel handyman doubled as a shuttle driver and chatted to Marcus as they drove down the long mountain road to the centre.

"Any recommendations for food and a decent beer?" Marcus asked.

The driver pulled over to the side of the busy street next to the Wagon Trail Grille.

"This place always gets good reviews," he said. "They do a great steak and good choice of craft beer. Call the hotel when you're ready to come back."

Marcus had decided to have a browse at the shops and tourist attractions before eating and so he wandered slowly along the hot, busy street. Every-other shop appeared to sell crystals, dream catchers and angel cards. All had a printed menu of Psychic Services much, he thought, like those you find in a salon; only these listed services he had never heard of like Soul Reading, Chakra Balancing and Radiant Energy Healing. He looked at the photographs of the numerous ethereal looking women and men, claiming to be psychic mediums, healers and visionaries. All were offering life enhancing experiences and he wondered how many, if any, of these people were authentic. He thought back to Vera and to Jeanie; gentle and self-effacing, modest but, seemingly, highly gifted. Neither had felt the need to adopt some mystical name like Angel-Bliss or Crystal-Light or, heaven forbid, Mystic Marvel.

Marcus walked back to the Wagon Trail Grille, ordered a pint and sitting on one of the high bar stools, wondered how the entirely uninitiated, like him, would even attempt to weed out the genuine spiritual talent from the many fraudulent opportunists. He smiled, as he realised his change in perspective: Only a few short months ago, he would have obstinately dismissed all suggestions that any individual claiming supernatural powers could be legitimate. He would have relished being able to use the blatant charade he had experienced in Las Vegas, as indisputable evidence to reinforce his dogmatic viewpoint; that all things spiritual are phony. Now, instead of regarding advocates, like his Ava, as misguided and gullible, he felt irritated and annoyed at the imposters and it made him more determined to find the truth.

The dining tables were all fully booked at the Wagon Trail, so Marcus ordered a burger and continued to sit at the bar and listen to the tourists chatter about their day.

"Can I get you another of those?" the bar man asked, pointing to Marcus's empty pint glass.

Marcus nodded and wondered if the workers and residents of Sedona paid for readings, or whether they preferred to leave the purchase of the psychic stuff to the cash-rich tourists.

"You live locally, Bill?" he asked the bar man, noticing the badge on his lapel.

"Not far; Cottonwood. 'bout a 20-minute drive." Marcus nodded towards the crowded restaurant tables. "So, do the locals buy into all this psychic stuff or is it just for the tourists?" Bill laughed, "Oh, we buy it but we're a little more, shall we say, discerning than most." Marcus waited for him to elaborate.

"You see, there's talent and then there's marketing," he said, looking towards the numerous posters, advertising psychics and mediums, which covered the diner walls. "I'm not saying they're fakes but many have more desire than ability, if you know what I mean?"

Marcus smiled, "So, if some open-minded but sceptical bloke wanted persuading that this stuff could possibly be legit, where would you recommend he goes for a psychic reading?"

Bill pulled the top sheet from his order pad and scribbled on it, "Here you go, bud. She doesn't advertise; doesn't need to. Tell her Bill at the Trail sent you."

Marcus rode the Dakar to his reading the following morning. Unlike many of the higher-profile psychics, Donna was a few miles north of the main tourist area and worked out of her home; a small wooden cabin on the edge of the mountain range.

Donna, Marcus guessed, was around 50 and wore cotton jeans and a plain, navy T-shirt. He was surprised at her appearance, which was in contrast with the people he had seen in the posters; all dressed, in keeping with the spiritual theme, in headscarves, beads or brightly patterned shirts.

"Marcus? Please come through onto the deck." Donna led him through the house and out of the double doors onto a wooden patio area, overlooking the valley. The heat was intense and Donna pointed to a chair at the edge of the deck, shaded by a large parasol.

"Thank you for seeing me," Marcus said, sitting down and glad to be in the shade.

"I only have today, as.."

Donna stopped him, "I know. You're off on your adventure again."

Marcus smiled nervously; pretty sure he had not mentioned his trip when he had booked the appointment the previous evening.

"Have you seen a medium before?" Donna asked. Marcus thought about how to answer. Technically he had seen two; Vera and Jeanie, but he did not want to mislead Donna into thinking he was anything other than an interested sceptic.

"Only as a support to a friend, a couple of times. This is my first reading."

"OK," she continued. "Let me tell you how this works. I listen; that's all I do, listen and say what I'm told to tell you. Some things will make sense right away and some won't, at least not yet. I can record our meeting, if you like. I can then burn it onto a CD or send it to your e mail, that way you can listen to it again and again until all of it is clear. Is that OK?"

Marcus nodded, surprised at how down-to-earth this lady seemed.

Donna stared over Marcus's shoulder and looked as though she was day dreaming.

"You've been on a journey, not the physical one here in America, although your journey is continuing here, but an emotional roller-coaster of a ride. Everything you thought you knew, well, it's melting and you're watching it. You're tossing books, school books, like the kids in first grade use to write in, on to a fire. Do you teach kids?" Marcus felt a flush of heat rise through his body. How the hell did she know he was a teacher?

"The great loss you have experienced was the catalyst for change. Randy, she's telling me Randy and she's laughing. That must be a nickname, is it?" Donna didn't wait for Marcus to answer, nor did she seem to notice the colour draining from his face. "She's saying it was on your blueprint. Would you know what that means?"

Marcus could not speak. He wanted to get up and run but he could not feel his legs. He reached for the glass of water next to the chair and drained it.

"Sorry, Donna," he said, hardly able to breathe, "Who is it that's telling you this?"

Donna did not reply. "She's showing me the flag of Peru. She has a pen in her hand and she's laughing, really laughing and she's drawing on the flag. It's a heart with an arrow going through it. Is she saying she, or maybe you, love Peru? Now she's holding a bird in her hand. Pretty little critter; it's red. She's telling you to, 'Look at my wing'." Marcus leant forward and put his head in his hands. He felt as though he was in a dream. Donna stopped speaking and waited for him to look up. "You OK to go on, honey?" she said, quietly. Marcus nodded.

"You're at a cross roads. You need to know you'll be guided to the right path and you'll help people in a way you never thought possible; even one year ago. 'Take the training, Randy. Take the training', she's saying." Donna went silent for a few seconds and looked as though she was concentrating hard,

253

"Eve, no, no, that's wrong. She has a strong accent, like yours. Eva, that's it, Eva she's telling me. Is that her name; Eva?" Once again, Donna did not wait for Marcus to respond. "She's laughing at me and handing me something. Let me see, Eva." Donna looked confused.

"OK, it's a pretty little silver cross." Marcus watched as Donna appeared to take something into her hand. "That's a strange thing to give to Marcus, Eva. He doesn't strike me as the religious type. Oh, OK, I'll tell him it's for Lyn."

Marcus sat dumbfounded, with tears running down his cheeks. His mind raced and his emotion flipped from elation, to confusion to frustration, as his logical mind tried to work out how this stranger had unearthed all of this deeply private information.

He paid Donna for her time and gave her his e mail address.

"I'll send the recording through tonight, honey. You can think about the messages and listen to them again, when you next look at your e mail." Marcus thanked her and turned to leave.

"Oh, Marcus, before you go, I have a message from a lady calling herself Vera. She says, 'Remember, they don't leave us, they just move to a different plane for a while'."

The sweeping roads through the red rocks and out of Sedona, provided the peaceful reflecting time which Marcus desperately needed. He was still shaking when he reached the junction of Interstate 17. He had previously gone out of his way to avoid the busy main routes and ride the more picturesque, isolated roads, but now he found himself craving traffic, noise, normality; anything which allowed him space to rationalise what had just happened.

The two-hour ride to Phoenix seemed to pass quickly. He kept playing Donna's words over and over in his head, trying frantically to take each extraordinary statement and find a logical reason for it. Some things were easier to attempt to justify than others.

Was mentioning his profession a long shot? It was, after all, August and the peak of the UK summer school holidays and maybe he really did have that teacher 'look'. Ava had, on occasion, ridiculed his clean, tame appearance. His short, neatly groomed hair and the customary Chinos and hacking jacket made him look more like a history teacher than a Head of PE, she had often commented. Perhaps, he concluded, Donna had made a lucky guess. Then there was the 'great loss' which the medium had confirmed he had experienced. Well, why else would I be here, 5000 miles away from home, alone? Again, he convinced himself, a calculated presumption on Donna's part.

The mention of the blueprint had shaken him. They, he knew, were Jeanie's words and he had heard them first hand, on Ava's regression tape. Ava had attempted to convince Marcus, on many occasions, that we all have a blueprint; a pre-life contract and plan, which we supposedly create for ourselves in order to evolve as beings. He had never heard the philosophy before, but maybe this was a recognised viewpoint among mediums and therefore, Donna may have known about it.

The message from Vera had caught him off guard and the irony of her timing had not gone unnoticed: Marcus recalled Vera's last uncomfortable 'door step' message, the first time he and Ava had visited the old lady. In his mind, he replayed the embarrassing reminder of his family name along with the message from Uncle Dom but, he thought, Vera was still alive in a care home in Brixton Hill, so Donna had got that one wrong.

Attempting to logicise each of Donna's remarks helped Marcus to feel more at ease but, in the pit of his gut, he knew there was no sound explanation for the accuracy of her comments. The drawing on the Peruvian flag, the reference to the red bird and Ava's wing-shaped birthmark were both, he conceded, impossible to blag, but most remarkable were the names. Eva, was far too close to be conjecture, as was Lyn, to whom the silver cross was to be given and finally, no one in the entire world knew Ava's mortifying abbreviation of Marcus's family name, Randy.

Marcus had a restless night. His sleep was fitful and his dreams animated and disturbing. Visions of Ava morphed into distorted, cackling images of Mystic Marvel and in an empty dark church, threatening shadows whispered incoherent messages. The air conditioning in the small hotel room was ineffective and Marcus woke, hot and uncomfortable, several times throughout the night. He was glad when the light of the Phoenix summer morning finally arrived.

The temperature was already 27 degrees when Marcus loaded his bike and set off for the Mexican border at 6am. He felt tired from his broken sleep and his mind was still churning the information from his reading with Donna, but he no longer felt confused or alarmed. Instead a sense of calm and a feeling that he was being watched over, protected in some way, made him feel safe.

He had risen early and looked briefly at his e mail. The usual junk and property details were accompanied by a short note from Donna, attaching the recording of his reading, and an unexpected message from Jeanie.

Hello Marcus, I hope you are finding peace on your trip. I know it would have been important to Ava, so I wanted to write and tell you that my dear friend, Vera McManus, passed away last week. I have a feeling you may already know. She's finally gone home. Jeanie x

Chapter 20 – The Spirit is Willing but the Flesh is Weak

The border crossings are generally unsafe; being havens for the notorious drug and sex traffickers. Only last week, two South African bikers were shot and robbed in Douglas, AZ, making the adjacent Mexico border crossing of Agua Prieta a good place to exit as soon as possible.

Marcus had read Steve Lloyd's MCN article again prior to leaving Phoenix and felt nervous about approaching the Mexican border. He had ridden the 230 miles, a hot and monotonous four-hour trip and stopped for refreshments only once, in the town of Tombstone. The town, famed for the Gunfight at the O.K. Corral, regularly re-enacted the famous Cowboys versus Lawmen shootout and Marcus had watched one of the performances before setting off for the small Mexican town of Moctezuma, via the infamous Agua Prieta crossing.

The queue for the crossing was long and the processing of papers tedious and uncomfortably hot but largely uneventful, much to his relief. Steve's article had also warned about the many topes, the steep and crudely made speed bumps, which marked the entrance and exit to every Mexican town. Marcus had managed to negotiate these, along with the dry and dusty potholed roadways, until he arrived tired and dehydrated in Los Hoyos, 27 miles from his motel in Moctezuma. The loud bang had startled him, as the front wheel of the fully loaded Dakar hit the rough topes and he just managed to stop the bike from falling.

When he arrived in the small agricultural town, he was physically and emotionally exhausted and the turbulent night he had spent in Phoenix only served to exacerbate his need for sleep. Tomorrow he would set off through the expansive and varied landscape of Mexico on the next stage of his journey.

The extremes of wealth and poverty in this vast country fascinated Marcus. His route along the coastal roads of the country introduced him to prosperous tourist cities as well as unnerving places within Sinaloa, North-West Mexico, the unofficial and dark centre of the narcotics trade. The colours, sounds and people in the towns and cities, captivated him and the places he chose to stay, during his journey through this country of paradoxes, were in stark contrast with the contemporary and law-abiding towns of Northern America.

The challenge of locating motels and specific travel routes no longer phased Marcus: His experiences and interaction with inspiring people so far, seemed to have fuelled him with the confidence that he was being protected along the way. There was no denying that his meeting with Donna had created a fundamental shift in him. His ability to rationalise every slightly curious occurrence, with structured reasoning, no longer felt possible or even important to him and his trip through Central and Southern America would only serve to further feed his spiritual growth.

Mexico, vibrant and at times menacing, had been an education. Steve had warned Marcus about the kidnap culture, which inevitably brought with it its multitude of heavy handed, armed bodyguards. He had shared many anecdotes about successful and wealthy residents of the country who had, habitually, altered their route to work each day to avoid abductors. While lone tourist bikers were not typically targeted by these criminals, Steve had advised Marcus to be vigilant.

The challenges which Marcus faced as he left Mexico and crossed the border into Guatemala, one of the poorest countries in Latin America, were less to do with organised crime and more immediately as a result of the weather. The recent heavy rains had caused landslides and many of the roads had presented him with the most arduous riding since the Dalton Highway. The taxing journey through Guatemala culminated in a needlessly overcomplicated and stressful crossing into Honduras. He had already experienced the swarms of local border-hopping 'helpers' at the crossing with Guatemala; forceful locals, insisting on expediting the formalities with the authorities, whilst demanding money. His inability to speak Spanish made him even more vulnerable and an easy target for the hustlers and while the crossing into Guatemala had been frustrating and unpleasant, the entrance into Honduras was even worse.

The aggressive and loud approaches from the border opportunists annoyed him and the realisation that these chancers could radically hinder his progress, if he did not comply with their demands, offended his sense of fairness. Having finally crossed the border, at significant emotional and financial expense, Marcus was then faced with the frequent stops by the local law enforcement officers. Claims that he had committed a variety of riding violations, in an attempt to extort as much money as possible from him, brought him to the firm conclusion that Honduras was a place to get out of, as quickly as possible.

Crossing the border into Nicaragua, his plan had been to take the lengthy but bike-friendly roads directly to Costa Rica. As he rode the long highway down towards the massive and imposing lake, the headache and mild nausea that he had noticed earlier in the day began to intensify and he made the decision to head, instead, for the Pacific Coast and rest at San Juan del Sur. The psychological and physical strain, which he had felt since leaving the relative normality of North America and encountering the cultural and geographical differences of Central America, were, he concluded, taking their toll.

Approaching the small fishing town, he became aware of a loss of power in the bike. Since beginning his trip, Marcus had religiously lubricated the chain, changed the tyres and managed the recommended oil changes, but his lack of technical competence prevented him from conducting anything more sophisticated. He decided to pull into the entrance of the first hotel he arrived at and as he did, the engine on the Dakar stalled and would not re-start. As he began pushing the bike toward the parking area, he started to shake. The outside temperature, cooled only moderately by the ocean breeze, was 35 degrees but Marcus was cold and shivering and the effort to get the panniers and luggage from the lifeless bike to the room was almost too great for him to manage. His sole objective was to climb into bed and sleep; the bike repair could wait until tomorrow.

He fell asleep almost immediately but awoke in the early hours of the morning, thirsty and aching. The rational explanation, that his sickness was caused by stress and exhaustion, seemed flawed at 2am and he was concerned that his symptoms could be those of Malaria or even Dengue Fever.

As he lay in his bed, damp with sweat, shuddering and fighting the urge to vomit, he wondered, for the first time, if this might be the end of his journey. He knew now that he had seriously underestimated the demands of the trip. He had naïvely thought that conquering the notorious Dalton

Highway would be his greatest obstacle and had failed to even consider the implications of the many miles through third-world countries, or the likely failure of either his body or his bike. Here, 5200 miles from home, Marcus felt vulnerable and alone and a further 8000 miles to Buenos Aires seemed an impossible dream.

He stared up at the ceiling and watched the ineffectual fan wafting the hot, humid air around the room. He thought about his father, his brother and Ava and wondered what they would say in response to his premature return home,

'Well, Alaska to Nicaragua is a pretty amazing achievement, Son.'

Marcus could imagine his dad's placating tone and felt crushingly disappointed.

'Shit, mate,' his brother would say, with a conciliatory slap on the back, '9000 plus miles, when you only passed your test in May? That's amazing, Bro!'

But Ava would not have let him off so easily,

'Come on Randy, you wimp! Get some rest, take a Paracetamol and fix the damn bike. You can do this and you'll never forgive yourself if you quit!'

Marcus knew she was right. No excuse would justify him abandoning his trip. He would get to Buenos Aires, he promised himself, if he died in the attempt.

At 9am, he woke from his uneasy sleep. He was shocked at how long he had slept and panicked at the thought of the broken bike awaiting diagnosis and repair.

While feeling significantly better than the day before, he was still weak and the uncomfortable echo of his headache was still making its presence felt.

The smell of fresh coffee met him as he sat at an outside table and looked at the breakfast menu. To his surprise and relief he felt hungry, having missed both lunch and dinner the previous day in favour of an early night. Surely a healthy appetite was a good indication of any infection or bug having passed, he thought.

The Dakar popped and spluttered into life, only to die again almost immediately. Initially concerned, Marcus was both grateful and reassured when the hotel Manager solicited the help of a local friend, able to diagnose and correct a fuel blockage. The intense, dry heat of Nicaragua had turned to heavy rain since Marcus's arrival, not unusual for the mid-summer months. Still a little frail, he decided to stay an additional two days in San Juan del Sur to benefit from some rest and recuperation, before recommencing his journey south into the environmentally progressive Costa Rica.

The negative impact of anxiety on his physical health had unnerved Marcus and, more conscious than ever of the fragility of his mental wellbeing, he had decided to seek out some treatment. As soon as he crossed the border into Costa Rica, he experienced a feeling of tranquillity and the ability of most of the individuals he came into contact with to speak English, made him feel far more comfortable and in control. Checking into the hotel in Tamarindo, he noticed a marketing flyer on a small table in the reception area and the headline caught his eye: *'Calm your mind, manage your anxiety and achieve your goals.'* Marcus picked up the leaflet and took it to his room and he was immediately intrigued by Rob, the American man who answered his call. He had briefly explained his trip and the impact his angst had had on his physical health, "I'm putting myself through some pretty serious challenges and I can't afford to let my mind hold me back. Do you think you can help me?" he asked.

"I don't know," Rob answered, "maybe, but that depends on if you really want to be helped or if you're just looking for an excuse to bail out and run," came the unexpected reply.

Marcus was caught off guard. Did he really want help to manage this phenomenal goal on his blueprint, or was he really looking for someone to hand him a professionally endorsed licence to quit? He thought for a second. "That's a really good question and I'm not sure how to answer you honestly," he conceded, "but I'd really value your guidance."

Robert's Centre for Clinical Hypnotherapy was a yellow, chalet style house in a cul-de sac off the main coast road. It was located only about a mile and a half from Marcus's hotel, so he had decided to walk to his appointment rather than take the bike. He was ten minutes early when he arrived at the front porch and waited without knocking, having read the sign on the door. *Hypnotherapy session in progress. Please wait.*

Exactly at 11am, the front door opened and a woman exited the house, leaving a middle-aged man standing in the doorway. "Hey. You must be Marcus. Please, come on in. I'll go and get us some fresh water."

Rob's studio was a converted garage to the side of the property and accessed through the entrance hall in the house. The room reminded Marcus of the treatment room in a hotel spa he had once had a massage in. It was cool and peaceful and the walls were covered with an impressive collection of Rob's certificates; NLP Practitioner, NLP Master Practitioner and NLP Certified Trainer, were nearest to where he was standing and he moved around the room to look at the others. Most were awards for hypnotherapy and psychotherapy, indicating competence at various levels and he was surprised to see one dated March 1998, confirming another of Rob's qualifications; Diploma in Past-Life Regression Therapy.

When Rob returned to the studio, Marcus spent quite some time discussing the reason for his Pan American trip and the increasing discontent he was feeling at the thought of returning to his old life.

"So," Rob asked impassively, "what does it look like when it's fixed?"

Marcus thought for a second, trying to assimilate what the man was asking so Rob reframed his question. "If your life was exactly as you want it; work, family, faith, leisure, everything, what would it be like? Let's take work first."

Marcus thought for a moment. "I like making a difference; you know, knowing that my interaction had made a positive difference to someone's day; that their life was better as a result of me spending time with them."

Rob listened and nodded his head. "I get that. Doesn't teaching make you feel that way?" Marcus sighed, "I just drifted into teaching, Rob. I can't remember ever making a conscious choice to be a Phys. Ed. teacher and as Head of Department, I'm more an administrator, playing politics, than an educator. The thing is, until Ava died, I had never questioned it. I've spent over 12 years on autopilot, doing something I don't feel passionate about. I've experienced how life can throw a curve ball and I don't want to waste any more time."

Marcus began to tell Rob about Ava; her care-free attitude and her unwavering belief that life is for learning and evolving. The conversation led him to tell Rob about Roisin and Linh and Ava's life-altering experiences with past lives.

"I noticed your diploma," he said, pointing to the framed certificate on the wall behind Rob. "Do you do many past-life regressions?"

Rob looked surprised, "In my experience, a significant number of the problems my clients encounter, are as a result of events from previous lives."

Marcus was amazed. He had thought past-life regression to be the domain of people like Jeanie; psychic mediums or at least eccentric free spirits. Here was an intelligent, educated and pragmatic man, talking about past-life regression as a solution to a problem, in the way a dentist might recommend a filling for a tooth ache.

"Doesn't that present you with some dilemmas?" Marcus asked, intrigued. "What if a client has a strong religious belief or is an old cynic, like me? How do you get them to consider the possibility that they've lived before?"

Rob smiled, "It's not my job to convince them. It's my job to present them with the evidence and let them make their own mind up. Most of the people I've used past-life regression treatment with have had a pretty rough time. Symptoms, like the ones you mentioned Roisin experienced, aren't unusual. I've helped people with crippling phobias, excruciating pain and irrational fears; often a debilitating fear of someone in their own family or friendship group. If it works, Marcus, that's generally enough to convince them."

Marcus's thoughts immediately turned to Isla, the distraught Scottish lady who he had met at the Grand Canyon and who had described to him, her pathological terror of her fiancé's father. He wondered if her problem could possibly be as a result of an event in a past life.

Rob looked up at the clock: "Time's up for today, buddy." He handed Marcus a small booklet. "Give this some thought, if you really want to make a difference with people. It might just help you scratch that old itch."

Marcus looked at the booklet,

'Introduction to Clinical Hypnotherapy, a two-day, interactive workshop covering the basics of hypnosis; creative inductions, deepeners and creation of therapeutic scripts.

with Doctor Robert Craven

The dates on the reverse of the marketing literature indicated that the next workshop was to run over the next two days; Saturday and Sunday.

As he set off on the walk back to the hotel, he recalled Ava's words from his reading with Donna,

'Take the training, Randy.'

Chapter 21 – Humble Pie and Coke

There were six people on the 'Introduction to Clinical Hypnotherapy' workshop. Marcus had struggled with the thought of attending; his new explorative self, battling with the former dogmatic Marcus; the one that dismissed the value of any cure which had not been written on an MD's prescription pad. It was also the old, closed minded Marcus who had created in his head, the typical profile of Doctor Robert's course attendees: alternative, meditating non-conformists, probably female, wearing hippy-style gear.

He was the second participant to arrive at the conference room at the Beach Hotel. The first was, to Marcus's surprise, a Consultant Psychiatrist from Dallas, named Bill. Rob pointed towards a table of coffee and pastries as he greeted his third delegate, Martha, a counsellor from New York City.

"Please help yourselves to some refreshments and get to know each other," he said, sending Martha over to join the two men.

"Pleased to meet you both," Martha said, holding out her hand first to Bill and then to Marcus. "What brings you both to hypnotherapy school?"

Bill explained how the increasing use of hypnotherapy amongst some of his colleagues, to address some psychiatric disorders, had piqued his interest. "Sur'nuff, they all seem to have gotten into this stuff so I thought I'd join y'all."

"Same here," Martha said nodding. "Most of my co-workers are re-training to include hypnotherapy in their portfolios. They've had some impressive results, particularly around addictions and weight loss. What about you, Marcus? What made you sign-up for the programme?"

Marcus was not sure where to start. He was astonished and a little ashamed of how inaccurate his blinkered view of hypnotherapy and its practitioners had been. He had allowed his own experiences, very limited though they were, to colour his view and dismiss the practice as fluffy and unsubstantiated. Now he was standing with credible and highly qualified professionals and was beginning to accept that he had been very narrow-minded.

Two more course participants joined the group and Marcus was relieved that Bill and Martha's attention had turned to them.

"Hi everyone, I'm Gary and this is my wife, Gill." There was a hum around the room as everyone acknowledged the couple and introduced themselves before turning towards Rob and the last of the six attendees.

"Don't worry too much about introductions," Rob said, raising his voice to be heard over the chatter. "You can all speak in just a minute and get to know each other properly."

Once everyone was seated, Doctor Robert welcomed the assembled group and outlined the two days. "As you can imagine, there will be a lot of practical work and opportunities to try some interesting new techniques."

Marcus was shocked to feel a little nervous. He had been front and centre, demonstrating sports skills and talking to large groups of students for years. Why was he suddenly feeling very exposed?

"Before we get going," Rob continued, "why don't we find out about each other? I'll start you all off. My name is Robert Craven. I have a PhD in Psychology and have been a Master Practitioner of Hypnotherapy, Psychotherapy and Neuro Linguistic Programming for six years. For the last three years I have been training people, from all backgrounds and professions, to use hypnosis in their own jobs. I'm excited to share some of my knowledge with you all this weekend and hope you really enjoy and benefit from this introduction to hypnotherapy programme." Rob smiled and turned to face the married couple.

"Hello again," Gill began, "my name is Gill Mills-Sharp and I'm here with Gary, my husband. Three years ago, Gary and I set up a retreat in Palm Bay, Florida for veterans suffering with PTSD. We offer access to all kinds of conventional and alternative treatments and really want to be able to offer hypnotherapy, as we've heard so many great things about it."

Gary nodded, in acknowledgement of his wife's comments and continued the couple's introduction. "Hi, yes, I'm Gary Mills-Sharp and, well, actually I'm the reason we set Bay Retreat up." The room went quiet. "I was in the military for 15 years and I've completed a number of tours of duty; Panama, the Gulf, Bosnia, you know. I came back pretty messed up five years ago and, well, my body healed but my mind needed some extra help and that was our inspiration for the retreat. We're starting to see some bad stuff from the Afghanistan war and Gill and I want to offer the emotional help to these poor dudes that I never got."

A mumble of approval circulated around the conference room. "Thanks, you two." Rob said. "Who's next?"

Bill and Martha were the next two to complete their formal introductions and a young woman, the last of the delegates to have arrived, spoke after them.

"Hi everyone. It's really good to be here with you all. My name is Lauren and I've just finished my internship as a Social Worker in Detroit. I'm starting my Masters and one of my Tutor Supervisors has used hypnotherapy with kids; abused and neglected kids. She recommended I sign up, so here I am."

The group welcomed Lauren and then all eyes turned to Marcus.

"Hello," Marcus swallowed hard. He had no real clarity about what to say to these admirable people, so he just said what came into his head. "I'm Marcus, Marcus Crane.

Until six months ago, I was a content but pretty dull Phys. Ed. teacher in a town in England and then my life changed." The room was silent. "My partner of 13 years died very suddenly. Ava was my complete opposite; gregarious, spontaneous and very spiritual. She also believed she had lived before and had experienced past-life regression, which I dismissed fairly ruthlessly, even though there was some very compelling evidence. When she passed away, I sold my house, learned to ride a motorbike and booked a solo trip from Alaska to Argentina and that's what brought me here, to Costa Rica. I'm sure I'm not the first person to completely lose the plot after a bereavement." Marcus smiled and the group laughed nervously, waiting for him to continue. "The trip has changed me; for the better I believe. I'm more open minded but I think I'm wasting the time I have on this planet and I need to change direction. That was the reason I initially came to see Rob."

The captivated group nodded approvingly. "I wasn't sure about the whole hypnotherapy thing but I have listened to you guys, all of you, and feel humbled and never more convinced that I need to explore this further. Maybe like you, I can use it to really make a difference." Marcus stopped speaking and the room broke into thunder of applause.

"Thank you, Marcus," Rob said, standing up, "Wow! What a way to finish the intros. Let's get going, shall we?"

The two days were both interesting and draining for Marcus and his fellow course participants. The plenary and slides, highlighting the different hypnotic inductions and deepeners, were followed by hours of practical application; some significantly more successful than others.

Marcus had been apprehensive about being the subject in any of his co-delegates' hypnosis attempts. He remembered his inability to concentrate for even the shortest of time, when trying the meditation tape which Jeanie had given him and he desperately did not want to let anyone down. Somehow, however, the credibility of these people enabled him to focus more easily and with the exception of the very quick shock inductions, Marcus managed to achieve a good state of relaxation, relatively quickly.

On Saturday night, the group were charged with creating their own deepeners in time for Sunday's practical; visual passages used, as the name suggests, to deepen the state of relaxation. Marcus had never considered himself especially creative and as he sat in his hotel room, he thought back to the dismal attempts he had made at descriptive writing as a teenager. A walk along the Tamarindo beach seemed to adequately address his writers' block and act as inspiration for a well-received visual passage and Marcus had thoroughly enjoyed the second day of the programme.

When the course had finished, the group all went their separate ways, promising to keep in touch and committing to attend further workshops. Marcus stayed behind to speak with Rob.

"So, has the course inspired you to take up hypnotherapy?" Rob asked.

Marcus had been pleasantly surprised at his apparent success in the practical exercises. He knew that this introduction to hypnosis had only enabled him to experience a tiny fraction of what hypnotherapy could achieve, but a part of him was a little disappointed that past-life regression had not been addressed, even though he knew that this very specialised practice was not a subject for a beginner.

"It's been a great couple of days, Rob. Thank you so much for opening my eyes to the power of hypnosis and giving me the opportunity of meeting those fabulous people. I guess I have a lot to learn." Rob smiled as he led Marcus to the door.

"I have some contacts in London, Marcus; some very talented practitioners who will help you to understand past-life regression therapy much better. I'll e mail their details through to you and you can maybe do a little more research. They'll be able to share some astounding, UK based case studies, which will help you decide if it's for you."

The rainy season was coming to an end and temperatures were a hot but bearable 27 degrees when Marcus crossed the border into Panama in mid-November.

Steve's article had reminded Marcus that he would need to arrange transport for his bike from Panama City over the border into Colombia. The Darien Gap, a 10,000 square mile, lawless wilderness of swamp and rainforest which spans the border between the two countries, was a definite no-go, Steve had warned. 'If the venomous snakes don't get you, the narcotic traffickers will.'

Marcus had considered the convoluted route by boat and had, instead, decided to fly the Dakar from Panama City to Bogota. As he arrived at the cargo terminal, he saw another biker waiting for the shipping of his Suzuki DR-Z400S to be processed. Marcus noticed the British number plate immediately and rode over to meet the rider. The biker was Ricky Finch, a 33-year-old Sales Director from Coventry and he was relieved to hear the familiar accent of another Englishman. Ricky had been waiting at the cargo bay for an hour and a half and was beginning to get frustrated when a Columbian woman with broken English came to complete the documentation.

The two men took a flight to Bogota later that evening and caught the complimentary shuttle to the hotel. Ricky was the first British rider Marcus had met in the six and a half months since he had left the UK and they had agreed to travel together to Mitad del Mundo or 'Middle of the World', a park which marks the precise location of the Equator, three days' ride away.

After that, Marcus would continue his journey into Peru while Ricky headed north east towards Venezuela.

Ricky had flown his motorbike into Chicago and travelled the 2448 miles along the original Route 66 before heading south. The entire journey, ending at the south-ern-most tip of South America, would take him around a year, he had anticipated. Like Marcus, he had already been travelling over six months and the trip, he was sure, had saved his sanity and probably his life.

"I was on a fast route to self-destruction; four stone overweight, working 20 hours a day and keeping myself fired on cocaine."

Marcus listened, as the strong beer fuelled Ricky's tale of woe. "I was fucked up. I couldn't function and eventu-ally lost my job, my wife and my kids. She couldn't take anymore of me being a complete arsehole and God, I don't blame her."

Marcus looked at the wretched man sitting opposite him. He guessed Ricky was around six feet tall and maybe 170lbs. He looked good and Marcus wondered how he had managed to shed the excess weight and kick the coke habit.

"She threatened to stop any access to the kids, unless I sorted my life out. They already think their dad's a complete loser and I wanted the trip to make them proud of me. I had to lose the weight before I could even attempt 25,000 miles on a motorbike so, having been sacked for snorting the nose-candy in the office loos, I hit the gym, lived on rabbit food and went cold turkey. It took me the best part of a year, but I made it."

Marcus was impressed at Ricky's phenomenal achievement but he also felt sorry for his new biking companion. His own life, leading up to his Pan American trip, could not have been more different. He had felt broken when he lost Ava and he could not begin to imagine Ricky's pain at losing his life partner as well as his livelihood, his children and his self-respect.

"So, what's the plan when you eventually reach Ushuaia?" Marcus asked.

"One day at a time. I've sent the boys pictures from every state and every new country, so they know I'm doing OK. I'm not going back to the old life though. Maybe I'll buy a coffee shop on the south west coast or drive a taxi. I don't know what the future will hold but I will get my priorities straight; work to live, instead of living to work."

Marcus and Ricky rode together for the next few days until they reached the tall column, indicating their arrival at the equator. There they exchanged contact details.

"Ride safe, my friend," Ricky said as he started up his bike.

"You too," Marcus replied. "Let me know what new path you decide to take and when we get back to Blighty, I'll let you know what's next on my blueprint."

Chapter 22 – JFDI

As Marcus left Quito and headed south towards the border with Peru, he thought about Ricky's improvised and spontaneous adventure and wondered if his old propensity for structure and deadlines was influencing his own trip too heavily. He had seen some incredible places during his 14000 miles of travel so far, but it was not unusual for him to spend six or more hours on the Dakar in a day and he was starting to feel it. The heat and long days of riding were taking a toll on his back and neck and something Ricky had said had made him think.

"When are you ever going to be able to take a year out again; go where you want, when you want with whoever you want? This is a one-off, mate."

He was right, of course. While Marcus planned some major changes in his life on his return to the UK, he did not anticipate a similar trip any time in the near future.

"The best adventures don't happen in straight lines," Ricky had insisted, when Marcus questioned his decision to ride nearly 700 miles from Bogota to the Ecuador Equator, only to retrace his steps in order to ride through Venezuela.

"You don't need to take the quickest route or spoil the journey with timetables, Marcus. Squeeze every last second out of this trip, mate."

Ricky's advice had convinced Marcus to slow down and enjoy the four remaining countries; Ecuador, Peru, Chile and Argentina and instead of taking the direct route to the Peruvian border, he headed west to Manta and the beautiful Ecuador Pacific Coast.

The three unscheduled weeks in Ecuador provided reflection and repair time for Marcus. The culture and history of Santa Elena and peace and tranquillity of the Puyango Petrified Forest were a welcome contrast to the seemingly endless nights of festivals and Latin American beach parties, on the build-up to the Christmas season. He was grateful to Ricky for his advice and valued the unrushed and anxiety free time he had spent dawdling slowly from town to town towards Huaquillas and into Peru. During his time in Ecuador, he had given some thought to his future, something which he had avoided doing during most of the trip, and he had made some fundamental decisions.

To: Brian Evans; Headmaster
From: Marcus Crane; Head of Physical Education
Dear Brian,
I hope all is well with you and with the school. I am now seven months into my Pan American trip and I am writing to you from the Galapagos Islands, having taken some time out in Ecuador.

While I know we discussed my taking a full academic year away from school, I am conscious that my absence will inevitably cause some instability and uncertainty, particularly within my own department. I am also aware of the expense, effort and lack of continuity which arranging supply teachers can incur. For those reasons, I feel it is only fair that I inform you of my decision to resign my position of Head of Department, with immediate effect.

I am so grateful that you permitted me the time away from work. Whilst still early days, a healing process has begun, which I am certain would have taken considerably longer, had I remained in the UK.

I would like to take this opportunity of wishing you and all of the staff a very happy Christmas and all the best for a successful 2003 and beyond.

Kindest regards,

Marcus Crane.

Marcus was surprised at how easy it had been for him to submit his resignation. He felt it was the right decision and he knew without doubt, that Ava would have been proud and supportive. He thought about some of the significant people he had met during his trip so far, who had provided the emotional impetus for his decisions: Grant, the discontented lawyer, his roommate in Deadhorse, who had inspired him; single dad Jake and his son Mikey, who had saved him on the Dalton Highway and introduced him to the amazing Kelly-Anne and her miraculous Reiki. He recalled his time with Steve and Karyn and his admiration for just how remarkably stalwart they were in the face of sickness, disability and bigotry and he thought of Ricky's direct but justified advice to, *"JFDI, mate! Just Fucking Do It!"*

It was the third week of December by the time Marcus approached Lima, the capital and largest of Peru's cities. He had been looking forward to visiting the country since receiving Jeanie's note, showing the Peruvian flag and an indication that Ava thought the place would be of significant interest.

As the chicken bus limped through the crowded roads on the outskirts of Lima, the heat was increasing and Cherie Rutherford wished she had left Pisco earlier that morning.

The journey from Pisco, about 145 miles and normally three hours south of Lima, had taken Cherie five and a half hours. The draw of the early morning boat trip to the Paracas National Reserve from Pisco, to see the marine life, had been too strong to ignore and Cherie had missed the direct Red bus and opted instead for a later but significantly more convoluted route, ending 15 miles short of Lima centre.

The yellow chicken bus was full of locals and seemed to Cherie to stop every couple of minutes to collect and deposit noisy, luggage laden people. She had, after a few minutes on the bus, managed to get a seat and give her back and shoulders, aching from the weight of her heavy backpack, a much-needed rest. As she gazed out of the dusty window, she thought about her mother and brother back in Christchurch and made a mental note to e mail them from Lima.

Cherie had been away from her native New Zealand for five weeks now. At 29, she considered herself a mature gap year traveller but reconciled her delay in travel with the knowledge that her family had needed her during her early 20s. Most of her friends had disappeared off to Europe or the USA for extended periods, some finding partners and never returning to their Southwestern Pacific home.

Her adventure had begun in Argentina and followed the history and wildlife of South America through Chile and into Peru. As her confidence grew and the ticks on her bucket list increased, Cherie became more immersed in the culture of these incredible places and her love for their people; their generosity and selfless kindness, never ceasing to amaze her.

The sound of raised voices stirred Cherie from her day dream and leaning forward to see what was causing the disturbance, she became aware of an altercation between the bus driver and a truck driver. She watched the animated argument as the two angry men shouted over each other in unintelligible Spanish and wondered what had happened to create the furore. The temperature was rising rapidly in the overcrowded bus and some of the passengers chose to terminate their journeys early, while others grumbled at the uncomfortable delay. Cherie fanned herself with a bus timetable and watched as the numerous cars, trucks and pedestrians continued along the road and pavement.

As the bus stood motionless, Cherie spotted a motorbike at the side of the road; the biker in deep conversation with a police officer. She watched for a while, having noticed the GB on the bike's registration plate and wondered how far the heavy laden and dirty bike had travelled. She strained, her face pressed hard against the grubby window, looking ahead and behind the bike for any sign of a biking companion but the man seemed to be travelling alone. Cherie wondered if the lone adventurer was experiencing the peace and serenity which she had enjoyed these last five weeks; not having to worry about, consider or plan around any other human.

The chicken bus jolted back into motion and Cherie was grateful for the gentle wafts of air, breezing in through the open door and windows. The gentle growl of the bus's engine was briefly smothered by the popping sound of a motorbike and Cherie watched as the lone British biker accelerated past her slow, clunky transport. A couple of miles further towards Lima, Cherie saw the biker, yet again stopped at the side of the road. Once again, he was in conversation with a police officer and this time the biker was clearly unhappy. Cherie chuckled to herself. She had been warned about the South American Police's propensity for ripping off unsuspecting tourists and was pretty sure that this poor biker would not be the last to fall victim to the authorities' false claims of road violations, today.

Cherie's journey into Lima terminated outside the Government Palace and feeling hot and sticky from her trip, she decided to find her accommodation and have a shower before exploring the historic centre of the city. The small hotel was a fifteen-minute walk and Cherie was relieved when she arrived in her clean, bright room. Her nights so far had been spent in hostels or dark, dirty rooms, which had been grossly misrepresented in the travel guides and Cherie had promised herself that her short stay in Lima would be slightly more luxurious. She stepped out into the warm sunshine of the late afternoon and wandered through the impressive official buildings and into a commercial area offering numerous shops, restaurants and bars. The rich smell of cooking emanating from the row of eateries, reminded Cherie that she had not eaten since leaving Pisco and she decided to stop for coffee and picarones, a Peruvian donut which she had been advised to try. As she continued her search for a refreshment stop, Cherie noticed the motorbike she had seen from the chicken bus, parked a little further up the road. Curious to find out if her suspicion, that he had been duped by an unscrupulous cop, was correct, she looked into the various shops and restaurants in the immediate vicinity of the bike. The bar, immediately next to where the bike was parked, had an outside seating area and Cherie quickly spotted the biker, now sipping a coffee while supervising his fully loaded bike.

She sat down at the next table. "Hi, I saw you being stopped earlier. I hope they didn't rip you off too much. I'm Cherie, by the way," she held out her hand.

"I'm very pleased to meet you, Cherie. I'm Marcus and yes, the robbing bastards took me for forty quid, twice!"

Cherie tried to look suitably sympathetic but somehow the thought of this strong, independent man being swindled twice, within a few minutes, made it difficult for her to maintain a serious expression and she started to giggle. Marcus initially looked surprised before joining Cherie laughing.

"Why didn't you just tell them you had no money?" Cherie spluttered, biting her lip in an attempt to stop giggling. Marcus thought for a moment and shrugged, "I have no idea. I'm a law-abiding citizen, Cherie and I didn't want to end up in chokey."

Marcus's strange choice of words combined with his strong, standard English accent, only served to fuel Cherie's laughter. "Robbing bastards? End up in chokey? You English sound so funny." Cherie had repeated what Marcus had said while trying, unsuccessfully, to mimic his British accent. Marcus tutted dismissively, "You order 'fush' and 'chups' instead of fish and chips and take a 'beth' instead of a bath and you say I sound funny?"

Cherie smiled and nodded, conceding defeat and drained her coffee.

Marcus was grateful for the company and light relief, which his new found friend had given him. His day had been stressful, not least due to his frustration at being taken for a fool by the police. He ordered two more coffees and the pair exchanged stories about their adventures before Marcus asked about Cherie's motivation for her trip.

"My parents owned a bar in Christchurch. They had it for years, all my life in fact, and my little brother and I helped out after school and at weekends. When I was 17, my dad left; dumped Mum and ran off with the Bar Manager. Mum was left alone to keep the place going and take care of two kids. It was a tough time for her."

Marcus listened as Cherie explained her decision for travelling later than she had originally planned. "He left the place in a lot of debt. Mum couldn't pay the staff we needed, so my plans for travel and uni had to be shelved and I became waitress, barmaid, cleaner, you name it. When Sean, my brother, left school, he took over the management of the bar. We ran it together for a while and took some risks; built an outside area and changed the menu and it paid off. It was doing fine until my father came back three years ago and wanted half of the business, in cash."

Marcus started to feel the frustration he was accustomed to, when faced with tales of injustice. "What happened? Did you have to sell?" he asked.

Cherie shook her head. "Nope, but we had to re-mortgage to pay the legal fees and get the old goat off our backs. It's taken another three years to get our heads above water again but it's doing OK and now was my chance to take the trip. How about you, Marcus? Why Peru on your lonesome?"

Marcus smiled, unwilling to spoil the atmosphere with his sad story of loss. "Boy, where do I start?" he said. "Very long story and too much for me to explain without a shower and a beer." Marcus paused and hoped his next question would not be misinterpreted, "How about I bore you with all the details over a bite to eat, later?"

Cherie smiled, a genuine smile which Marcus noticed reached her eyes and lit up her whole face. "Great idea. How about I meet you back here in two hours?"

Marcus's hotel was a ten-minute bike ride away and by the time he had parked and unpacked, he had less than an hour to shower, shave and get back to the bar to meet Cherie. He looked at his watch as he approached their meeting spot; 19.20.

Marcus had always been fanatical about punctuality and knew it was an obsession passed down from his father.

"Being late," Terry Crane would remind his two sons, *"is like saying 'you aren't important enough to be on time for' and it's very disrespectful."*

Ava had always been late and Marcus had taken to telling her that any important event was beginning 30 minutes before the scheduled start, in an attempt to get her there on time.

When Marcus reached the bar, Cherie was already there. "I haven't been here since you left, honestly," she said laughing, "I just have a real aversion to being late, so I'm always super early. I think it comes from running the bar. No one wants to turn up for a cold beer and find the place shut."

Marcus smiled. "What do you fancy to eat?" he said, as they wandered along the street, filled with tourists.

The restaurant was almost full when Marcus and Cherie arrived and they sat at the bar with a beer until their table was finally available. The small, traditional eatery was decorated with lights and garlands; the only things in the warm, humid evening, which reminded Marcus of the imminent Christmas celebrations.

"So," Cherie said, raising her glass, "here's to travel and Peru and the abolition of crooked cops." Marcus clinked his glass against Cherie's. "Cheers! I'll drink to that."

"OK, the sign on the door says the restaurant is open until half past midnight. By my calculations, that gives you five hours to tell me your long story. Think you can manage that?" Cherie asked, sipping her wine.

"Hmm." Marcus pulled a face. "Well, I guess I could make a start."

The evening seemed to pass in a heartbeat and Marcus had managed to find a way to tell Cherie about his beloved

Ava and his motivation for his Pan American trip, without dampening the atmosphere too much. When considering how much information to share with this relative stranger, he had not intended to discuss the more unorthodox aspects of his story; the past-life regressions, the spiritual messages and the wholly inexplicable reading he had attended with Donna, in Sedona. To his surprise, the discussion had naturally progressed into all of these areas and Cherie listened, without interruption or any sign of doubt or disbelief. She smiled as she looked Marcus in the eye. "Sounds like this lovely lady of yours is directing you, Marcus. How fantastic to have an advocate and guide on the other side. She'll keep you safe on your trip. You really are a lucky guy and you need to listen to what she has to say. You won't go far wrong, I'm sure."

Marcus walked Cherie back to her hotel and agreed to meet at 9am for breakfast the following morning, before planning to visit some of the must-see tourist attractions over the next couple of days. As he walked back to his accommodation, he felt a totally unexpected wave of guilt. For the first time since May, he had enjoyed the company of another human, without feeling the churning knot of sadness in his gut. Was it bad, he wondered, to enjoy the company of a woman, only eight months after Ava had died?

He knew there could be no thought of romance for him but Cherie was funny and beautiful. She and Marcus had the same sense of humour, the same values and intolerance of lateness, injustice and prejudice and Marcus felt he was betraying Ava by wanting to spend more time with her. By the time he had reached his room, he had made the decision to tell Cherie that he was leaving for Chile and would not be accompanying her on her exploration of Lima.

Marcus lay in his bed and thought about Ava and how she would feel about his evening with Cherie. He knew she would have encouraged him, selfless and generous as she always was, but to Marcus it felt disloyal and he pushed the thoughts of Cherie from his mind as he drifted off to sleep. In the morning, he staggered out of bed, his eyes still closed and as he walked towards the bathroom, he was aware of something rustling under his foot. As he looked down, he noticed the torn page which Jeanie had given him. Wondering how it got from the closed bag inside a pannier onto the floor of his hotel room, he picked it up and looked at it, for what must have been the 1000th time since Jeanie had sent it. The drawing of the motorbike sticker seemed an obvious reference to his trip but what about the flag of Peru? He had visited 11 countries so far, all fascinating and beautiful in their own right, so why had Ava specifically indicated Peru?

"What are you trying to say to me, Ava?" he muttered to himself. "Is there something I need to see here? Are you telling me to stay for a while longer?"

Marcus left the hotel at 8.30am and walked along the quiet street, the tourists still sleeping and the shops still closed. The city felt so different at this time; peaceful and calm, but the quarrel inside Marcus's head became louder with every footstep he took towards the breakfast café. 'Only eight months. It's not appropriate for you to laugh or have fun.' The self-rebuke was compelling and Marcus felt the heaviness of disappointment, as he wrestled with his uncomfortable internal dialogue. 'But Ava would hate you being miserable. She would want you to get the most out of every day of your trip and clearly, there's something she wants you to discover in Peru. Feeling some joy doesn't mean you love her any less.'

The reassurance felt good. Marcus realised he wanted to be persuaded and the sound of Ricky's clear instructions to, *'JFDI, mate,'* certainly helped.

"Morning. I've ordered coffee and eggs." Marcus smiled at the sound of the Kiwi accent, as he entered the café, "Iggs?" he laughed, "Sounds good. Let's eat and then we can plan our tour of Lima."

Chapter 23 – All Good Things..

The little motor boat travelled quickly through the crowded water off Peru's coastline and although the day was overcast and grey, the sea breeze was pleasantly warm.

As the boat neared the sharp, dark rocks of the Palomino Islands, the noise became deafening and Marcus likened it to the cheers and jeers in a crowded football stadium. Thousands of barking sea lions covered the rocks and played in the ocean, as tourists in bright yellow life jackets shared the teeming water.

Cherie felt a little apprehensive as she sat on the edge of the boat, Marcus bobbing in the murky water and waiting for her to take the plunge. The strong smell reminded Marcus that this isolated area was the habitat of 8000 of these playful and friendly aquatic creatures. He wondered how hygienic it actually was to swim here but he did not want to spoil the experience for his companion. Cherie had heard a couple of the swimmers complain about the temperature of the water. "Just how cold is it in there?" she shouted to Marcus, who was now surrounded by a group of curious sea lions. "Not nearly as cold as the Dalton Highway," he laughed. "Stop dithering and get in."

Marcus and Cherie had exhausted the top attractions in and around the city centre; the atmospheric squares and the famous architecture with ornate, wooden balconies and the Spanish inspired palaces and mansions. With Christmas now only three days away, they had decided to make the most of the dry weather and constant 25 degrees and travel a little further afield. The boat trip to the Palomino Islands, to swim with sea lions, had been Cherie's idea. It had been something she had wanted to try during her marine trip in Pisco, but a fear of open water had stopped her being comfortable swimming alone. The experience was also a huge step out of Marcus's comfort zone, but one which he had ultimately been delighted he had taken. A Peruvian cooking course and traditional yoga class, neither of which Marcus had been especially adept at, had made him laugh more than he had laughed in the last eight months.

As anticipated, most of the main city was closed on Christmas Day and Marcus spent much of the day calling his family, catching up on his e mail and watching festive films with Spanish sub-titles. The vast majority of the e mails were property details from Hemel Hempstead based estate agents and Marcus realised that, having resigned from his job, there was no longer a need for him to live in Hertfordshire; a county he hardly knew and where he had few friends. He tried to think about where he would like to live on his return to the UK but the thought of registering with agents and trawling through mountains of house details fatigued him. "That can wait until I get back," he told himself.

One of the emails looked like the standard junk mail which Marcus was always confronted with on opening his mail box. He usually pressed delete without even opening them but the subject on this one had caught his eye: 'International School of Clinical Hypnosis'. After his weekend workshop in Costa Rica, he had briefly looked online for UK based Hypnotherapy training providers but he did not remember requesting information or registering his details with any. He wondered if the newer, more sophisticated internet search engines could identify key words and phrases and automatically trigger these marketing e mails.

The website looked professional and was headed, *'A leading International Hypnotherapy Training Centre'*. Marcus clicked on the Foundation Course curriculum and noticed the programme content was very similar to Doctor Robert's workshop. Their Professional Diploma Course, held over 12 weekends in London, culminated in both a written and practical examination, which impressed Marcus. He was aware that the practice of hypnotherapy was currently unregulated in the UK and this had both surprised and concerned him. The ISCH appeared to be offering a highly regarded qualification, requiring proof of completion of an Introduction to Hypnotherapy programme and offering many more hours of practice than most of the other schools he had read about. The testimonials page glowed with accolades; *'enthusiastic and very capable trainers'* and *'wonderful'*, *'enjoyable'* and even *'life-changing content'* and Marcus started to feel more excited about continuing his hypnotherapy training. Finally, he looked at the faculty profiles; all of them with impressive backgrounds and experience and most with significantly more letters after their names than in them.

The next Diploma course was due to begin on 15th February 2003 and uncharacteristically for the reflective and cautious Marcus, he completed the details form on the contact page immediately and submitted his application to join the programme. "That is it then," he thought. "I need to be back home by the beginning of February."

That evening, over Christmas dinner in the hotel, Marcus told Cherie about his application to hypnotherapy school and the conversation prompted him to disclose more details about Ava's and Roisin's experiences with past-life regression. He was interested to know how Cherie felt about the prospect of having lived numerous lives and completing a self-designed blueprint each lifetime.

Cherie thought for a second. "We've never really been into that stuff in our house. Mum and Dad never went to church and I've never met anyone like Vera or Jeanie. I guess I just thought this was it, you know, one life, live it."

Marcus thought about the stories he had just told Cherie; of Roisin being a Suffragette and Ava, the Vietnamese mother of her high school History teacher and felt suddenly awkward at how ridiculous he must have sounded. Having been silent for a minute, Cherie put down her knife and fork and looked at Marcus. "Makes a lot of sense though, doesn't it?" she said, "what's the point of going through all this hard yakka just to get old, kick the bucket and push up daisies, end of?"

Marcus was not sure whether to feel relieved that Cherie did not appear to think he was a complete wierdo or burst out laughing at her very Kiwi colloquialisms.

"Hard yakka?" he snorted, struggling to stop a mouthful of red wine spurting over the table.

"Yakka, work, graft, you know?" Cherie joined Marcus laughing. "Seriously though, I think there's probably something in this past-lives stuff and you should find out more."

Having spent over a week off the bike and sightseeing in and around Lima, Marcus and Cherie agreed that their last tour together should be to Machu Piccu; the ancient wonder, perched in the mist-covered forests of the Peruvian Andes. While Cherie took a Red bus to Cusco, Marcus loaded up the Dakar and set off on the 712-mile trip and smiled to himself as he realised he would be riding some 500 miles out of his way to visit this famous place. He remembered the hard time he had given Ricky for doing exactly the same and recalled his friend's wise words, *"The best adventures don't happen in straight lines."*

Two days later, Marcus and Cherie boarded the shuttle bus from Aguas Calientes, up the winding road with breath taking views of the Urubamba River, to the lost city of the Incas. As Marcus stood with Cherie and stared at the amazing steps, terraces and ceremonial shrines of this beautiful and spiritual place, he felt a wave of emotion which no other place had ever created in him and as Cherie took his hand, a single tear ran down his cheek,

"Is this it?" he said. "Is this what Ava wanted me to experience?"

Marcus spent the first two weeks of the new year making his way along the Chilean Pacific Coastal road. The road quality was better than he had expected and the temperatures an acceptable 23 degrees. He had set himself a limit of three hours riding each day, so he could really absorb the atmosphere of each place and find decent accommodation with safe parking for the Dakar and internet facilities, and he felt content. His long journey and time with his unexpected Kiwi companion had been cathartic and Marcus knew that his father had been right; he had started to heal.

On the 15th January, Marcus crossed the border, east of Santiago, Chile, into Argentina; his 13th and final country. The 226-mile route to Mendoza offered him and the Dakar little in the way of suitable lodgings and Marcus decided to break his own rules and ride the five and a half hours to reach the vibrant city and home of Malbec, his favourite red wine.

Having arrived in Argentina, Marcus felt under pressure to initiate arrangements for his return journey to the UK and make some decisions about his life. He took advantage of the business centre in the hotel and logged into his e mail and as he scanned the 24 new messages, he realised his disappointment that none were from Cherie. He recognised that his new fixation with internet access was little to do with estate agents or hypnotherapy schools and more about updates from his Kiwi travel buddy. He missed her company and the ease he had felt, talking with her about Ava and his plans for the future. He had grown accustomed, over the last couple of weeks, to receiving her short, funny messages each time he logged into his account. He knew that she was due to be back in Christchurch, having flown back on 13th January and he hoped she was safe and happy to be home.

Marcus spent a further two weeks in Argentina, much of which was in Buenos Aires. He had felt an incredible sense of achievement on his arrival at the Argentinian capital, having completed almost 19,000 miles, in all weathers and over every kind of inhospitable terrain. He loved the cosmopolitan city with its presidential palace and grand opera house but the freedom he had felt, up until his arrival in Lima, was now replaced with a sense of emptiness, as he wandered the sights alone and he knew, it was time to go home.

His flight landed at Heathrow on 28th January and Terry and Gwen Crane were waiting at the airport when he arrived. Marcus was glad to be back in safe, predictable England and realised that he had not fully appreciated how sheltered and protected his home country was, until he had been exposed to the corruption and exploitation of some of the less developed locations on his trip. He was looking forward to sharing his travel adventures with his family, although remembering he had never told his biking-averse mother about the Dakar, he wondered how she would react to the news that her son had secretly ridden some of the world's toughest roads on a motorbike.

Marcus had planned to stay with his parents until deciding where to eventually buy. He had granted his father temporary power of attorney to enable the completion on his Buckinghamshire home in his absence and the house had been sold months before.

"Any idea where you might like to base yourself, Son?" Terry Crane asked, as he poured himself and Marcus a beer. "You know your mother and I would love you to be back in Gloucestershire and there's some decent stuff on the market."

Terry reached into the sideboard cabinet, pulled out a pile of papers and handed it to Marcus. The details of the properties which Gwen Crane had printed off, indicated that they were all situated in the small towns and villages around Cheltenham. Marcus flicked through the pile, looking at the pictures and locations; Winchcombe, Stow-on-the-Wold, Bourton-on-the-Water, Painswick, Leck-hampton, Stroud. It had been 16 years since Marcus had left his home county and he liked the thought of returning. His brother Neil and his wife lived in North-leach, just 11 miles south east of Cheltenham and as his parents approached their mid-sixties, Marcus could see the advantages of being closer to them. Ava had frequently commented on how beautiful the Cotswolds were and the couple had even looked for work opportunities there at one time. Marcus could probably have found teaching work but nothing suitable in publishing had ever presented itself to Ava. Now Marcus was thankful that they had never lived there together.

Neil arrived at 6.30pm and Marcus spent the early evening telling his family about his trip. The Dakar had arrived back in the UK three days before Marcus and Neil had organised its transport from the airport. Having nowhere to store it safely, he had arranged for it to be delivered to Terry and Gwen's garage.

"Your Father had some serious explaining to do when that flaming thing arrived here," Gwen said, shaking her head. "I can't believe you did that hideous journey on a motorbike. Good job you didn't tell me. I wouldn't have slept for nine months!"

Marcus had transferred most of the hundreds of photographs he had taken, onto his laptop and as he clicked through them, he remembered how his faith in humanity had been regularly restored by the amazing people who, he believed, fate had sent his way. He showed his interested audience the pictures of Grant Bruton, his Deadhorse roommate,

"This guy was loaded and had every material thing he could ever have wanted," Marcus told them. "He intends to face the wrath of his suffocating father and then give it all up to help the disadvantaged. He was such an inspiration."

Marcus clicked through a number of photos of the Dalton Highway, describing the scenery and extreme weather and deliberately omitting the pictures of the Dakar laying on its side in the thick mud. In his hurry to skip through the accident pictures, he was reminded of the red bird, the 'Wing', Mikey had called it; how it had reminded him of Ava's small, red, wing-shaped birthmark and how its arrival had made Marcus feel that Ava was with him. He wanted to tell his family how kind Jake and his son had been, so he decided to be economical with the truth.

"My bike had a problem and Jake and Mikey drove me all the way back to Fairbanks, where Jake had the Dakar fixed. Kelly-Anne sorted out my aching back and introduced me to Reiki. The whole experience was a bit mind-blowing, to be honest."

Marcus had taken many pictures of Seattle and his phenomenal hosts, Steve and Karyn. He described the brave, awe-inspiring couple and was surprised how angry he still felt about the insensitive and prejudicial treatment Karyn had received, when people made unfair and inaccurate judgements about her disability.

Terry Crane smiled at his sons. "I do believe Marcus has learned, in the first few weeks of his trip, what years of Sunday school didn't manage to teach him."

The next half an hour was spent in raptures of laughter, as Marcus emulated the flamboyant and affected performance of the Mystic Marvel in Las Vegas. "The man was a complete fake," Marcus objected, still outraged by the bogus medium.

"I can't actually believe that the Marcus we know went to see a psychic medium," Neil mocked. "Who are you and what have you done with my cynical, dogmatic brother?"

Marcus described Donna's uncomfortably accurate reading in detail and when Neil questioned her validity, to his surprise, Marcus found himself fervently justifying and supporting her comments. "Honestly Bro, she couldn't have known this stuff," he objected, "I've got the recording on my laptop. You really need to listen to it."

When Marcus reached the photographs of the Ecuadorian Equator, his family listened with fascination to Marcus's story of Ricky Finch. Neil had always had a tendency to prioritise work over both health and family time and the story made him reconsider just what his objectives should be.

As the final few images of Ecuador flashed upon the screen, Marcus was aware of feeling uncomfortable and realised that most of his pictures of Peru featured Cherie. The old feelings of guilt, that he had spent so much time in the company of a lovely woman, came flooding back and Marcus felt ashamed. "Shall we look at the rest some other time?" he asked, dropping his eyes to his laptop.

Terry looked disappointed. "I want to see Machu Picchu, Marcus. It's supposed to be very holy and I've always wanted to go. Come on. Show us the pics."

Reluctantly, Marcus clicked through the pictures of Lima, The Palomino Islands, the Christmas meal and the stunning Incan Citadel, "Who's the girl, Bro?" Neil asked. "You've smiled more in the photos of Peru than all the others put together. Shit mate, you look like the old Marcus here." Neil pointed to a picture of Marcus and Cherie on the boat, on the return journey from their sea lion swimming adventure. They were both wet and wearing their bright yellow life jackets. Marcus had his arm around Cherie's shoulder and both of them were laughing. Marcus remembered the photo being taken and had thought about it a number of times since. One of the tour guides had offered to take a photograph of them and had encouraged him to get awkwardly close to Cherie. He had been a little embarrassed but had rebuked himself later for being secretly glad of the pushy photographer's demands,

"She beautiful, Senor. Get much close."

Marcus briefly told his family about meeting his Kiwi travel companion. "She was great," he said, dismissively. "She listened to me bleat about Ava and my plans and then she went back to New Zealand and I finished my trip."

Terry and Gwen seemed nonchalant about Marcus's brief liaison but Neil's smirk did not go unnoticed by Marcus and when his parents left the room to finalise the evening meal, Neil probed a little deeper. "Come on mate, I've known you all my life and I can read you like a book. What's with this Cherie lady, then?"

Marcus surprised himself with his reply, "She's lovely. Total opposite of Ava but funny and pretty and kind and if I'd met her in any other circumstances, I'm not sure I would have let her leave."

Neil smiled, "OK, so you feel guilty, like you're betraying Ava and I get that. How much of your reluctance to talk about her is because of what people will think?"

Marcus did not need to consider his answer. "I loved Ava more than anything in the world. I would have changed places with her right up to the end and I thought my life was over when she died, Neil. I spent seven months genuinely wondering how I was going to live the rest of my life without her, so what kind of person am I to even think about enjoying time with anyone else?"

Neil left the armchair he was sitting in and sat next to his brother on the sofa. "Think about the people who have suddenly turned up on your trip, out of the blue, to make you see what's important." he said. "Think of all the messages, the weird shit that you couldn't explain and the almost water-tight evidence that both Ava and her birth mother had lived before. Think about the stuff that the old psychic woman, what's her name, Vera, said to you and the medium in Sedona: Do you really believe that Ava had nothing to do with you meeting Cherie? Come on, mate. Think back to all the messages you got. There must be something to convince you that Cherie was another thing that was meant to happen?"

Marcus swallowed hard. He didn't want Neil to see that he was close to tears. "The flag, Neil. Ava drew a heart on the flag of Peru. I think she probably knew all along I was going to meet Cherie."

Chapter 24 – Physician, Heal Thyself

To: Crane, Marcus
From: Rutherford, Cherie
29ᵗʰ January 2003

G'day Marcus. If you're reading this, good on ya, you made it through your long trip. I think you said you were due to fly back home yesterday, so I wanted to say Hi and welcome home.
The bar was fine while I was away; no disasters, so I think I'll go walk about again soon. I really miss the heat in Peru; it's cold and hosing down here. So much for summer! Write me and tell me how life is back in Blighty.
Cheerio
Cherie x

Marcus was happy to receive Cherie's e mail and wrote back straight away, telling her about his journey home, his evening with his parents and Neil and his decision to move to Gloucestershire. He attached a couple of pictures of properties he had found online and asked what Cherie thought about them, hoping the question would encourage her to reply quickly.

As the weeks passed and the novelty of reminiscing about the cheeky sea lions and the Peruvian meals, during which they playfully ridiculed each other's accents, faded, the communication between Marcus and Cherie settled into a regular weekend occurrence. The short, funny notes, about nothing in particular, became longer e letters, telling each other about family and friends and the events of the previous week. Marcus looked forward to reading about Cherie's life at the Christchurch bar and the seemingly endless stories of humorous customers. He told Cherie about his house-hunting adventures and his mail to her on 5th April included a picture of the house he had bought in Bibury, a small Cotswold village on the River Coln, about 15 miles from his parents' home.

Marcus's new home was a stone built, Grade II Listed cottage, just off the centre of the pretty village. The rooms were small, but the exposed stonework, wooden beams and open fireplace, with a wood burning stove, gave the building a homely feel and Marcus loved the character of the place. The dining room was a converted cellar which could be accessed without having to pass through any of the other rooms and Marcus had felt, immediately on viewing it, that it would make a great hypnotherapy studio. The cottage had a fenced garden with a small lawn and patio area and the mature borders housed an abundance of rose bushes, which also covered the lower walls of the cottage. They were starting their spring growth when Marcus moved in on 9th April and he thought about how much Ava would have loved them.

Marcus was over half way through his Diploma in Clinical Hypnotherapy by the time he moved to Bibury. He had been taking the train from Kemble, 12 miles from the village, into London Paddington every Saturday and Sunday morning for the last seven weeks and had a further five to go before sitting a full day of examinations. He had intended to spend the weekdays getting his new home into some semblance of order and had arranged for the belongings he had put in storage to be delivered the day before he moved in. It was only once the furniture had been delivered, that he had realised most of it was either too modern or too large to be suitable for the little cottage.

Conscious of the dent in his savings, as a result of the bike trip, the Hypnotherapy course fees and the purchase of a new property, Marcus had also added his details to the Gloucestershire register of available supply teachers. He had not expected that there would be a significant demand for temporary PE teachers and was surprised when he was contacted immediately and asked to work three days a week at a Cheltenham based secondary school, until the end of the summer term.

Marcus was enjoying his studies but had initially been shocked to realise that there were 42 delegates in his cohort; his Foundation workshop in Costa Rica having had only five other participants. He had imagined a similar number attending the diploma course in London and wondered if the much larger class size would impact negatively on his learning. The group was very diverse, with representation from the medical professions and counselling organisations as well as individuals, like Marcus, who were considering setting up in private practice.

As he had expected, the first couple of weekends revisited the content he had previously covered; different kinds of hypnotic inductions, creation of effective deepeners and an introduction to Neuro-Linguistic Programming. Each of the subjects was covered in more depth than Marcus had experienced before and the volume of both practical work and home-based reading was considerable.

The benefit of the larger, disparate cohort, Marcus quickly realised, was the increased opportunity of being exposed to a wide range of motivations for learning. Many of the delegates had very personal reasons for joining the programme and a sizeable number had previously experienced hypnotherapy in an attempt to treat their own issues; phobias, weight loss and smoking cessation, being the most common.

Marcus worked hard to understand and master the numerous hypnotic tools and techniques and was surprised that the vast majority of the people he worked with, during the many practical sessions, complimented him on his gentle but authoritative approach.

Like most of his class, Marcus enjoyed some of the syllabus components more than others, but his interest had always been in reaching the Sunday of weekend nine, when the group was introduced to past-life regression.

Nicola James was the Programme Director and most of the modules had been run by her, but this weekend the group was introduced to Bernie Hudson. Bernie was one of the faculty whose impressive bio had encouraged Marcus to apply for the programme and he was curious to see her in person.

Like all of the other modules, this one began with a demonstration from the tutor. At the beginning of each new topic, one of the students joined the specialist on the raised platform at the front of the lecture room and was the subject for the hypnosis practical. Marcus had been disinclined to volunteer to be the class guinea pig up until now, preferring, as he did as a school boy, to merge inconspicuously into the crowd. Today was different. He wanted to experience this, first hand; to know, indisputably, if this thing was for real or not.

"I know this might be a sensitive subject for some of you," Bernie said, as the group settled into their seats. "A few of the group have requested not to take this module and as it is an optional component of the course, you may choose instead to move to the break out room and practise some of the techniques which will feature in your examination, instead. If you would prefer to do that, please leave now and we can reconvene after lunch."

A mumble of voices echoed around the room before seven people left and the rest of the group waited for Bernie to continue.

"I decided to specialise in past-life regression 12 years ago, having experienced it myself. It's not for everyone and even clients who you may suspect would benefit considerably from this intervention, may not entertain it. What I can say is, for me, this is the most exciting and fascinating part of my role as a Master Practitioner of Hypnotherapy."

The mumble of voices started again and Marcus smiled to himself as he noticed a number of the students sink down into their seats, in fear of being selected, as Bernie arranged the chairs on the stage in readiness for the practical demonstration.

"OK. Anyone fancy.." Marcus did not let Bernie finish her sentence before his hand was up and as he realised he was the only willing participant in the group of 30 plus, he felt a little like the over enthusiastic swots he had hated at school.

Bernie looked delighted. "Excellent. I usually have to bribe my volunteers with chocolate. Please, come and take a seat." The class laughed nervously, as Marcus stepped up onto the raised platform. He sat in the chair opposite

Bernie and waited until she had explained the process which the group was about to observe. She asked Marcus which induction technique he felt he would be most receptive to and asked one of the students to switch on some music, conducive to relaxation.

Marcus responded well to the induction and deepener, having by now had a significant number of hours of practice. He focussed on Bernie's gentle, melodic voice and became quickly unaware of the captivated, silent audience.

"Now you're relaxed, so relaxed and you're going to feel yourself floating. That's it, light as air. Now you're drifting, drifting upwards. Can you feel that, Marcus?" Marcus was silent for a second before exhaling deeply and nodding his head.

"That's good. You're doing so well. Keep drifting upwards and in a second you'll feel yourself stop. Let me know when that happens." Again, Marcus was silent and after a few seconds, he whispered, "I've stopped now," and Bernie continued.

"You're so relaxed, so comfortable. Just floating in mid-air. Now, in a second I want you to look down and when you do, you will see a line stretching in front of you. Look now and see the line. Can you see it?" Marcus nodded and Bernie spoke again, "Notice that the line has markings and next to those markings are dates. See them now, stretching out in front of you, 2004, 2005, 2006. This is your future, Marcus. Now feel yourself turning around. See the date you are standing on is 2003. Can you see it?"

Once again, Marcus nodded. "Excellent. Now see the dates of your past, 2002, 2001, 2000, 1999. I'd like you to go back to a significant date in your past. A really important date. Feel yourself floating along the line of your past and tell me when you're there."

Almost immediately Marcus nodded. "I'm here," he said, quietly.

"Good, now float down into that time and tell me where you are." Marcus's lip began to tremble and a tear ran down his cheek and dropped onto his jeans. "It's May 2002. I'm at the hospice, with Ava. She's going and there's nothing I can do."

Marcus described the scene in minute detail; the smells, the sounds, even to the petals which had fallen from the roses in the vase next to Ava's bed, before Bernie stopped him and brought him back to his position, standing on the line at 2003.

"You're doing so well, Marcus," she said quietly. "Now, I'd like you to go further back, further back in time. See the numbers under your feet and watch as they count down. Now they're moving quicker and you're standing over the date of your birth. Can you see it?" Marcus nodded. "What date is it now?" Bernie asked.

He swallowed, "It's 1969." Bernie spoke again. "OK, see the numbers count down again, 1968, 1967, 1966. Now go to a significant time; a time before this lifetime. See the numbers counting down again and tell me when they stop."

Fifteen seconds passed and then 20 and Marcus was still silent. Bernie waited for a few more seconds before repeating her instruction. "Can you go to a significant date before this lifetime, Marcus?" Marcus shuffled in his seat. "I can't. I just can't see anything. I'm sorry."

Bernie asked him to, instead, come forward in time and back to 2003 before gently bringing him out of trance state. Marcus looked embarrassed and shrugged as he addressed Bernie and the class, "Sorry guys. I guess it doesn't work for everyone."

Bernie smiled reassuringly. "It's not unusual to have difficulty at first. Why don't you and I catch up after class?"

Marcus returned, disappointed, to his seat and watched as one of the younger women in the group, replaced him on the stage. Bernie used the same timeline regression technique and the woman seemed to have little trouble accessing a memory of being a nurse in a French wartime field hospital in 1916. Marcus was not really paying attention to the regression and was still thinking about his own dismal attempt. He did not want to return to his previously sceptical feelings about past lives, but he was disheartened and decided to join the small group in the breakout room rather than watch the remainder of the demonstration.

When the group reconvened after lunch, the energy in the room was tangible and the enthusiastic discussion centred around Bernie's second demonstration. After Marcus had left the lecture room, a number of easily verifiable particulars had emerged, including specific names, dates and events. The audience was suitably impressed and the woman who had experienced the regression, fully intended to check the validity of the details.

At the end of the afternoon, the class dispersed quickly. Marcus remained seated until Bernie had finished talking with one of the other students and she beckoned for him to join her on the platform. "I have a feeling that this module was of specific interest to you. Is that right?" Bernie asked. He told Bernie about Ava's and Roisin's past-lives and how he had gone from being an obstinate cynic to receptive scholar.

"I guess I just, naïvely, expected it to be easy and I feel a bit deflated that I couldn't do it. Have you had clients that were unable to be regressed before?"

Bernie pointed to the chair which Marcus had sat in earlier and took a seat opposite him.

"OK, so let me explain a couple of things," she said gently. "Firstly, everyone can be regressed and so can you. You had no problem going back to 2002, did you? That was a difficult memory for you and the technique that I used encouraged you to be associated with the pictures and feelings; you were part of the action, if you like. Perhaps you were uncomfortable that the next memory would cause a similar pain, so you resisted going there. That's not unusual. You were possibly also a little conscious that you were being watched by thirty-odd, expectant students and that's enough pressure for anyone.

I think, if we were to remove those obstacles; have no audience and I use a technique which enables you to be dissociated with the images; you know, as if you're watching yourself on a screen, it would really help. Fancy giving it a go?"

What Bernie was saying seemed very logical. The scene he had revisited at the hospice had been so detailed and distressing and Marcus knew he may well have been resistant to feeling more pain. "OK, I'm up for it, if you think it will work," he said, settling into the chair.

Bernie guided Marcus into a deep state of trance before suggesting that he was holding a TV remote control and sitting in a comfortable armchair in front of a large screen.

"When you're ready, Marcus, I would like you to press rewind and stop at a happy memory in this life. Let the image appear on the screen, as if you are watching yourself in a movie.

Marcus quickly began describing a wedding he had attended in 1998, with Ava.

"There are lots of our uni friends around us. We're laughing and I'm watching myself looking at Ava. She looks beautiful."

Bernie asked him to let the scene fade. "OK, that was very good. Now press rewind again. Let the time run backwards, backwards and past 1969, past your birth and beyond. When you're ready, press stop and a significant time; a time before this lifetime will open on the screen. You're just watching it and you can press stop at any time. OK? When you're ready then."

A few seconds passed before Marcus's facial expression suddenly changed.

"I can see a man. It's me. I'm hurt and my leg, my left thigh is bleeding."

"What's your name?" Bernie asked. Marcus was silent and Bernie spoke again, "Do you know what year it is? Tell me where you are."

"I'm in prison," Marcus replied, "I look cold. It's 1839 and my name is Thomas Wilson."

"Why are you in prison? What did you do?" Bernie asked and watched as Marcus slowly shook his head. "I was caught stealing. They shot me and now I'm in prison."

Bernie interrupted, "OK, press rewind and go back further, further in time to when you were really happy in this lifetime. Let the scene open up, when you're ready,"

Marcus was silent for a second or two before smiling. "What can you see?" Bernie asked.

"I can see myself getting married. I'm getting married to, to Neil." Marcus sounded confused and Bernie asked for clarification. "Neil? Thomas is marrying Neil?" Bernie asked.

Marcus nodded. "Yes, it's Neil but it's not really Neil.

Here she's Martha and I love her very much. I can see other people in the crowd that I know but here they look different."

Bernie could sense Marcus's confusion. She had witnessed this before; people recognising friends and family in past lives, but often they were different genders or had a different relationship to the one they had with the client in their current life.

"Who else do you recognise?" Bernie asked,

"Mum!" Bernie jumped at Marcus's excited exclamation, "Mum is there but she's, she's really Martha's dad and I can see Ricky, only here he's Mr Bronson. He's my boss, he owns the Estate and he's with Mrs Bronson. Mrs Bronson doesn't look happy. She doesn't like me. I know her too; she's Cherie."

The session continued for a further 60 minutes, with Marcus explaining that Thomas Wilson had been a farm hand in the 1800s. Having married his childhood sweetheart at 17, he and Martha lived happily until she died in childbirth. Distraught, Thomas had taken to the road, surviving by stealing, as he travelled from town to town. He had been shot in the back of his left thigh when escaping through the window of a house, having stolen jewellery and food and had been imprisoned in 1839. Thomas became ill and had died in prison in 1843.

Marcus could remember most of the regression, when Bernie brought him out of trance state, and he felt confused.

He wondered if he had just dreamt the entire story.

He had never been especially creative and thought it unlikely that he had spontaneously invented Thomas Wilson and his wife, Martha, who was coincidentally, his brother Neil, in his current life. Why did he think his mum and Ricky Finch and Cherie were there? They did not even look like themselves, but he knew, instinctively, that it was them. Surely, he was just visualising what was uppermost in his mind? How likely was it really, that this was a previous existence?

Marcus had asked these questions during his debrief, expecting Bernie to be able to provide conclusive answers.

"Who knows?" Bernie said, smiling. "Some of my clients have been able to verify names and dates and one even used a few Russian phrases in his regression, having never known the language before. It's not unusual for people to have weakness from injuries carried over from previous incarnations, and birthmarks or moles, where wounds have been inflicted in earlier lives. It actually doesn't matter to me if it's true or not. What's important is that regression therapy has been used to successfully address pain, both physical and emotional and people have been able to live a better quality of life as a result."

Marcus thought about the regression all the way home; Thomas's injury and the people who had played very different roles in that life, if that's what it was. He was still unconvinced that his regression really was proof that he had lived before. The evidence was certainly not as compelling as either Roisin's or Ava's had been and Marcus was disinclined to spend time researching some random farm hand, who may have lived in the 1800s. But, to his surprise, verifying the story was not important and he shared Bernie's magnanimous acceptance that, if healing was achieved, it did not really matter.

Marcus returned home tired and with a headache and decided to soak in a hot bath and take a couple of Ibruprofen. He was due at school the following day with a full timetable of PE lessons and he was not looking forward to it. He knew he had put a few pounds on since returning from his trip and did not feel especially fit. He climbed out of the bath and towelled himself down before stretching round, looking in a full-length mirror to see if his previously toned body looked as out of shape as it felt. As he did, Marcus saw a small mole on his left thigh that he had never noticed before. He remembered Thomas Wilson's bullet wound, Ava's wing-shaped birthmark and Bernie's words, and he smiled.

"It's not unusual for people to have ……..birthmarks or moles where wounds have been inflicted in earlier lives."

Chapter 25 – Never Too Broken to Heal

On 31st May, Marcus and 34 of the original cohort received their Diplomas from The International School of Clinical Hypnosis. Marcus had been advised at the beginning of May that he had passed the course with distinction, but the awards and celebratory drink had not been scheduled for a further three weeks.

Marcus had called Cherie to let her know he had successfully completed the course.

"I'll be getting together with the group to celebrate on the 31st. Dad can't make it, but Mum and Neil are coming to the award ceremony and then I need to start clocking up some hours of practise."

Cherie was excited to hear from Marcus. She had been aware of his exam date and knew he was apprehensive, having not sat a written examination since his university finals.

"What a fantastic achievement, Marcus. I wish I could be with you to celebrate but I'll raise a glass in the bar for you."

The ISCH usually hired a room at the Mandarin Oriental for the award ceremony and a well-known practitioner from the field of clinical hypnotherapy was always present to hand out the diplomas. Students could invite up to four guests and champagne and photographs followed before the group disbanded, usually to enjoy a private celebratory meal. Marcus's mother and brother had gone into London early to shop and Marcus had arranged to meet them at the hotel just before the event started.

Appropriately suited and booted, he arrived, predictably, forty-five minutes early and decided to buy a coffee at the nearest Starbucks rather than be the first at the venue. With ten minutes to go he walked into the large, opulent room and looked among the seated crowd for his guests. Gwen Crane waved from the third row of the neatly placed chairs and Marcus walked along the central isle to join them. As he got nearer, he noticed his father was sitting with his mother and Neil. Pleasantly surprised that he was able to make the ceremony after all, Marcus leaned past his mum and Neil to shake his father's hand and as he did so, noticed a familiar, beautiful face sitting in the middle of his giggling family.

"G'day Marcus. I decided to go walk about and see my Pommy friend graduate."

Gwen and Terry Crane had been delighted when Cherie had written to them to tell them she would appreciate their help in surprising their son. He had mentioned his Kiwi friend a few times since his return from his trip and like Neil, they had wondered if the relationship could, one day, develop into something more than a friendship.

Terry Crane had picked Cherie up at Heathrow the day before the award ceremony and Cherie had stayed with the couple in Cheltenham for the night. They had spent the evening discussing their sons and Cherie was grateful of the opportunity to ask about Ava. Marcus had, of course, mentioned his girlfriend; her illness and subsequent death; and how it had been the catalyst for him travelling but that was all. Cherie had wanted to know more but had been concerned that her interest may have seemed insensitive to Marcus, so had avoided the subject during their time together in Peru.

"She was his first and only girlfriend," Gwen had explained. "They met at university and were together 13 years."

Cherie had wondered why Marcus had never married. "Did they ever talk about making things, you know, more official, Mrs Crane? Thirteen years seems a long time to be dating." Gwen nodded. "Terry and I lived in hope," she said smiling, the smile not quite reaching her eyes. "I think Marcus would have liked to get married and have a family but it wasn't what Ava wanted."

Terry was aware of the mood becoming heavy. "Anyway," he said, changing the subject, "what about you, Cherie? Tell us about life in New Zealand."

Cherie shared the story about her father leaving the family home and business. She explained how working at the bar and supporting her mother and brother had caused the delay in travelling and the abandonment of any ideas of further education.

"Like Marcus," she continued, "I had a childhood sweetheart but he went to uni in Auckland at eighteen. We tried to make it work but after the second year he stopped coming back to Christchurch. I guess my life, running a small bar in our home town, wasn't very exciting for him. I heard he'd got married about four years ago and I've been too busy rebuilding the business to think about men."

"And the student with the highest score in this Spring intake at ISCH and achieving Distinction, is Mr Marcus Crane."

The entire room clapped and cheered as Marcus left his seat and walked to the front of the room to receive his certificate. The highly regarded Professor Donald Gilberson, Lecturer in Psychiatry and early advocate of Hypnotherapy, was the special guest presenting the students with their certificates, having been advised of each of the graduates' names by Nicola James. As Marcus approached the front of the room, Bernie Hudson, the past-life regression specialist, took Nicola's place and whispered to Marcus as he passed, "Come and find me after the ceremony."

As the final speech of congratulation from Professor Gilberson finished, the laughter and chatter in the room replaced the silence and the gathered crowd stood from their seats and began to leave for their champagne and photographs.

Marcus hugged Cherie. "I can't believe you came all the way over here to see me graduate. Now you'll get to see the cottage and the new hypnotherapy studio and actually, there's someone I'd like you to meet."

Marcus took Cherie's hand and led her over to Bernie.

"Congratulations, Marcus," Bernie said cheerfully, patting him on the arm and smiling at Cherie, "your young man is going to be a very talented hypnotherapist."

Marcus was embarrassed at Bernie's assumption and he could feel the dreaded prickling on his neck, indicating the unsightly blotching, which had always been the bane of his life.

"This is Cherie, Bernie, my friend from New Zealand and Cherie, this is Bernie, my past-life regression tutor."

The two women smiled and shook hands before Bernie turned to Marcus. "I understand you met a very dear friend and colleague of mine on your travels. It's no wonder you want to be a past-life regressionist if you've trained with Doctor Robert."

Marcus was amazed. Robert had said he would put him in touch with someone in the UK who could help him with this very specialised practice, but what were the odds of his tutor in Costa Rica being close friends with his tutor in the UK?

"Anyway," Bernie continued, "you know that ISCH requires you to accrue a number of complimentary hypno-therapy hours before you can begin to charge for your services. I have a feeling that you would prefer for most of those hours to be with past-life regression clients, so I have a list here of people I have worked with and who would all be happy to continue therapy with you. I'll be your Supervisor and we can meet once a month. You OK with that?"

Marcus was delighted. He had wondered how he would find the requisite number of practise clients and did not relish the thought of attempting any kind of therapy on his family or close friends. He thanked Bernie for her kindness and turned to walk away. Bernie smiled at Cherie. "You've got a special one there, my dear. I'd hang onto him, if I were you."

The celebratory meal, which Neil had arranged at one of his brother's favourite Thai restaurants, was the first opportunity for Cherie, Gwen and Terry Crane to divulge their subterfuge, as they told Marcus about the secret calls and e mails to arrange the surprise visit. Marcus was impressed at how comfortable Cherie seemed chatting with his family and realised how happy he was to see her and hear that endearing accent again. He watched as she laughed with Neil, shared stories of their trip to Machu

Picchu with Terry Crane and supported Gwen in her disapproval of the motorbike.

"I'm with you, Mrs Crane," she said, winking at Marcus. "He must be mad as a meat axe, riding that thing for thousands of miles."

They had all laughed at Cherie's humorous simile and with the red wine starting to take effect, Marcus surrendered to the knowledge that he felt something more for Cherie than just the affection of a travel companion and long-distance pen-pal. He loved the way her eyes glistened when they caught the light from the floating candles on the table, the little creases at the corner of her eyes when she laughed and the perfect cupid's bow of her plump top lip.

"Why don't you come back with us tonight?" Gwen asked Marcus, as they got on the return train at Paddington. Marcus had wondered about the plan for overnight accommodation and had anticipated his mother's question.

"Thanks Mum, but I promised Cherie she could experience the metropolis that is Bibury and there's plenty of room at the cottage. I think we'll jump out at Kemble and get a cab, if that's OK?"

Terry caught his wife's concerned expression and put his hand on Gwen's. "Let him find his own way, love. He needs to get on with his life," he whispered.

The old cottage was cold when the couple got home and Marcus lit the log burner and poured two glasses of brandy. He had day dreamed about this moment; he and

Cherie alone in the cottage with the log fire sending a golden glow into the room. In the cold light of day he had felt a little nervous at the thought, but the ease of conversation and the protective warmth of the alcohol seemed to have rid him of any anxiety as he sat on the small, soft sofa next to the beautiful Kiwi. They discussed the events of the evening and Cherie's stay with Terry and Gwen, before the conversation turned to Peru and their journey together to Machu Picchu.

"It was one of the most amazing days of my life," Marcus said, taking hold of Cherie's hand. "Looking at that phenomenal sight with you by my side." Marcus took a deep breath, "I miss you, Cherie. If I'm honest, I missed you the second we went our separate ways in Peru. I didn't want to admit it because I felt guilty: guilty that I could have feelings for someone when Ava..." Marcus stopped speaking and Cherie squeezed his hand. She could feel that familiar tingling at the top of her nose as the emotion in her rose and her eyes filled with tears. "I've missed you too; every day. I know losing Ava has left a huge space in your heart. You clearly loved her very deeply and I'm not saying I could ever entirely fill the gap that she has left but, if you'll let me, I think I could help you to heal and maybe love again."

Marcus gently held Cherie's face in his hands and kissed her cheek, as tears spilled over the long lashes of her dark blue eyes and ran into his hand. He could feel his heart thumping as he leaned forward and gently kissed Cherie's soft lips. Her kiss felt different to Ava's, soft but passionate, and Marcus could feel the electricity running through his spine as he pulled her into his body. The sweet taste of the brandy on her breath and the smell of her perfume were intoxicating and as Cherie ran her long fingers through his hair, Marcus realised he had been willing this moment to happen for some time.

The faint sound of the bells in the clock tower of the village church signalled midnight and as the final flames in the log burner faded, Marcus stood and held his hand out to Cherie.

"Shall we go to bed?" he asked.

As the church bells chimed their 7am melody, Cherie climbed out of bed and opened the curtains, letting the morning sunlight fill the room. The bedroom door was slightly ajar and Cherie could hear Marcus in the kitchen. Slipping on one of his T-shirts, she walked down the narrow, wooden staircase to find him sitting at the kitchen table, sipping a mug of coffee.

"G'day. I thought you'd abandoned me." Cherie said smiling. Marcus laughed and pointed to a small tray next to the oven, holding a glass of orange juice, a slice of toast and an empty egg cup. "You beat me to it," he said, nodding at a sauce pan bubbling on the hob, a single egg dancing in the boiling water. "I thought you might be hungry. Come and sit next to me."

Cherie walked over the cold stone floor and kissed Marcus on the top of his head before sitting at the table and taking a sip of his coffee.

"I know you have things to do today so I thought I might go into London; you know, do some touristy stuff." Cherie said, looking for Marcus's reaction.

"Sounds like a good idea," he replied, walking over to the hob and spooning the boiled egg into its cup while putting the single rose he had cut from one of the bushes in the garden into another egg cup and placing it on the tray. "I'll drop you at Kemble station. Let me know when you're on your way back and I'll come and get you," he said, placing the tray in front of Cherie.

"Sweet-as and thank you for making me breakfast. No one has done that for me since I was about six," Cherie said, cheerfully.

Marcus sat with Cherie and watched as she ate. He noticed how small and vulnerable she looked, dressed in only his T-shirt, her long, fair hair still ruffled and uncombed. He could sense his feelings for her developing and the thought of her going back to New Zealand caused an almost physical pain; a pain that reminded him of loss, crippling, excruciating loss. The pain he had felt when Ava had died.

While Cherie was in London, he had intended to contact some of Bernie's past-life clients and arrange sessions, but the events of the previous day were occupying his mind and he decided, instead, to meet Neil for lunch.

"Hey Bro!" Neil called, waving from a seat by the window in the Puesdown; the old coaching Inn and Neil's local hostelry.

Marcus ordered a beer from the bar and went to join his brother. "Hi, thanks for meeting me, mate."

Neil shrugged. "No probs. If you hadn't called me, I'd have been at the cottage banging on the door. Come on buddy, tell me everything."

To Neil's surprise, Marcus sighed and, his elbows on the table, rested his head on his hands.

"Shit mate," Neil said, reaching to put his hand on his brother's shoulder, "what happened? I was certain you guys were in for a big night and let's face it, she's gorgeous. How did you manage to stuff that one up?"

Marcus shook his head, "I didn't stuff it up. She is gorgeous and kind and the whole night was incredible."

Neil interrupted, "So? What's the problem?"

Marcus didn't look up, "It's exactly one year, two weeks and four days since Ava died. It nearly broke me and I genuinely never thought I'd ever feel any kind of affection for any other woman, as long as I lived." Neil waited while Marcus tried to work out what he was trying to say. "And then I met Cherie. Nothing happened, in Peru, I swear mate, nothing; but what kind of man am I that I wanted it to? I think I love her Neil, but the guilt is overwhelming me and the last thing I want to do is hurt Cherie."

To Marcus's surprise, Neil rolled his eyes and leaned back in his chair, crossing his arms.

"Just remind me, Marcus. Didn't you say that Ava sent you a message via that psychic woman? What was her name? Oh yeh, Jeanie. Didn't you say Ava sent you an image of the Peruvian flag and, oh yes, she just happened to have drawn a heart with a big arrow going through it? Doh! I think there might be a clue there, don't you?"

Marcus could hear the frustration in Neil's voice. "Listen, mate, ultimately you have to do what you want. You can wear the hair shirt, feel resentful that you were dealt a shit deal and spend your life alone, or you can acknowledge that life goes on. Ava would be the last person to ever begrudge you finding happiness; that's why she sent you that message. Cherie clearly makes you happy and she wouldn't be here if she didn't feel the same about you. Wake up and smell the damn roses, Marcus. You're meant to be with Cherie."

At 7.25pm, Marcus arrived at Kemble Station and waited the fifteen minutes for the train from Paddington to arrive. His mind was racing and he was nervous about Cherie's reaction to what he had planned to say. Regardless of what Neil or anyone else said, he knew he had to do what his gut told him to.

Cherie was buzzing with stories of her day in London. She had visited numerous museums and art galleries and had bought far too many souvenirs to take home to her mother and brother in Christchurch. As they arrived back at the cottage, Cherie realised that Marcus had said very little, as she had chatted enthusiastically about her day. "You OK? You're very quiet," she asked, cautiously.

Marcus turned to the concerned young woman and took her hands in his, "I've had a tough day," he muttered, "and I've had some big decisions to make."

Cherie looked away, fearing what Marcus might say.

"I love you and I don't want to be thousands of miles away from you, Cherie. Please say you feel the same."

Chapter 26 – The Changing Face of Fear

"Hi Isla, It's Marcus Crane. I was thinking about you yesterday and I've got an idea."

Marcus had kept in touch with all of the people he had spent time with during his Pan American trip. He frequently exchanged e mails and photographs with Steve and Karyn in Seattle and got regular updates from Grant, his impromptu roommate in Deadhorse, who had finally escaped the suffocating control of his father and the family Law firm and was now working for a missing persons charity in Massachusetts. He had written to them all to tell them about his new venture as a clinical hypnotherapist and had received a congratulatory note from all except Isla, his troubled friend from Scotland, who had told Marcus, during his stay at the Grand Canyon, about the inexplicable fear she had of her fiancés father.

Isla had written to Marcus a couple of times since her return from the USA. Marcus could tell that things with her future father-in-law were still not good and the engagement was, temporarily, on hold. He had frequently thought of Isla and her paralysing fear of the seeming innocent and innocuous man and could not help feeling that some regression therapy might uncover the cause of the extreme reaction.

"Hi Marcus, how lovely to hear from you. Congratulations on your studies, by the way. I meant to text or e mail you but, well you know how it is, time got away from me."

Isla sounded preoccupied and Marcus wondered if he had called at a bad time.

"Thanks, yes, I was pleased to have passed the course. Er, is now a good time to talk, Isla?"

Marcus could hear sounds of people talking in the background, perhaps on the TV and Isla sounded as though she was moving somewhere a little quieter so she could speak to him.

"That's better," she said, the background chatter now gone. "Luke is watching the news and I couldn't really hear you."

Marcus was relieved to hear that Luke appeared to still be in her life. She had mentioned that her fiancé was becoming increasingly intolerant of her totally unprovoked dislike of his father and Marcus had wondered if he would stay the course.

"How's it going?" he asked, letting Isla decide how to interpret the question.

"It's a little tough, if I'm really honest. We used to argue a lot and it wasn't nice but at least we were speaking. Now Luke won't even talk about it and somehow that's even worse."

Marcus could hear the tremor in his friend's voice and guessed she had not been able to discuss the problem for a while. He had deliberated about making the call, as Isla had suggested, while they were in Arizona, that she did not really believe in any of the less orthodox therapies and he did not want to make her feel uncomfortable.

"Look, I know you're not really into this stuff. I wasn't, but I've seen some really amazing results from hypno-therapy; particularly regression. Please let me try to find out why you have such a problem with Luke's dad. There's no guarantee it'll work but surely it's worth a try?"

Marcus had anticipated Isla declining his offer with the customary claim from the uninitiated that, 'she would not be able to be hypnotised'. He had heard this frequent objection debated in class and was well versed in the recommended response that 'all hypnosis is self-hypnosis. Nothing is 'done' to you and hypnotherapy is simply a deep state of relaxation.' He was prepared with his reply but to his surprise, it was not required.

"Right now, Marcus, I'd try just about anything, if it would help me to sort this dreadful mess out. When can I come down and see you?"

Marcus was thinking about Cherie when Isla arrived on the 8.30am commuter flight from Edinburgh. Cherie had returned to Christchurch to tell her mother and brother about her intention to join Marcus in the UK.

"I'll need to find someone to help in the bar. As soon as I've shown them the ropes, I'll be back," Cherie had said. That was three weeks ago and he missed her. He spoke with her every day; long, affectionate conversations, when they talked about their future and how much they wanted to be together. But in his quiet moments, the insecurities he suffered in his teenage years came flooding back and he found himself worrying that Cherie might ultimately change her mind and stay in New Zealand.

He looked up at the arrivals screen and noticed that Isla's plane had landed seven minutes before. He knew that travelling on a domestic flight with no luggage, she would be through quickly and by the time he had purchased two cappuccinos from Costas, she was in the arrivals' hall. He thought Isla looked pale and thin, the healthy golden tan from her holiday in the States now faded.

On the journey back to Bibury, Marcus chatted to Isla about his studies, the cottage and Cherie. He did not want to pressure her into talking about Luke too quickly but, as the minutes passed, he could sense Isla's reluctance to make small talk and decided to broach the subject, which was clearly weighing on her mind.

"So, things were pretty difficult when I spoke to you last. Tell me what's been going on." Marcus waited for Isla to speak, even though the initial silence was uncomfortable for them both.

"When I got back from the US, Luke expected everything to be fine. Apparently, he'd been telling himself and everyone else that I was stressed and simply needed a holiday. He just doesn't get it. It's like he's in denial."

Marcus had thought a great deal about Isla's dilemma and could understand Luke's frustration. "Has he spoken to his dad about it?" he asked, interested to know how Luke had explained Isla's refusal to meet with his father.

"Oh, he has indeed," Isla replied, a bitterness in her voice that Marcus had not heard before. "Do you know what his dad said? He said I was neurotic and thought that Luke should dump me while he still had the chance."

Marcus could feel Isla's anger. "This all emerged in one of our many rows. I know it's hard for him to understand," she admitted, her tone softening, "but I'm actually feeling a bit betrayed."

Marcus felt sorry for her but he could also understand how both Luke and his father might respond defensively to Isla's extreme and unjustified reaction.

"Just explain to me again, in as much detail as possible, the feelings you had when you were near Luke's dad," he said, knowing he may need to be able to use Isla's specific feelings and phrases in her regression.

Isla took a deep breath. "OK, I've thought about this a lot, so I could try to help Luke to understand. Think of your worst fear. No, not just fear; terror. Think of a hideous nightmare or a horror film that has had a particularly strong effect on you; one that has taken your breath away and made your heart race and you can't get out of your head. That's how it felt when I met him. It's like I've escaped from someone trying to hurt me only to realise that the person I've escaped with, and I'm now hiding in a tiny, locked room with, is really the bad guy and he's going to kill me." Isla sounded drained. "I know it doesn't make any sense but even the thought of him on the phone to Luke freaks me out."

Not so long ago, Marcus would probably have shared Luke's father's opinion, that Isla may well need psychiatric help for her illogical emotions. Now he did not doubt that there was, in fact, a rational reason for her feelings and he was eager to help Isla find the root cause.

He made her comfortable in the studio and gave her a coffee before spending some time writing a hypnotic script, which he hoped would begin to uncover the reason for Isla's feelings.

Having explained what hypnosis was and put Isla at ease, he talked about the technique he would use. "Contrary to popular belief," Marcus said, smiling, "you won't be in some zombie-like state, nor will you be unconscious and if anyone was to shout 'fire', you'd be out of that door before me, so don't feel that you'll be out of control in any way. Just relax and enjoy the experience and if nothing else, you'll have a good rest. OK?"

Isla nodded and closed her eyes, as she leaned back into the soft leather of the reclining chair.

Recording the session on his laptop, Marcus played some gentle meditation music and asked Isla to concentrate on her breathing, before asking her to imagine a special, peaceful place where she felt relaxed, safe and happy. Isla recalled a field of buttercups which she had played in as a child and described lying in the field and watching the patterns and shapes which the clouds had made. Remembering his own reticence during his first, aborted attempt at regression with Bernie, Marcus decided to use the technique which both Jeanie had used with Roisin and Bernie had used, during the second regression attempt with him, and allow Isla to watch herself on a screen.

"You have full control, Isla. All you have to do is press stop, if you'd like to, OK?" Isla nodded and Marcus could see her hand holding the imaginary remote control.

"See yourself on the screen. You're here with me, in the cottage. See us chatting in the kitchen. Can you see the image on the screen?" Once again, Isla nodded. "OK. Now I want you to press stop. Can you do that?"

Marcus watched as her index finger moved. "Now, when you're ready," he continued, "I'd like you to press rewind. See the images moving in fast motion, backwards,

backwards in time, really fast and when you're ready, you will press stop. On the screen will appear images of a really happy day for you. A day in your past that makes you feel safe and in control. Can you do that?" He waited for a few seconds and could see Isla's expressions changing and then a smile appearing on her face,

"What can you see?" Marcus asked.

"I'm with my dad. He's holding the bike while I sit on it. I've never ridden a bike before and I was a bit scared but I'm not now because I know he'll keep me safe. I can see my mum standing in the driveway watching. Now we're moving but Dad's still holding me. He promised he'd hold me until I was ready and now, now I feel strong. I can see that he's let go but he's running with me."

Marcus asked her to let the scene fade and press stop, on her remote control.

"OK, you're doing so well, Isla," he said, impressed at how vividly she could recall her happy memory. "In a moment I'd like you to press rewind again and when you do, the images will go back to the first time that you felt the fear, the fear which you experienced when you met Luke's father. OK? Tell me when you're there and let the image open up on the screen. Remember you can press stop at any time."

He waited, having seen Isla's finger press the remote. Once again, he noticed her expression change but this time, as he expected, she looked scared.

"I'm in the bedroom at Luke's dad's house. I can see myself standing with my back to the door. I can hear a voice. It's Luke's dad asking if I need anything. I can't breathe and I feel like I'm going to collapse. Please don't come in. Please go away." Marcus could see Isla's breathing had become faster and shallower. He had hoped she would have described the event which had caused the fear, a time before her ill-fated meeting with Luke's father, but he let her continue.

"Just relax. Press pause, if it helps." Isla took a deep breath.

"Why are you afraid? What is it about Luke's dad that makes you feel this way?"

"It's his eyes. Something about his eyes that I've seen before but I don't know where." Marcus felt excited that Isla seemed, at least, to have been able to identify something about Luke's father which had triggered a memory.

"When you're ready, try to see his eyes on the screen. What is it about his eyes that scare you? Remember, it's just an image on the screen and you can turn it off at any time."

Isla gasped and looked distressed. "Pause the image and describe those eyes to me."

"They're blue, really light blue with tiny, tiny pupils. The skin around the right eye is all creased with a scar. I can see where there has been stitches and it makes the eye lid droop." Marcus noticed Isla's face becoming pale, almost grey. "I feel sick," she said, trying to sit up in the reclined chair. He asked her to let the scene fade and relax.

"You're doing so well. There's nothing and no one to bother you. No one will hurt you and you're in complete control."

Marcus regressed Isla to a further couple of times in her childhood which held happy memories, one of which appeared to be when she was an infant and was lying in the sunshine in her pram. During his training, he had not experienced anyone recalling memories from before they could either speak or realistically interpret what they were seeing and Isla's detailed descriptions of her sensations amazed him.

"I'm really happy. I remember it so well. I watched the birds flying over me and landing in a huge tree that I was shading under. Every so often I could hear the sound of a plane and I tried to move so I could see it through the branches."

Marcus was fascinated and wanted to know more. "How did you know what a plane or a tree or a bird was?"

Her reply shocked him. "I knew from before. From when I'd been here before. Planes were rare and different but birds weren't and trees; I loved trees before."

Marcus wanted desperately to probe further but was conscious of his objective to uncover the cause of Isla's irrational fear and reluctantly, asked her to let the scene fade.

"OK, now I'd like you to press rewind and go back to the very first time you saw those blue eyes; the eyes you said had scared you so much. It may be in this life, or it may be before your life as Isla. Take your time."

He watched as she pressed the invisible remote control and she seemed relaxed.

"What can you see? Tell me what's on the screen?" he asked, gently. Tears ran down Isla's cheeks before she spoke, "I'm never getting out. None of us are," she whispered.

"Getting out of where? Marcus asked. "Where are you?" he waited for Isla to speak.

"This place; the prison camp, Auschwitz. I'm in a hospital bed. I'm so still. I don't think I can move."

She started to sound anxious and Marcus reminded her that she could stop the scene at any time before asking for more details.

"What's your name and why are you in hospital? Are you sick?"

She shook her head, "Moshe, my name is Moshe and I'm not sick. They brought me here with Mendel, my twin brother. I don't know where he is now. He's not in the hospital."

As a child, Marcus had watched the World at War documentaries on a Sunday afternoon with his father and knew very well of the inhuman and devastating experiments which had been inflicted on identical twins in the concentration camp. He was almost nervous to ask for more details. "Mendel is your brother? Does he look like you, Moshe?"

Isla nodded, "Yes, we're identical twins. I'm seven minutes older."

Keen to understand the link between this experience and Isla's fear, Marcus probed further.

"Tell me about what's happening to you in hospital and who you see there."

Isla seemed remarkably calm. "He gives me injections. I fought him, at first, but he hit me and then he gave me something that stopped me being able to move."

Marcus had noticed Isla's reference to a male presence. "Who is 'he'? What does he look like?"

As she thought about his question, Marcus noticed a shift in her emotions and she seemed to become angry and aggressive. "I hate him. He's a doctor but he doesn't care about us. He's evil and he kills innocent people."

Marcus repeated the second part of his question. "What does he look like? Describe his face to me."

A few seconds passed before Isla spoke again. "He has a scar down his face and his eye is crooked. He's about thirty or maybe thirty-five and his eyes are very blue and mean; he has really mean eyes."

Marcus felt elated. Could this experience have been what had caused such problems for Isla in her current life?

"I'd like you to go to the very last few moments of your life as Moshe and let the scene open up on the screen. Can you do that?"

Again, her index finger pressed the remote in her lap. When she spoke again, she was calm. "It's OK now," she murmured. "When he looks at me, I'm not scared anymore. I know I'm dying and I don't care now. It'll soon be over."

When Marcus was planning the script for Isla's regression, he had anticipated a single, initial sensitising event which he had hoped he could reframe to help her remember the traumatic incident more positively. Moshe seemed to have experienced a terrifying number of invasive and abusive experiments, with no specific event standing out, so Marcus decided to focus on the abuser's face.

"I would like you to see the screen filled with the doctor's face. See his eyes, piercing blue, and see the ugly scar on the right, distorting his eye. Notice all the details and then watch the scene change, just as I'm going to describe to you. Can you see the face?"

Isla took a deep breath and nodded her head.

"OK. See the eyes, cold and mean. Now watch those eyes darken. See them become soft brown with long, beautiful eye lashes and see the large, black pupils. See them sparkle and notice the scar on the right eye shrinking and disappearing, leaving soft, clear, flawless skin. Notice, as it does, that the eyes become symmetrical, warm and kind. Notice the face, hard and cruel, become gentle and compassionate and as it does, feel any fear melt away. Remember the feelings when your dad held you on your bike; protecting and loving you. Feel those feelings now, when you see this new face and know that that old face and those old feelings have all gone, forever. Just absorb the new feelings. Can you feel them?"

Isla had not mentioned Luke's father's physical appearance and Marcus wondered if her description of him, while she had been under hypnosis, had been accurate.

"Yes, he's bald now but he's fair skinned and has very blue eyes. He does have a small scar on his eye but it's not disfiguring and he's actually not a bad-looking guy," she said, sipping a glass of water. Marcus immediately noticed the lack of any emotion, as she described Luke's father, and hoped it was indicative of the reframing having worked.

Isla could only remember her recollections from the current life regression and Marcus had to explain the details about Moshe and his twin brother, Mendel. She shook her head in astonishment. "Dad used to watch films about the Holocaust and I could never watch them with him," she said. "Now I know why."

She wondered if she had created the entire story in her head and asked Marcus what he thought. He recalled Bernie's wise words after his own regression and knew he should probably have said to Isla what Bernie had said to him, but curiosity got the better of him.

"You say you didn't want to watch programmes about the Holocaust but did you study it at school?"

Isla shook her head. "No, I dropped history at 14 and we never covered 20th century stuff anyway."

"And what about the accurate details," Marcus asked, "like the experiments on twins or the traditional Jewish names which you and your brother had? Were they things you might have read or seen somewhere?"

Isla shook her head and Marcus shrugged and smiled as he heard himself, finally, share Bernie's words,

'It actually doesn't matter to me if it's true or not. What's important is that regression therapy has been used to successfully address pain, both physical and emotional and people have been able to live a better quality of life, as a result."

Chapter 27 – The Last Piece of the Puzzle

25th July 2003 saw the end of the summer term and Marcus was relieved that he could now focus more on his hypnotherapy. He had been grateful for the money from the supply teaching work but his life had changed so dramatically since his days as Head of Physical Education in Hemel, that he had felt like an imposter.

He had completed two-thirds of the requisite pro bono hypnotherapy but still had a couple of Bernie's clients to conduct sessions with and now his teaching work was complete, he could arrange to meet them. He was flicking through his diary when Cherie called from upstairs. "Hey love, could you come here for a sec?"

When he got to the spare bedroom, he found Cherie sitting on the floor in the middle of the room, surrounded by books and papers.

"I'm trying to find a home for all this stuff but the place is chocka, love. I just wanted to check with you before I dump some of it."

Marcus walked over to Cherie and knelt down, putting his arm around her waist and kissing her on the side of her head. He was so happy to have her back with him and now that they had been together in the cottage for a month, he could not imagine being here without her.

"This lot here," Cherie said, pointing to a pile of envelopes and papers, "this is for chucking but I didn't know which of this stuff you wanted." She moved her finger so it was pointing to another stack of papers and Marcus stood and walked over to the heap. As he lifted the papers on the top of the pile, he noticed a black box file underneath. Cherie saw him looking at it. "Oh yes, that has some pictures and letters in. I think it might be something to do with Ava so I'm guessing you'll want to hang on to it?"

Marcus pulled the box file out and tucked it under his arm. Having browsed through the remainder of the books and papers, he smiled at Cherie. "All that can go, honey."

An hour later, Cherie went downstairs to join Marcus and found him in the sitting room, looking through the contents of the black box file. Ava had added the letters and recordings, which Vera had given her after her birth mother's death, to the box of photographs and documents which Roisin had sent to her. Ava had mentioned some of the letters but Marcus had never read them. It was only now, having seen Roisin's one and only letter from her mother, dated 8th May 1970, that he realised that

Roisin's parents had probably never even known of Ava's existence. He knew that Roisin had been just 19 or 20 years old when Ava was born and that would make her 52 or 53, had she still been alive today, he thought. He did the maths in his head and guessed that Roisin's parents would probably be in their late 70s, if they were, indeed, still alive.

Cherie sat down next to him. "Going to tell me what's in the box?" she asked.

Marcus handed Cherie the old black and white photograph, which had been taken outside the Swatragh General Stores. "This is Ava's birth mother and her family," he said. "This is Roisin at about seven or eight years old. She had two brothers, Fergus and this little chap."

He pointed to the small child in the wheelchair. "This is Roisin's younger brother, Liam. He had a few problems and died very young."

Marcus had mentioned Roisin when he and Cherie were discussing past-life regression in Peru. He handed Cherie the copy of Eveline Lytton's birth certificate, which Roisin had tucked inside the cover of a book about the Suffragettes.

"This is who Roisin thought she was in a previous life. It's so sad that her parents never knew about this or Ava or her drug problem or.."

Cherie put her hand on Marcus's arm and stopped him in mid-sentence. She looked shocked. "What, love? Roisin's folks never knew she was pregnant? They never knew they had a granddaughter? That's dreadful, Marcus. Someone needs to tell them."

Marcus was ashamed to admit that he had never given any thought to Roisin after Ava's death. The old, obtuse, small-minded Marcus reigned; refusing to acknowledge anything remotely spiritual until after Ava's illness. His trip had occupied his mind immediately after her death but Cherie was right; Mr and Mrs Collins needed to know.

The 30 miles from Aldergrove Airport to Swatragh seemed, to Marcus and Cherie, to take a very long time. The small stretch of motorway out of the Belfast suburbs soon ran into single lane roads and given the agricultural nature of the area, they found themselves crawling behind tractors and a variety of other slow farm vehicles, for much of the journey. Marcus had never been to Northern Ireland before; its reputation for political and religious unrest and the associated violence having made him disinclined to visit. The province had been in the news earlier in the year, as US President George Bush and UK Prime Minister Tony Blair had met in Belfast for discussions about the fighting in Iraq, and Marcus had realised that he knew very little about that part of the UK.

As he drove the small hire car along the country roads through Castledawson and Maghera, he noticed the multitude of small, grey or white single-story dwellings. Most were standing in their own grounds and many had a barn or farm buildings within close proximity and cattle or sheep in an adjoining field. The smells of slurry and silage drifted into the car as they drove through the pretty country-side from village to village. Marcus noticed the fields were much smaller than in England. They were clearly divided by fencing or thick hedgerows and he assumed that the decades of Protestant and Catholic conflict had made land a coveted commodity and an indication of power and dominance.

It was 1.30pm when Marcus and Cherie arrived in Swatragh and the outside of the General Store, in the centre of the village, appeared to have changed little since the old black and white photo had been taken, some forty-five years earlier.

Marcus had not provided the Collins with much detail in his letter, preferring to make a calculated judgement about exactly how much of the significant news to share with the elderly couple.

4th August 2003

The Cottage
High Row
Bibury
Dear Mr and Mrs Collins,
A good friend of mine had the privilege of meeting your daughter, Roisin, a while ago and has left some documents and information which I felt I should return to you.
My partner and I are planning to be in Northern Ireland 16th – 18th August and we would welcome the opportunity of meeting with you.

*You can contact me on the address above or, alternatively,
we will be staying at the Staff and Flag B&B in Maghera.
Perhaps you could let me know if it would be possible to
meet?*

Kind Regards,

Marcus R Crane

Annie Collins wrote back to Marcus by return and the
tone of her letter had both shocked and disappointed him
and Cherie.

6th August 2003

Swatragh General Stores,

Swatragh,

County Derry,

Dear Mr Crane,

Thank you for your letter.

*We have not seen Roisin since she left Belfast for London
33 years ago and were only aware of her passing when
Mrs McManus, Roisin's landlady, kindly wrote to us.*

*Roisin turned her back on her family, her faith and her home
and chose an unholy path of self-indulgence and immodesty.
We, as practising Christians, forgive her and hope that she
has found her peace in Christ.*

*We would, of course, be pleased to welcome you and your
partner to our home on 16th August.*

Yours sincerely,

Annie Collins

Marcus was incensed when he initially read Annie's letter and without Cherie's intervention, would have cancelled his planned trip to Northern Ireland.

"What kind of person doesn't try to get in touch with her only daughter for 33 years?" he seethed. "Unholy? Self-indulgent? The poor bugger was addicted to heroin, Cherie. She was alone in a strange country, living in squalor and they did nothing to help her."

Marcus was surprised at how vehemently he felt about the Collins treatment of Roisin, when they professed to be religious people. He thought about his father, a caring and kind Christian Lay-Minister, who could see the good in everyone and would do anything to help another human being in need. He, Marcus thought, was a credit to his religion.

"Didn't you say that Roisin was raised mainly by her grandmother, love?" Cherie asked. "Sounds to me like Annie had issues of her own. Maybe, with a seriously disabled son, she wasn't able to care for her other children and you know how people are about religion; if the Good Book says she's a 'sinner' and her parents felt guilty about deserting her, maybe blaming her is the easiest way to justify their neglect?"

When Cherie and Marcus entered the general store, a young woman standing at the cash desk was the only person in the shop. Cherie smiled and asked if Annie and Francis were home and the woman disappeared through a door behind the checkout.

"Granny, Granda, you have a visitor!" she shouted.

A few moments later, an elderly looking man appeared and held out his hand to Marcus.

"Hello, Mr Crane, I'm Francis Collins and this is Cara, Fergus's wee girl." Marcus nodded at Cara. "And this must be your wife," the old man continued. "What's your name, pet?"

Cherie ignored Francis's inaccurate assumption and smiled. "Cherie, Mr Collins. Lovely to meet you."

Instead of taking Marcus and Cherie through to the back of the store, Francis led them to the front and towards the house adjoining the shop. He stopped before entering the house.

"We were surprised to hear from you, Mr Crane. Please don't be offended by my wife's harsh feelings about Roisin; she took her leaving quite badly."

Marcus caught Cherie's eye and noticed her look of trepidation and he wondered if this visit had been a bad idea.

When they entered the sitting room, Annie Collins was waiting for them, a huge tray of sandwiches and cakes sitting on the coffee table in front of her. Francis pointed to the sofa,

"Make yourselves comfortable and I'll bring the tea," he said, exiting the room.

Marcus was surprised to see Annie looking nervous. Her eyes were wide and he wondered if the way she was perched precariously on the edge of her chair was to make for a rapid escape, should she deem it necessary. She looked uncomfortable, as though she was posing for a portrait and Cherie felt sorry for her.

"Thank you for letting us visit, Mrs Collins," she said, smiling.

Annie appeared to relax a little. "Please," she said, handing her visitors a china plate, "help yourself to some lunch. You must be hungry."

Marcus looked at the impressive spread in front of him and wondered if Francis and Annie were, perhaps, expecting the rest of the family to join them. He wondered how to turn the conversation to Roisin.

"So, you knew our Roisin?" Annie asked, before he could speak. "How did you get to meet her? Was it through her music?"

Marcus bit into an egg sandwich to buy himself some time, as he thought about how to respond.

"Er, Mrs Collins, Roisin's daughter, Ava, was my partner for 13 years. I learned about Roisin from Ava." He held his breath as he waited for the news that Annie had another grandchild to register with the old woman. To his surprise, her expression did not change.

"And did she ever make anything of her music?" she continued; her tone austere.

Marcus reached for the large, brown envelope he had brought with him and pulled out a picture of him and Ava when they were at university.

"This is Ava, Mrs Collins. She was born a few months after Roisin arrived in London. She was adopted when she was only a few weeks old and at eighteen she decided, with her adoptive parent's help, to find her birth mother. Roisin was having a difficult time, so the relationship didn't have the opportunity to develop but Ava was a special person. You would have loved her but she sadly died 16 months ago and Cherie made me realise that you may never have known about her." Marcus noticed that Annie did not look at the photograph,

"Did you, Mrs Collins? Did you know you had another grandchild?"

Annie Collins did not look at Marcus and her awkward position on her chair remained unchanged as she spoke,

"'Put to death therefore what is earthly in you: sexual immorality, impurity, passion, evil desire and covetousness, which is idolatry' Colossians 3:5."

Marcus could not believe what he was hearing. He could feel his pulse increasing and heat rising in his neck. "Mrs Collins, you had a grandchild; a beautiful, kind woman and.."

Still staring at the floor, Annie Collins interrupted, her voice now raised, "'No one born of a forbidden union may enter the assembly of the Lord.' Deuteronomy 23:2"

Cherie put down her plate of sandwiches and stood up, looking at Marcus. "OK, I think it might just be a good time to leave."

Marcus shook his head and putting the photograph back into the envelope, pushed passed Francis Collins, who had been listening at the doorway.

The Staff and Flag was a small, traditional public house in a town five miles from the Collins store. The rooms were small but clean and comfortable and the place reminded Marcus of the Green Dragon, where he had stayed before his trip.

Marcus had hardly spoken since leaving the disastrous meeting with Annie Collins and was still infuriated at the old woman's dismissal of both her own daughter and her granddaughter.

"Come on, love. Let's go down to the bar and get a beer," Cherie said, cheerfully.

Marcus looked at his girlfriend from where he was sitting on the bed,

"I'm so sorry you had to experience that, honey. It's hard enough for you to hear me talk about Ava without being exposed to that."

Cherie bent down and kissed Marcus. "We all have baggage and I think old Mrs Collins has more than her fair share," she said, softly.

The bar was busy when Marcus and Cherie went down stairs and looking around for an empty table, Marcus spotted a familiar figure sitting at a table in the window.

Catching Marcus's eye, Francis Collins walked over to the bar.

"I wanted to apologise for earlier," he said, looking embarrassed. "She's not done well since our Liam passed. She has a lot of guilt, you know."

Cherie joined Francis at the small window-table while Marcus ordered beer for him and Cherie and a lemonade for teetotal Francis.

Marcus felt sorry for the old man and wondered for how many years of their decades of marriage, Annie had been so sanctimonious and unpleasant.

"Did she know Roisin had had a baby, Mr Collins?" he asked.

Francis dropped his head. "She knew, right enough, son. Roisin wrote to her a number of times, asking for her to visit. She was having terrible nightmares and she thought making up with her mother might help but Annie only wrote back once, to tell her about wee Liam passing. I tried to encourage her to get in touch but she would just get angry and I was worried that she would end up in the hospital again, you know, with another breakdown, if I contacted Roisin. I was wrong, wrong and weak. I know that now but it's too late."

Marcus felt a wave of emotion as he looked at the despairing old man and knew Francis must be carrying an unbearable burden of guilt. He put his hand on the old man's.

"She really was an amazing person; Ava, your grand-daughter, Francis."

Francis reached into the inside pocket of his tweed jacket and pulled out a picture.

"This is our Roisin just before she went to England. The boy she's with is Jim O'Connor and they met at Queen's. He came from Carrickfergus. The address is on the back here."

Francis pointed to a handwritten address on the back of the photograph. "He came to see us a few months after Roisin had left. He was planning to finish his studies in Dublin and Annie wasn't very kind to him; I think she blamed him for Roisin leaving and we never saw him again."

Marcus looked closely at the faded photograph. He could immediately see Ava in her father. Her face was the same shape and her smile was exactly like his.

"Thank you, Francis," Marcus said. "This is the final piece of the puzzle."

Francis finished his drink and stood up, holding his hand out to Marcus.

"Sorry about Ava, Marcus. 13 years is a long time but I'm so glad you have found yourself a beautiful wife."

Cherie chuckled as Francis left the bar. It was the second time that he had called her Marcus's wife. Marcus smiled and took her hand.

"Beautiful wife," he said, "I'd like that." He leant forward and kissed Cherie.

"Would you darling? Would you like to be my wife?"

Chapter 28 – I Will Be Here

"I got your invitation today, man. I'm so excited for you and are you kidding, I wouldn't miss it."

Marcus was surprised to get the call from Grant. His Deadhorse roommate mailed him regularly but they had only spoken on the phone once since he got back to the UK.

He had invited a number of the special people he had met on his trip to the wedding and had been surprised to have had enthusiastic acceptances, so far, from Jake and Mikey, his Dalton Highway Samaritans and his Equator riding buddy, Ricky Finch.

Now heavily involved in his missing persons' charity and with significantly less disposable income than before he left the family law firm, Grant had been a long shot on the wedding invitations list but Marcus was delighted that he would be joining them for the small gathering in December, at the Trout Hall Hotel in Bibury.

Marcus noticed that Grant sounded much happier and more relaxed than he had back in Deadhorse. He remembered the despondent young lawyer telling him about an encounter in Delhi, which had left him feeling he was not on the life-path intended for him. His words had a lasting impression on Marcus and they still rang in his ears,

'I know I've lived before. I feel an unrelenting, uncontrollable empathy when I meet people who have been unfairly treated, sometimes even ruined, by wealthy people who can buy victory when they don't deserve it. I know that my destiny is not to be a corporate lawyer; it's just not what I'm here to learn.'

"So, leaving the family firm seems to have done you good, mate. How is your new job at the charity coming along?" Marcus asked.

Grant chatted about some of the people he had been able to help with his legal expertise but Marcus had a feeling there was something else that Grant wanted to talk about; the reason a phone call had replaced his customary e mail.

As the chat about Grant's work and Marcus's wedding plans drew to a close, Marcus could hear his friend take a deep breath,

"Oh, and I got married," Grant blurted out.

"What? Bloody hell, mate!" Marcus shouted, excitedly. "That's quite a bombshell to drop, mid-conversation. Shall we start this call again?"

Grant joined Marcus laughing. "Yeh," he said, "Sorry about that but, actually, I'd like to bring Dalia with me to the UK. Is that OK?"

Marcus felt so overjoyed for Grant; this kind and inspirational young man who had found the courage to walk away from an easy, privileged life so he could help those less fortunate.

"Absolutely not," Marcus said, firmly, before laughing again, "not until you've told me every single thing about this wonderful, brave woman who has had the balls to take you on."

Grant began to tell Marcus about Dalia, a 28-year-old African American defence attorney and their chance meeting at Plymouth County Correctional Facility, where they both had pro bono defendants awaiting preliminary hearings.

"She is beautiful and strong and I would certainly not want to be on the prosecution team when she's doing her thing," Grant enthused. "She's everything I admire. She had none of the advantages, or the opportunities for nepotism, that I had. Her family are loving and hard-working; her father's a car mechanic and her mother's a nursing assistant. They never had much money but what they did have they used to encourage Dalia and her brother to make the most of their lives. Her parents have shown me more love and kindness in one year than mine have in thirty."

Marcus listened to his friend's ebullient and adoring description of his new wife and felt happy that his life had changed so much since they met nearly 16 months ago. He had often wondered about the serendipity of Grant turning up that night in Deadhorse and telling Marcus about his experience in Delhi.

'I'm not sure where to start; you see, I believe I've lived before, dude. Actually, that's not true: I know I've lived before.'

"So, what about the past-life experience you had in Delhi?" Marcus asked. "Have you told Dalia about it or will she think I'm a complete weirdo for choosing to be a past-life regressionist?"

Grant went quiet for a few seconds and Marcus wondered if the line had been disconnected, "Grant? You still.."

Grant interrupted, "Yeh, yeh, sorry, man. Actually, I wanted to ask you a favour." Marcus waited for him to continue. "I told Dalia very early on about the feeling that I'd lived before. Her parents are Christians and I was nervous about her reaction but she was actually really cool about it. In fact, when I told her about your experience, you know, Ava and Linh and the whole Vietnamese connection, she suggested that I ask if you'll regress me to find out more. What do you think? You up for it? Say no if you're not cool with it, dude."

Marcus had always been a little apprehensive about involving people he knew in his hypnotherapy practice. He had achieved great results to date but he was concerned about disappointing friends and family who would, understandably, have significantly high and often unrealistic expectations. He recalled Isla's recent session and her remarkable Auschwitz recollections. "Of course, mate. You know I'm no expert so I can't promise any earth-shattering breakthroughs but sure, I'll do my best."

The second the phone call ended Marcus started to regret his agreement to hypnotise Grant. "What if it doesn't work and they think I'm a complete idiot?" he said to Cherie.

"Why should Grant's experience be any less useful than Islas, love?" Cherie said, noticing Marcus's concern. Marcus was grateful for Cherie's support but whilst Isla's session had been fascinating, he did not yet know if her regression had enabled her to address her discomfort with Luke's father.

Marcus sat at the kitchen table and thought about Grant and how his brave decisions had been the catalyst for his entire fortunes changing. His thoughts drifted to his own decisions to abandon his career and his home and step out of his comfort zone with a 20,000 mile motorbike trip across the Americas. He realised how those uncomfortable steps had enabled him to find his new vocation, the cottage and his wonderful Cherie and he smiled as he saw the parallels between his own choices and Grant's. Perhaps this really was all on the blueprint, he thought; written a lifetime ago.

The sound of a knock at the front door stirred Marcus from his daydreams and he smiled to himself as he heard

Cherie greet the visitor to the cottage, "G'day. How's it going, mate? Cheers for that. Have a good one."

Cherie mumbled to herself as she made her way into the kitchen, "What the b'jeepers? You been shopping, love?"

Marcus watched as his fiancé negotiated the small, wooden-framed kitchen door with a large, brown paper wrapped parcel and a handful of letters.

"There's some more replies from the wedding invites here Marcy-boy, and this."

Cherie put the large, flat parcel on the kitchen table and looked at Marcus for an explanation. He thought for a moment.

"I don't think I've ordered anything, honey. It looks like a picture. Do you think it could be an early wedding gift?"

Cherie looked excited and put her arms around Marcus. "A talented hypno-hubby and gifts as well," she said excitedly, waiting for Marcus to open the parcel.

Marcus stripped the brown wrapping paper from the package and stared at the scene looking up at them. The thirty-six by twenty-four-inch framed oil painting was of a field of bright yellow buttercups. A small child lay, looking skyward, in the centre of the painting, the clouds forming shapes and pictures in the otherwise bright blue sky. At the far-left side of the exquisite painting was the silhouette of a woman.

Marcus looked at the picture and realised immediately, it was a depiction of Isla's 'safe place', during her regression. Tucked into the back of the frame was an envelope and Marcus opened it and read the hand written note inside.

My special, special friend,

You told me that everything happens for a reason and it is all part of our 'blueprint'. Now I know why I was meant to travel to the US and the incredible Grand Canyon and bump into the kindly biker who would spend an entire evening listening to what, to anyone else, would be crazy ramblings.

I want you to know that you have truly changed my life for the better. My debilitating fear is now nothing more than a mild discomfort but more significantly, I have recognised that Luke's blueprint offered him the choice of learning and support or ignorance and denial: Maybe he has a few more lives to come; to live and learn.

I am so delighted that you have found happiness, my friend and I hope, one day, I will too find someone who can help me be the best person I can be, as I complete this life-time's blueprint.

Being with you when you marry Cherie will be my absolute pleasure. I hope you like your wedding gift and will get as much pleasure from the picture of the 'special place' you helped me to find, as I did painting it for you both.

See you in December,

Much love,

Isla

Marcus was speechless; his emotions part elation, with the knowledge that the regression had been successful and part sadness, at Isla's realisation that Luke was not her 'happily ever after'.

"Wow," he said, "I guess the regression did its job. Funny the picture arrived just as I was feeling uncomfortable about agreeing to Grant's hypnotherapy."

Marcus noticed that Cherie did not reply and turned around to look at her. Cherie's eyes were red as tears streamed down her face. Marcus smiled and pulled her close.

"Don't be sad, darling. Isla is lovely and she'll find someone special."

Cherie tore a piece of kitchen towel from the roll on the windowsill and dried her eyes.

"Fifteen minutes ago you doubted your ability to help the people you work with. Then this amazing gift turned up, reinforcing not just your amazing skills as a hypnotherapist but your kindness and ability to give people hope." Marcus wrapped his arms around his sobbing fiancé as she whispered through her tears, "I can't wait to be your wife."

Marcus stood at the front of the elegantly decorated room with Neil and was surprisingly nervous.

"Don't worry, she'll be fashionably late," Neil said, noticing Marcus looking towards the back of the gathered multinational crowd.

"No, she won't," Marcus replied. "Cherie doesn't do late, any more than I do. She'll already be here and waiting around the corner."

The wedding hall was full, with every ribbon-adorned chair occupied and every important person in Marcus's life, waiting for Cherie to arrive. Marcus looked around the room and seeing his parents, Isla and Grant and Dalia, he wondered if he would be able to get through his vows without being overcome with emotion. Mikey and Jake had hugged Marcus as he arrived at the hotel and Ricky and his new girlfriend, just arrived, waved from the back of the room. Marcus looked at his watch: 15.56 and with his eyes fixed on the rear of the room awaiting his fiancé, he felt his breath leave him as Karyn's electric wheelchair entered the room, followed by Steve.

It had been many months since Marcus had stayed with these wonderful people in Seattle and while he had longed for them to come to the wedding, he had not dared hope that Karyn would be well enough to make the 13-hour flight. Steve caught Marcus's eye and waved and the smile on Karyn's face could not have been a more perfect precursor to Cherie's arrival.

At exactly 4pm, the music, which stood every hair on Marcus's body on end, began to play and as he listened to the words, Marcus could feel Cherie walking towards him.

'Tomorrow morning, if you wake up and the sun does not appear, I will be here.

If, in the dark, we lose sight of love, hold my hand and have no fear, I will be here.'

Chapter 29 – Wings; and the Courage to Fly

"See the long hall of mirrors stretching as far as you can see in front of you. Lots of full-length mirrors to your right and left. Notice they all have different frames; some gold, some wooden, all ornately carved, others brightly coloured. Can you see them, Grant?"

Unlike Roisin or Isla, Grant had not experienced any particular strong symptoms or emotions to suggest he may have suffered a trauma in a previous life. He had visited a hypnotherapist in Delhi a couple of years previously, in the hope that she might be able to help him cope with anxiety, exacerbated, he was sure, as a result of his deteriorating relationship with his mercenary father. The hypnotherapist had recorded the session and had felt that some of Grant's comments, under hypnosis, hinted that his feelings about his father may have initiated in a previous existence.

"He was the same before. He hasn't changed this time. Everyone hated him before," Grant had protested.

The Indian hypnotherapist had probed further. "When was 'before'?" she had asked, "Before you worked for him? Before you joined the firm?"

"Before I was Grant. When I was one of the others."

Grant had begun to sound distressed and the hypnotherapist had felt it inappropriate to investigate any further at that time. She had played the recording for Grant and suggested that he may wish to explore the possibility that he had experienced a previous life.

Grant had replayed the recording numerous times since and when Marcus wrote to tell him that he had achieved his diploma in hypnotherapy, with a specific interest in past-life regression, he knew he needed to delve deeper.

Grant had responded quickly to Marcus's induction and deepener and had described his safe place as a wooden cabin in a forest, filled with dry heat and surrounded with bird song.

When Marcus suggested that Grant now find himself in the hall of mirrors, he was interested to see if the Indian hypnotherapist's instinct had been right.

Grant breathed deeply and at one point, Marcus wondered if he had fallen asleep. After a few seconds he nodded and spoke. "I see them; hundreds of mirrors in a long, thin, dark hall."

"Excellent," Marcus said, encouragingly. "Notice that above each mirror is a date. The nearest mirrors have the most recent dates. Find the one with 2003 above it, Grant, and look into the mirror. Can you do that?" Grant nodded.

"Describe what you can see," Marcus prompted. Grant was quiet for a few seconds before smiling, "I'm in a suit. It's my wedding gear."

Marcus spoke again, "Now step into the mirror, into the scene and tell me what's happening."

Grant continued to smile. "It's my wedding day. I have a glass of champagne in my hand. I can see Dalia chatting to our guests." Grant's expression changed suddenly, "Oh no, Dad is talking to Dalia's father. I really hope he's not being an ass. He can be such a jerk at times."

Marcus asked Grant to step out of the scene and back into the hall of mirrors.

"Now see yourself walking down the hall; mirrors either side of you. Notice as you walk along the hallway, the dates above the mirrors decrease. See 2000 and now see the one with 1990 above it." Marcus waited for Grant to acknowledge he had found the mirrors.

"Now find the one with 1973 above it and look into the mirror, Grant. Can you do that and let me know when you're there?" Marcus waited until Grant nodded, "OK, what can you see?"

"Mum, I can see Mum. She's in a hospital room. There's a doctor and nursing staff and she's holding me. I've just been born."

Marcus let Grant absorb the scene before speaking, "OK, you're doing really well. Now look again at the hundreds of mirrors stretching out in front of you. I'd like you to think of your feelings for your father. Remember, all those feelings you have for him. I'd like you to go to the mirror which has the date, before 1973, that is most relevant to those feelings. Can you do that?"

Grant was quiet but Marcus noticed a puzzled expression on his face. "Can you find the right mirror?" Marcus asked. Grant stayed quiet but his head was moving from left to right.

"Lots of mirrors. Many, many years," he finally muttered, before his head became still.

"Here it is. I'm here. I'm at the right mirror now."

"Excellent," Marcus said. "What year is above the mirror, Grant?" Grant responded immediately, "It says 1619."

Marcus asked Grant to see himself in the mirror, as he was at that time and to describe what he could see.

"I'm black, black and strong and tall; I must be six feet three or four." Grant said, hesitantly.

Marcus asked Grant to step into the mirror. "Take your time and describe what's happening." Grant sounded scared and his voice was raised,

"There are lots of us. I know some people but most, most are strangers." Marcus waited for Grant to continue, "Men with guns have tied our hands and there are ropes around our necks. They're kicking us and pushing us with rifles and we're all tied together. I don't understand what they're saying and they're wearing strange clothes."

"What's your name?" Marcus asked, "and, where are you?"

Grant paused, "Kwame, my name is Kwame and I'm in Angola. There's a ship and I think they're taking us to the ship. I have a family here and I don't want to go on the ship. I'm frightened I won't see my family again." Grant began to sound distressed and was writhing in the reclined hypnotherapy chair, as if he was fighting to release himself.

"Step out of the mirror," Marcus said gently. "Take some deep breaths and tell me when you're ready to step back in." Marcus noticed Grant become calm, the panic gone from his face.

"OK, now when you step back into the mirror, it will be a few days later. Remember those feelings you have for your father when you step back in and go to a day that is significant."

When Grant acknowledged that he was back in the scene, his arms were fixed tightly by his side as though he could not move.

"Describe where you are," Marcus instructed.

"I'm lying in the bottom of the ship. There are many, many of us here. It's hot and people are lying on me. The smell is terrible and people are dying; many people are dying. Our women and our children are dying."

Marcus was keen to understand the connection between this distressing scene and Grant's father. "Who is keeping you there, Kwame?" he asked.

"The men with pale skin. They put us here," Grant replied.

Marcus had guessed that Kwame had been captured and was now on a slave ship and he wanted to establish what had happened and if Grant's father had played a part in the past-life.

"Step out of the mirror and move to the mirror marked 1625. Can you do that for me?" Marcus asked. Grant was still for a few seconds before speaking, "I look old. I'm only 24 but I look so old."

Marcus asked Grant to enter the scene and describe it.

"I'm in Virginia," he said, sounding tired, "and I work for the Master. I've been here for years now and I miss my family. I know they will think I have died."

Marcus was interested to hear more about Kwame's owner, "Tell me about the Master, Kwame. Is he a decent man?"

"He's very rich but his money comes from dishonest means. He has many slaves and anyone who does not obey him is beaten. The Mistress is a cruel, deceitful woman. She treats us as she would the cattle and the pigs. She lies about us to her husband, if she is displeased." Grant sounded nervous. "Jami, the slave they call Kit, forgot to address her as we had been instructed. She told the Master that Jami had cursed at her and the Master had Jami beaten. He never recovered and will never get justice for his treatment."

Marcus was interested in Grant's choice of the word justice, as it was a word he had used frequently in his criticism of his father's firm. Once again, he asked Grant to step out of the mirror. "Step out, but when you look back into the mirror, see the Master and the Mistress. Can you do that?"

Marcus was fascinated by Grant's change of posture and facial expression. He almost looked like a different person, as Kwame became Grant and he became dissociated from the scene.

"Look closely at the Master and his wife. Do you recognise them as anyone in your life as Grant Bruton?"

Grant was silent, as if scrutinising the faces in the mirror. "I don't recognise the Master but," he paused, his lips became thin and Marcus could see his face redden, "the woman, the Mistress, she's my father, ruthless and dishonest and cruel."

Marcus knew there was no specific event which he could attempt to reframe, with the aim of improving the relationship between Grant and his contemptible father. But he felt giving Grant and perhaps Kwame a voice, may help take the edge off Grant's resentment.

"See the Master take a step back and let the Mistress come to the front of the mirror. Have you done that?" Grant nodded, his face still red and angry.

"OK, now that she can't hurt you, take this opportunity to let the Mistress and your father know how you feel."

Marcus could see Grant's fists clench and his nostrils flare and waited for the spew of hatred and the torrent of accusations.

"I want you to know that I feel sorry for you. Anyone who can be so oblivious to the pain and injustice that they proliferate has much to learn; too much to learn in one lifetime. One day you will suffer for the hurt you have caused to others and you will feel the agony of the vile prejudice you have shown to those who have not bene-fitted from your privilege and when that day comes, I will pity you even more. I have escaped from you now and you will never be in a position to poison me with your hatred and inhumanity ever again."

Marcus was astonished at Grants eloquent and moving monologue and knew his honest but compassionate speech would be a deep therapy for his friend.

At Grant's request, Marcus played the recording that evening with Cherie and Dalia captivated by the poignant recollection of Grant's past life as a slave.

From his first meeting with Grant in Prudhoe Bay, Marcus had felt a close bond; the kind of love and admi-ration usually reserved for a family member or a close friend, built over many years. He wondered if, perhaps, Grant had featured in one of his own past lives and smiled to himself as he imagined being Grant's son or maybe his niece or even a parent; perhaps hundreds of years ago and in an entirely different country or continent.

"Anyway, enough about me and my weird past lives. What's it like to be Mrs Crane, Cherie?" Grant's question broke into Marcus's thoughts and he turned to his wife to watch her reaction. "Well," Cherie said, smiling at Marcus, "I fell in love with a motorbike-riding school teacher in Peru and I married a MG driving hypnothera-pist in a tiny village in Blighty but, yeh," she said kissing Marcus, "he'll do, I guess."

Marcus and Cherie had decided to spend some time in New Zealand for their honeymoon. Mrs Rutherford and Sean, Cherie's brother, had both attended the wedding but their visit to the UK had been fleeting as they had needed to return to Christchurch to supervise the running of the bar.

Cherie had been disappointed that her mother had not had the opportunity to get to know her new husband and was delighted when Marcus had presented her with two return fight tickets to New Zealand on their wedding night.

Marcus had imagined a small, suburban pub, when Cherie had described the bar and was surprised to see what he would have described as a large, town-centre bistro with an inside and outside seating area and a pretty extensive menu.

The bar was busy when Marcus and Cherie arrived, following their long flight from London, and Marcus was touched when he noticed the balloons and banners welcoming him and Cherie home. A loud cheer filled the bar as Cherie entered and Marcus was amazed as customer after customer surrounded them with greetings and gifts. He had always wanted to visit New Zealand; his parents having described it, after a holiday there, as God's own country. As he watched his beautiful wife take centre stage in the impressive business, which she and her brother had fought so hard for, he knew he would be spending more time here in the future.

As Marcus sat, beer in hand and watched Cherie chat to her customers, he realised that the strange coincidences and messages he had experienced prior to meeting her, had stopped. He wondered if Ava, having guided him through his trip, his reading with Donna and his meeting with Cherie, had now progressed to her next incarnation and he considered if, perhaps, he might somehow encounter her again in this life.

He thought about the people that were important to him and smiled to himself as he imagined the roles they might have played in his previous lives. He knew that Neil had been his wife, in his incarnation as Thomas Wilson and that his mother, Ricky Finch and Cherie had all featured, in some vague way, in the same past life but he thought about Ava and wondered what kind of relationship they might have had before this current life.

While Marcus had been waiting for his wife, he had been appreciating the unusual cover versions of some of his favourite songs, playing over the sound system in the bar. When Cherie finally came to join him he asked her who the vocalist was.

"That's Wing Han Tsang," Cherie said. "She's a big hit in New Zealand and we just call her The Wing."

Chapter 30 – Faith; the Light that Leads Us Through the Darkness

"How was the café, honey?" Marcus asked, as Cherie slumped down on the lounge sofa.

"Good," Cherie replied, dropping her head on to Marcus's shoulder, "but I'm done. In fact," she continued, "I feel a bit crook."

Marcus felt a wave of fear shoot through him. Returning home to find Ava sick in bed, nearly three years ago, had created a devastating anchor which he was sure he would never be free from.

"Crook, honey? What kind of crook?" Marcus asked, struggling to sound calm.

"Oh, nothing, just a bit sick and really, really tired."

Marcus thought back to the symptoms Ava had described that fateful day before his life changed forever; weakness, breathlessness and violent nose bleeds.

He looked at his precious wife as she dozed on his shoulder and consoled himself as he noticed the pink in her cheeks and her steady, unlaboured breathing.

The following morning Cherie felt much better. "Bye, love. Shall we eat out tonight?" she shouted, as she opened the front door of the cottage.

Relieved that his wife appeared to have shaken whatever had made her feel ill, Marcus booked a table at the Mayflower, Cherie's favourite Chinese restaurant.

Friday night was always Marcus's favourite night. Cherie had managed to find an experienced hospitality manager to take care of their café on Saturday and they always enjoyed a meal out and several glasses of wine, knowing they had a lie in the following day.

"Red or white, honey?" Marcus asked, pondering the extensive wine menu.

"Er, just sparkling water for me please, love."

The familiar stab of fear shot through Marcus; Cherie never wanted just sparkling water. Maybe she was still ill and trying to spare Marcus the anxiety?

He took a deep breath. "Are you OK, honey? You always want a glass of wine on a Friday."

Cherie took Marcus's hand, "Sweetie, you have to stop worrying about me. It's really not unusual for a woman in my condition to avoid the pop."

Cherie reached into her handbag and pulled out a pregnancy test; the two bright blue lines clearly displayed.

"You're going to be such an amazing dad," she said.

"Now, I don't want to spoil the surprise, but would you guys like to know if you're going to have a Miss Crane or a Master Crane?" the sonographer asked.

Marcus had been completely blown away when he saw his child at the 20-week scan. Cherie and he had agreed that they would like to know the sex of their first child, so they could plan names and decorate the nursery.

"Oh yes please," Cherie said. "We can't wait another 20 weeks, can we love?"

Marcus smiled at the young woman awaiting their answer. "It really would be special to know," he said, squeezing Cherie's hand.

Marcus watched as the ultrasound moved over Cherie's abdomen, "This is an arm and this here, is a leg. Yep, he has all his bits and pieces, guys."

Cherie pulled Marcus close. "We're having a little boy, love. I hope he's just like his awesome daddy."

Marcus's hypnotherapy practice had developed significantly, since qualifying two years previously. Having returned to the hypnotherapy school to complete his Master Practitioner training and his Certificate in Supervision, the ISCH had asked him to become the past life specialist on the diploma course, following Bernie's retirement.

Marcus found it amusing that somehow, the universe had managed to get him back to teaching. He had not missed school for a second and had no desire to return to education but he had to admit that training willing, enthusiastic adults in regression, was markedly easier than forcing reluctant kids to run cross country, in the pouring rain. He looked forward to his occasional practical demonstrations for the hypnotherapy school and rarely had difficulty finding a willing volunteer, ready to discover their past life.

The past-life module, for the summer 2005 cohort, was due to run in early August. As always, Marcus had arrived in the lecture hall early to prepare his presentation and check the technology was working. Nicola, the Programme Director and the same lady who had lead Marcus's Diploma classes, popped her head around the door to check that Marcus had everything he needed.

"Have a great session," she said. "Oh and by the way, one of our international tutors might be joining you for the session. He was particularly keen to attend the past-life practical. Hope that's OK?"

Marcus smiled obligingly, while secretly feeling a little irritated at the thought of another tutor observing his class. He was never averse to adlibbing during the practical sessions, if circumstances called for it. As long as he was professional and safe, the result was more important than the purity of the method, he had frequently told himself, and the presence of a member of the faculty made it more difficult for him to go off-piste, should he deem it necessary.

At 9.15am, the students began to fill the room. This summer's Diploma cohort was 45 strong and was a diverse group, with medical practitioners, counsellors and alternative therapists joining the usual throng of people simply wanting a career change. A couple of the delegates had travelled from mainland Europe, one being Polish and one French; and while Nicola had informed Marcus that both had strong English capability, he had made a mental note to speak clearly and regularly check their comprehension.

As the room filled and Marcus felt the tingling of the butterflies, which he always got just before his session began, a young girl approached him on the raised platform,

"Hi, Mr Crane," the girl said, nervously, "I have really enjoyed the course so far but to be honest, this week, the past-life module, was the main reason I signed up."

Marcus was pleasantly surprised and flattered. He remembered that he had felt equally passionate about the somewhat unconventional practice and understood the girl's enthusiasm. "That's really kind of you, er," Marcus looked, uncomfortably for the girl's missing name badge.

"Georgia," the young girl said. "I really wanted to ask; when you do the demonstration, could I perhaps be the volunteer?"

Marcus knew that ISCH best practice suggested that all delegates were given the opportunity to volunteer, but he also recalled how eager he had been to experience the regression with Bernie.

"When I ask the group, Georgia, make sure your hand goes up." Georgia smiled and returned to her seat.

As the assembled group chatted to each other while waiting for their tutor to speak, Marcus checked his laptop and was just about to introduce himself when the door opened.

"Well, well, Mr Crane. Who would have thought it?" Marcus turned and looked towards the familiar American accent. "Doctor Rob! What are you doing here?" he exclaimed.

Robert Craven joined Marcus on the platform and hugged him.

"The ISCH have asked me to set up a sister-school in Costa Rica. This is part of my induction and when Nicola told me who was running the past-life module, well, I couldn't miss it, could I?"

"Well, good morning, everyone." Marcus waited for the hum of chatter to die down.

"I'm delighted to be here with you all today."

Marcus introduced himself and acknowledged Robert, who the delegates had met when he had attended previous modules, earlier in the course. He then made the customary offer of a morning of induction practice in the break-out room, as an alternative for anyone not comfortable with the subject matter.

"I'd like to start the day by conducting a past-life regression. Is there anyone who would like to be my willing guinea pig?"

The class laughed and Marcus was surprised that most of the delegates raised their hands.

"Wow has Nicola bribed you all?" he said smiling as his gaze fell on Georgia.

OK, well given there are so many willing volunteers, maybe we could do another practical later but for now, would you like to join me on the stage?"

Georgia smiled and sat in one of the chairs which Marcus had positioned earlier.

Marcus had, over the last couple of years, created a number of his own inductions and deepeners which were not strictly in line with ISCH content. Sitting in front of 40 plus students and his mentor, he briefly considered being overly compliant but knowing Doctor Robert's mantra, 'If it works and doesn't hurt, do it', he stuck to what he had planned.

"Feel the soft cinema seat underneath you, Georgia. Feel the velvet of the chair arms and feel comfortable in the peace, no one around. Now feel a remote control in your hand. It has a start and stop button and it also has rewind, fast forward and pause. Can you feel that? Take your time."

Georgia had initially struggled to visualise her safe place and Marcus had used an additional deepener to take her into a deeper state of trance. He waited for her to acknowledge her position in the empty cinema with the remote control.

"I can feel it," she said, quietly.

Marcus was relieved. Aware of his talented observer, he was eager for the session to go well.

"Excellent, you're doing really well. Now, in a second, you'll notice numbers on the cinema screen. When you press rewind, the numbers will count backwards from ten to one; just as they did in the old films. When they reach one, an important scene from a previous life will appear on the screen. When you're ready Georgia, you can press rewind. OK?"

The young girl's hand moved in her lap, as though pressing the invisible remote control.

"Can you see the numbers?" Marcus asked.

Georgia said nothing, for what seemed to Marcus to be much longer than ten seconds but before he could speak, Georgia started to pull at the sleeve on her T-shirt.

The class sat in silence as the young girl's left hand continued to tug impatiently at the shirt.

"It hurts," she said suddenly. "My dress is digging into my arm and it hurts."

Marcus watched the girl for a second before speaking. "Can you tell me about yourself?"

Georgia nodded, her feet turned in towards each other, making her posture appear like that of a small child. "I'm six and I'm the big sister. I can feel the splashes from the road, that's why I sit here. It feels funny on my legs."

Marcus was surprised that Georgia was describing a scene she seemed to be a part of. In his experience, the cinema technique enabled the participant to remain dissociated from what was happening, while watching themselves on a screen. He waited for Georgia to stop talking and asked for more details.

Georgia described sitting on the roadside in a poor part of Liverpool; discarded water mixed with rain water from overflowing drains running under her bare legs and splashing up at them. She was not sure what the year was, but her description of the few cars and the clothing of passers-by made Marcus feel it was probably the 1940s or '50s. The material she described as sacking, from which her dress was made, was cutting into her upper arm and she could hear her frustrated mother shouting at her younger siblings from the terraced house behind her. Marcus asked what she could see around her.

"I can see women walking. They walk past every day. They climb the hill to the big house and they look clean."

Marcus was interested by Georgia's choice of words. "Clean?" he asked.

"Yes, they're clean. They have white hoods and long black dresses with rope belts. I want to be clean."

Marcus asked Georgia to press fast forward and move forward in time to another significant time in that life,

"I'm a novitiate now," she said, her voice soft, "and when I take my vows, I will be Sister Gabrielle."

Georgia described how one day she had followed the nuns to the convent. There she had learnt about the Catholic faith and life in a religious order. She described her devotion for her faith and Christ, in a way which made Marcus and many in the stunned audience feel overwhelmed with emotion. Her meticulous descriptions of the chapel, her cell and the convent gardens were exceptionally detailed and Georgia carefully explained the routine of the day, the roles of the various sisters and her desire to devote her life to the church.

Having asked Georgia to come forward to the final day of her life as Sister Gabrielle, she smiled and described herself in bed with her bible and rosary beads in her hands and other nuns and priests around her,

"I'm ready now. I'm ready to go and meet my Lord," she whispered.

Marcus brought his young volunteer out of trance and waited for her to acknowledge that she was, emotionally, back in the room.

Georgia could remember her regression with clarity.

"I can still feel the water on my legs and the soreness around my arm," she said, giggling.

The class was interested to know if Georgia was a religious person.

"My parents don't believe," she said, shaking her head. "I've never been inside a church in my life but as I was describing praying in the chapel, I felt complete adoration for my faith; like nothing else in the world mattered. It was very, very strange."

Marcus was delighted with how well his practical had gone and he and Robert discussed it in detail, over dinner at the cottage that evening.

"I'm so glad you decided to train, Marcus," Robert said. "You really are very good. Maybe you could come and do a demo for me in Costa Rica?" he winked at Cherie. "Wait until you need sleep because Baby Crane has you exhausted, then come over."

"Letter for you, love," Cherie shouted, as she shuffled slowly into the kitchen, her hand pressed to her lower back. Marcus giggled as his heavily pregnant wife made her way to where he was sitting.

"He's going to be a bruiser, honey. That bump is bigger than you."

Cherie smiled and manoeuvred herself into the chair next to Marcus.

"The return address is Dublin, love. Who do you know in Ireland?"

Marcus looked at the back of the white envelope before opening it and reading the short note out to Cherie:

14, Craig Court,

Dublin

Ireland

Dear Marcus,

I can't thank you enough for getting in touch.

My mother forwarded your letter and photographs of Ava to me and you can imagine my surprise when I received them: I had no idea that Roisin had been pregnant.

I am so sorry that I was not able to support Roisin through what must have been a very difficult time. I want you to know that I did try to contact both Roisin and her parents on a number of occasions but, reluctantly, had to accept that she no longer wanted me in her life.

My heart breaks to think that I had a beautiful daughter who I never met; my wife and I have two great sons and I know they would have loved to have had a big sister.

I am so sorry that you, like me, never got to spend enough time with her and wish you and your lovely wife every happiness for the future.

If you have any additional photographs or information about Ava, we would so dearly love to receive it.

Perhaps, if you are ever in Dublin, we can meet up?

Thank you, once again,

Kindest wishes,

James O'Connor

'Come on, Cherie. You're doing just great," the midwife said, cheerfully.

Marcus had never felt so nervous. He had expected the arrival of their son to be stressful and the antenatal appointments painted a very honest picture of a messy and painful experience but seeing his precious wife in such discomfort terrified him.

"Not long now. Wait for the next contraction and then give me a huge push," the midwife continued.

Marcus held Cherie's hand and could feel her grip tightening as the next wave of pain indicated another contraction.

"That's good, keep it coming, Cherie."

Marcus noticed a change of expression on the midwife's face and felt his heart beat quicken as she pressed the Nurse Call button, above the bed.

"Baby's heart rate has dropped a little," she explained, "and I can see a little meconium; that's baby's first bowel movement, which means he is getting a little distressed. Nothing to worry about but I just want to be cautious."

Cherie looked exhausted and scared and Marcus knew she needed him to be strong, even though he felt he was holding back a wave of panic. Fifteen minutes later, Cherie was in theatre and Marcus, gowned and masked, was sitting by her side.

"It's going to be fine, honey," he said, kissing Cherie's forehead.

The wait, as the surgeon worked to deliver their son, seemed endless and for the first time Marcus realised the words which were going over and over in his head were, in fact, a prayer.

"Congratulations, Mr and Mrs Crane. You have a perfect baby boy."

Marcus heard the cries of his son and felt the tears stream down his face. One of the theatre nurses lay the screaming bundle on Cherie's chest and Marcus felt as though his heart could burst as he looked at his beautiful wife and child.

"I am so proud of you, darling. Look at what you have given us. Welcome to the world, baby Thomas."

Cherie had suggested the name. "When you were Thomas Wilson, you never got to meet your baby. I want our son to be the baby you never got to hold in your previous life."

Marcus was amazed at how quickly Cherie had gone from exhausted and in pain, to the funny, relaxed woman he loved so much.

"He's a great weight," the midwife said. "He's got all his fingers and toes and he's a handsome little chap."

Marcus smiled at the midwife as she handed the sleeping baby back to Cherie.

"Oh, and that little birthmark, here, just below his ear, this little red mark, shaped like a bird's wing, that's what we call a salmon patch. It'll be gone by the time he's two."

The End

. . . .

Printed in Great Britain
by Amazon